Anthropomorphic

An Experience in Consciousness

Runda Books

Edited by Sarah Giustra
Cover design by J.R. Incer
Front cover photo from Shutterstock
Back cover photo from Freepik Premium

ISBN 978-0-9885288-5-7 (paper)
ISBN 978-0-9885288-6-4 (digital)

This book is a reference work based on research by the author. The opinions expressed herein are not necessarily those of, or endorsed by the Publisher.

Printed in the United States of America

For my wife, Deirdre, with love.

Contents

Part 3: It's All in Your Dreams

Acknowledgments

Writing this book has been a personal journey of discovery, in the course of which I have met many kind souls who have helped me along the way. I would have never started this journey without their kindness and willingness to share. Their amazing experiences inspired me to write and develop my own short stories. I hope this book inspires many others to seek and find the priceless treasures that the storytellers of the world hold in their hearts.

It would have been impossible to start this book without the support and love of my wife, Deirdre, and my mother, Veronica. I have deep appreciation for the teaching and wisdom of El Maestro Santiago Aranegui and Professor Flavio Campos, that will always guide me forward.

In the process of collecting these real life stories, I have drawn on the time and support of Teresina Incer, Jorge Blanco, Veronica Gutierrez, Chrissie Tannian, and Bart Tannian.

A special thanks to Sarah Giustra, copy editor, who stepped in at the right time to edit this book and kept me from appearing foolish. Thank you to Simona Boggio, for her skillful translation to German.

I am grateful to my friends, Dr. Miguel Angel Gonzalez, Luz Dari Orozco, Ron Vazquez, Guillermo Leon, and my brother-in-law Shane Tannian for their moral support. I am also hugely grateful to all of my clients. Their courage and strength to face overwhelming life challenges have taught me that the human spirit can never be extinguished.

Over the years, I've shared an important life lesson with my clients. In order to take control of our lives, we have to take responsibility for our thoughts and actions. Therefore, just as we need to take credit for all of the positive events and achievements in our life, we also need to take responsibility for the failures and conflicts that we face. For this reason, any lack of substance or interest in these stories which you are about to read, is due to the author's way of expressing them.

When I close my eyes,
I awaken to peace,
In complete stillness,
Then I remember,
We rest in Unity.

A sense of pure restful happiness,
There is something beyond what we call light,
It is the perfect state,
It is the perfect home,
Where all is One.

This is where We belong,
Safe and joyful We rest,
A timeless state of consciousness,
Forever alive We wander no more.

Then I open my eyes,
I return to a dream,
Where somehow I have a body,
Walking through time,
And traveling great distances.

The mind filled with frightening thoughts,
And a never-ending flow of emotions,
Illness or danger around every corner,
Thousands of forms in a single glance,
Not one permanent nor everlasting.

While dreaming,
The mind aimlessly drifts,
The past brings great sadness,
And the future paralyzing anxiety,
But the strangest belief in this dream,
It's a thought that seems to rule above all,
The thought of death.

– J.R. Incer

Introduction

*"I closed my eyes, and I heard a voice whispering
the title of this book into my ear."*
— J.R. Incer

Have you ever experienced a force or a drive that felt to have come from beyond your conscious self? Perhaps you have labeled this force as a career calling, higher calling, or a life mission. Well, throughout history, this force has been called many different names. But there is one term that is quite intriguing. That term is the "daemon." According to ancient Greek belief, a daemon is a divine supernatural being. Many historical figures have claimed to have been guided by daemons. Socrates claimed that during crucial moments, a daemon would advise him what not to do. The famous author, Rudyard Kipling, even wrote about daemons. He wrote, "When your daemon is in charge, do not try to think consciously. Drift, wait, and obey." Nietzsche wrote, "In looking back, everything seems to fit so well that it's as if a guiding spirit has been showing me the way."

From a Jungian school of thought or teaching, the daemon concept can be thought of as an unconscious core pattern of emotions, ideas, and perceptions that exist beyond our conscious awareness. Throughout my career as a clinical hypnotherapist, meditation teacher, and life coach, I've been fortunate to have the opportunity to work with many people who have been diagnosed with terminal illnesses or life-threatening diseases. Over the years, I have noticed that these individuals who were given this type of devastating diagnosis, go through a profound transformation. After the initial shock, they come to understand what really matters in life. Things that they considered important before, all of a sudden are meaningless, trivial, and a waste of time. On the other hand, people or relationships that before were a bother, unexpectedly become extremely important.

In most cases, when a person comes face to face with their own mortality, an overpowering shift in consciousness occurs. Our mind flips from ego identity to Self-focused (Self with a capital "S" refers to the higher Self or higher consciousness. Not to be confused with self-expression, which is the expression of our own personality or ego). Everything takes on a different meaning when we witness the world from the Self. All pretentiousness and falsehood is shed away and replaced by a sense of authenticity and purpose. We start to listen to our daemon. When I work with clients who were given life-altering diagnoses, we not only focus on the mental shift, but also on turning this new perspective in life into actions. Now, in some cases, something truly special happens, and the person who goes through this process of inner awakening is able to recover from their illness. Suddenly, the medical treatment that was not giving positive results starts working. It seems as if the suppression of the important things in life and the focus on the meaningless causes some type of unbalance or disturbance, both at the mental and physical level. These disturbances eventually express themselves as a chemical imbalance in the brain (mental illness) and/or physical symptoms (physical illness).

The truth is that we truly don't understand how our mind and body work. So how are we supposed to honestly believe that we know how the universe really works? For example, were you ever told that there are no such things as the afterlife, out-of-body experiences, other dimensions, past lives, or that dreams are just puzzling metaphors that the unconscious mind manufactures on its own? It's unfortunate that even today, with all the technological, medical, and information advancements that we have achieved, the world, at large, is still skeptical of these phenomena. What is more incredible is the fact that there are millions of cases, reported by mentally healthy individuals, who have themselves experienced such occurrences. However, their claims are met with disbelief, mockery, and in many cases, hostility. The evidence shows that all the data on ESP (Extrasensory Perception) indicates that our perception of reality is quite limited.

The fact is that at the root of our Western society lies a deep-seated fear to explore what modern science cannot measure or understand. The real cause of this stubbornness toward embracing an expanded extrasensory life experience as everyday reality is the fact that our worldview is highly material. Behind this materialistic ideology also stands a fear toward the unknown, something that the field of psychology has identified as a common trait in human nature. This is the reason why a large portion of the population resists change and expects the world to remain the way they think it should be, even if it is highly dysfunctional and destructive. Of course, the motivation for this is the fact that we want to be able to anticipate and have control over what happens. Otherwise, we would live in a constant state of anxiety. After all, who likes uncertainty?

The motivation to write and publish the material in this book is in the hope that in the near future, conventional science, medicine, and our culture, as a whole, will expand their perception, knowledge, and understanding to the true and complete nature of existence, beyond the physical, to enter an era of Self-enlightenment. Now, I clearly understand that the work that I present here would never be considered scientific evidence or proof of concept. However, the stories that I relate can't be dismissed as meaningless. The truth is that all the stories, (which are based on real-life experiences), were told with plain sincerity, and with great effort to avoid sensationalism. From my part, as a chronicler, I tried my best to be as objective as I could be, by relaying the events as they were told. But to the reader, I ask for you to be as open-minded as possible. After all, it can be difficult to accurately report the incident when even the individuals themselves who experienced the events had a hard time describing or understanding what occurred.

Another reason why I decided to produce this work is to encourage others to share their experiences. I believe that not only are extrasensory occurrences commonplace, but they are a natural process of the human experience. Almost everyone, at one time or another in their life, had an incident where they received profound insight or even precognition, while dreaming or in an altered state of consciousness. Throughout history and across all cultures, these "supernatural" experiences have been recorded repeatedly, (in many cases, by society's most influential and admired people). Some of these individuals have claimed that much of their success was due to the fact that they embraced these expanded extrasensory abilities, sometimes referred to as a "gift." For instance, the following historical figures experienced what could best be described as extrasensory perception:

• *Nikola Tesla:* Inventor and engineer known for designing the alternating-current (AC) electric system. Throughout his life, he experienced blinding flashes of light, accompanied by visions. He would often visualize mechanical and theoretical inventions, spontaneously.[1]

• *Niels Bohr:* The Danish physicist, who is referred to as the father of quantum mechanics, had tried many times to understand the structure of the atom, but none of his configurations worked. One night, he dreamt of an atomic nucleus with electrons spinning around it. His dream led him to the discovery of the structure of the atom.[2]

• *Ernest Hemingway:* During World War I, Hemingway was caught in an assault and was hit by 28 pieces of shrapnel. He saw a blinding light and, as he later described it, "I died then. I felt my soul or something coming right out of my body, the way you'd pull a handkerchief out of the pocket by its corner. I flew around and then came back and went in again, and I wasn't dead anymore."[3]

• Elizabeth Taylor: During an interview on CNN's "Larry King Live," the British-American actress shared her experience of having "died" on the operating table, while undergoing surgery, and of passing through a tunnel towards a brilliant white light.[4]

• *Johnny Cash:* In 1988, after having emergency double coronary bypass surgery, Cash developed double pneumonia, and his life suddenly hung in the balance. At that time, he reportedly caught a glimpse of heaven, during a Near Death Experience, but was brought back. He described traveling toward a "peaceful light," but became very angry at having to return. His NDE convinced him of the reality of heaven. "I just don't have any fear of death."[5]

• *Carl Gustav Jung:* Psychiatrist and psychoanalyst who founded analytical psychology. While in the hospital, he suffered a heart attack. Treated with oxygen and camphor, he lost consciousness and had a near-death and out-of-the-body experience. He found himself floating 1,000 miles above the Earth.[6]

• *Emanuel Swedenborg:* The Swedish Lutheran theologian, scientist, philosopher, and mystic, who, in the last twenty-eight years of his life, published eighteen theological works. During this time, he began to experience dreams and visions where he would travel to other realities and speak to angels, demons, and other spirits.[7]

• *Salvador Dali:* The Spanish surrealist painter claimed that many of his masterpieces were renditions of actual dreams. They were referred to as "Hand-painted dream photographs," and included works such as his famous melting clocks entitled , "Persistence of Memory."[8]

• *Louis Stevenson:* The 19th-century Scottish novelist and travel writer was already a successful author, when he dreamt about a doctor with a dissociative identity disorder. Stevenson documented the scenes from his dream and then went on to write the first draft of his novel, *Dr. Jekyll and Mr. Hyde,* in less than three days.[9]

I hope that *Anthropomorphic, an Experience in Consciousness,* will help renew the reader's interest in expanding his or her consciousness. You could say that ultimately my goal is to inspire people from all walks of life to dig deeper, until they can finally break free from the fear and uncertainty that has kept humanity imprisoned and separated from its infinite and unlimited nature.

So, if you were ever told that such things as spirits, past lives, precognition, or extrasensory experiences do not exist, please follow me, and I will demonstrate that only the self-deluded can make such ridiculous claims.

Forewords

*"If you want to find the secrets of the universe,
think in terms of energy, frequency and vibration"*
— Nikola Tesla

In one way or another, each of us has experienced the flow of energy, within and outside of our bodies. We perceive it in many different ways, from the subtlest to the most palpable. Sometimes it is difficult for us to accept this because we cannot see it. Therefore, we reject it because we fear the unknown. However, this energy within us connects us to a larger energy field that encompasses everything and everyone and makes us one with it, Oneness. It goes beyond our body and our conscious mind, and although it may not seem like it at times, it is also connected to the lessons of compassion and love that we have come to learn in this lifetime, here on Earth.

I have known the author, José Incer, since we were children. We've always shared a common interest in the paranormal experiences of people who we know mutually, and individually, in our own lives. We have shared experiences that go beyond the understanding of this physical plane, of this dimension we call "reality." We also share the desire to continue expanding the field of the healing arts through the practice of NLP, coaching, hypnosis, energy therapy, and other methods. José has always inspired me to expand my knowledge, learn more, and to see what is not so easy to see and understand with the naked eye.

When José told me that he was writing a book on this theme, I found it to be fascinating. I was intrigued to read its contents. The stories and reflections that José has captured here will immerse you in a transformative process that allows us to see and feel this larger energy field from another angle, and beyond what we are used to perceiving. The book is divided into three sections, that if read with an open mind, can demonstrate that our true nature is not physical, but spiritual. According to *A Course in Miracles*, a miracle is a change in perception. Throughout the pages of this book, you will have the opportunity to connect with a different type of energy. Perhaps, you may also have a change in perception regarding life and the experiences shared here. We can compare these experiences with what happens in the universe, whose ninety-six percent is invisible to our eyes. Not even the most sophisticated devices can detect or identify some of these unseen elements. However, today we know that these forces do exist because we are aware that light is cut off when it passes through ultra-dense objects, (which are also in and of themselves full of energy). And in that vast field of darkness, we can see the stars, planets, moons, and galaxies.

This book was written in a period of great uncertainty. We ended 2020 and started 2021 in the middle of a pandemic. Millions of people have died alone, and their families have not had the opportunity to say goodbye. Many countries have taken drastic measures to lock down citizens to prevent the virus from spreading. Thousands of companies have suspended functions or gone bankrupt. As a result, millions of people have lost their jobs. Although many countries give economic aid to their citizens, it is not enough, and thousands are in dire need. In many countries, an already volatile social and political climate was thrown into chaos by the pandemic.

During this challenging period, it has become clear to most of us how much all of these things around the world affect us. No matter where on the planet we happen to be, there is a butterfly effect, (a distant butterfly flapping its wings in one continent can cause tidal waves in another). And it is with this understanding that we are all connected, and we share Oneness. It is this concept that challenges us to see beyond what we perceive with our five senses. Life is full of causalities and not mere coincidences. And the fact that you are holding this book in your hands today means that there is something you need to remember to continue evolving, and you can find it in these pages. Be very attentive while reading.

The stories you will find in this book are funny and serious, short and long. They are full of wisdom, love, and knowledge that will transport you into various experiences. If you allow it, these stories will open your eyes and guide you from doubt to discovery. All you need to do is have an open mind and let it expand as much as possible, so that this wonderful journey into the unknown can begin.

The tales in the first section, "Something Extraordinary," help us to understand that the body contains neither the mind nor the soul and that both can be manifested without the need of the body. It is important to remember that these experiences related by the author allow us to leave the ordinary and enter a sacred world, which is not governed by time or space and goes beyond all the limits that we have established as rational. In my case, they have reminded me of my own experiences, and how they have helped me to expand my consciousness, showing me, from an early age, that we are all interconnected in that energy field and that we are manifestations of energy.

The second section, "Stories to Tell," reminds us that we are what we believe in, and we ultimately create what we believe. Here, the author tells us about the thoughts, feelings, and emotions that create our reality. Shamans have taught us that time is not linear. It does not manifest itself as an arrow that goes from the past to the present and into the future. Instead, it can be circular, or spirals, figure eights, or infinite shapes. This concept of time makes the miracles of synchronicity possible, giving us the opportunity to break free from the chains of causality. Therefore, we are not the product of our past, but we can be a creation of the future and we can live in a world where everything is possible.

The third section, "It's all in Your Dreams," reminds us of how our dreams are weaving what we perceive and that we yearn to form what we experience while our conscious mind rests. This section has to do with congruence, the concept of what we think we are, and the truth of what we really are. This congruence dictates our life. It fulfills us or makes us feel like impostors. It infuses us with energy and gives us the strength to achieve what we desire, or it fills us with fears, judgments, and doubts. At the same time, it connects us with that state in which we can perceive the energy of other beings around us, and it becomes entangled. We are more than the labels we put on ourselves and others.

Each section of this book shows us that reality is more expansive than our limited awareness allows us to perceive. It is an open invitation for each of us to open our minds and allow these stories to become a collection of transformative possibilities. As Dr. Brian Weiss said in his book *Miracles Exist*, "An understanding of our higher nature, (that we are the soul, not the body or the brain), leads to profound changes in core values and aspirations. And then the most important transformation begins. The conscience is awakened, which opens its divine but lethargic eyes and distinguishes its spiritual path." Treat this title as a tool to discover your full potential.

— Waleska Guerrero

Something Extraordinary

"Reality is merely an illusion, albeit a very persistent one."
– Albert Einstein

The following true-life stories demonstrate that reality is far more expansive than our limited conscious logical mind can conceive. Perhaps by reading the content in this section of the book, the reader will understand that the identity of Self can exist in the material world, whether it possesses a physical body or not. In other words, consciousness does not end when "it leaves the body," as in the case of out-of-body experience or physical death. We have been conditioned to believe that our brain does all the thinking. This is not the case. Under certain conditions, consciousness or awareness of self can be perceived above, beside, or even far away from the body.

Consider the following analogy. Imagine that the human body is a drone and the mind (not the brain) the pilot. If the drone ceases to function (it dies), does the pilot also cease to exist? Of course not. That is because the pilot is not the drone nor lives inside the drone. In today's highly material world, some individuals get confused and truly believe that they are the drone. But in reality, all the pilot has to do is wait for the right time and conditions to get a new drone to fly again. This metaphor represents the process of how consciousness utilizes different vehicles to navigate multiple realities, including the physical universe.

As you read the following stories, keep in mind that every individual possesses unique qualities, perception, and abilities that they might not understand completely. For this reason, no two experiences will be alike, and no two narrations will follow the same pattern. However, the sequences of events that occurred are closely represented to what transpired, according to their report. Some of the names of the individuals in these stories have been changed to respect their privacy.

Whispers

It is hard to describe on a written page, the experience that we encountered in Castle Darcy. You, the reader, might focus on the site itself or the frightful events that took place, but to really understand what happened, you need to put yourself in our shoes. Pay close attention to all the small details, and try to imagine the feelings and emotions that we experienced. This is the only way that you will be able to understand the undying eeriness that existed in our first home, Castle Darcy.

Fear has the power to hold you, to embrace you, to reject, and to undermine any sense of safety or security. Have you ever had an uneasy feeling without knowing the cause? Have you ever felt weak or threatened without really knowing why? If you have, then you know exactly what we experienced. It was overwhelming.

It was 1962 and we had just gotten married. Bart, my husband, had made, what seemed at the time to be a risky move. He purchased a beautiful site next to the ocean to build our first home, in a small town called Lahinch, on the west coast of Ireland. He had to take out a loan of fifteen hundred pounds to purchase the land and build our house. All of our friends and family told us that we were crazy to borrow that kind of money. In the end, it turned out to be a wise decision.

I was so happy that in less than fifteen months, we were going to have our lovely home, across the road from one of the most beautiful and little known beaches in the whole of Ireland. However, this meant that we had to find a place to stay while they finished building our home. We inquired into renting, and looked at a few properties, and that is how we came across Castle Darcy. We were fortunate, we thought. This relatively large residence was affordable, spacious, and just a short walk from the site that we had purchased. It made perfect sense to stay at Castle Darcy. We would save money and check on the progress of our future house.

We moved in, and in a short amount of time, we settled into our temporary home. Bart began working as a pharmaceutical sales rep. This meant long working days. I was in the process of finding a job as a teacher, so it was up to me to take care of most of the household chores. It was a Monday afternoon, just a couple of weeks since we had moved in, when strange things began to happen. I was cleaning the kitchen counter.

"I see that. Shhh."

I heard a muffled whisper, followed by distant laughter. Shivers ran down my spine. I instinctively turned around and pressed my back against the kitchen cabinet. My heart sank, as cold air filled my lungs. My two hands held tight to the edge of the wooden frame. I looked around in a panic but saw nothing and heard nothing. What would you have done?

I can tell you from experience, a situation like this one can leave you feeling confused and questioning your sanity. The silence seemed to last an eternity. I knew I was alone in the house. It would be several hours before Bart would be home.

"Who is there?" I purposelessly asked out loud to break the chilling stillness.

There was no answer to my desperate inquiry, which came both as a relief and a frightening mystery.

After a few minutes, I cautiously began inspecting each room, even the bedrooms on the second floor. Next, I went outside to look around the house. There was no one there, except for the cold drizzle that you would expect on an autumn day in Ireland. I went inside again and sat at the kitchen table. My logical mind began to rationalize what had just occurred. It was probably the voices of one of our neighbors, carried by the wind.

By the time Bart arrived, I was calm. I told him about the incident over dinner. He agreed with me that it probably was the voice of one of our neighbors, carried by the wind. We finished our meal and got ready to go to bed. Back then, we did not own a TV set. However, we did own a new gramophone. In those days, I had no problem falling asleep. So, in a matter of a few minutes both, Bart and I were peacefully sleeping. It was two forty-five in the morning.

"He is behind you now."

A whisper woke me up in the darkness. Then I heard a faint giggle outside of our bedroom door. Imagine that for a moment. Imagine that you awaken in the middle of the night to a strange voice whispering. How would you feel?

I looked around in a daze. It was pitch black.

"Bart, Bart, wake up, wake up," I said, shaking him by his shoulder.

"What, what, what?" exclaimed Bart, in confusion.

"There is someone in the house. I just heard someone outside the bedroom door," I answered hastily.

I heard Bart stumble around, as he made his way to the wall switch. The light bulb extinguished the blackness of night. He stood still for a moment, by the door. Our eyes fixed on the bedroom door. Bart slowly reached for the door handle. He warily opened the door and stepped out. I heard him walking as he inspected around. I was petrified with fear. He came back after a few minutes.

"There is no one in the house. All the doors are locked," he remarked.

He reassured me that everything was fine, and suggested that I could have dreamt the whole thing, but I was not one hundred percent convinced. It's not hard to guess that I got very little sleep that night. The next morning, during breakfast, we discussed what had occurred. Just for the sake of my peace of mind, we both agreed that these highly unusual incidents were just merely a matter of nerves and anxiety. Bart always had a way of making things better. He left for work, and I focused on my daily chores. By early afternoon, I was exhausted. The lack of sleep from the previous night caught up with me. I reluctantly decided to take a short nap on the living room couch. I started to drift into a haunting dream. There was a priest, or bishop, or some sort of man of the cloth looking directly at me. He gave me a gentle smile and whispered, "You're not asleep. Shhh," followed by laughter. I woke up after just a few minutes of rest. I sat on the couch for a moment, as I contemplated the bizarre dream.

Bart arrived home earlier than usual that day. He told me that he was a little worried about me. We put on our coats, and we went for a walk. It was cold but not freezing. We passed by our future home. The workmen were leaving. We were both surprised at how far along they had come in just a few weeks. We walked down to the beach and enjoyed the fresh ocean breeze. We could not have been happier. Somehow, we knew we had made the right decision on where to live. The ocean was choppy, and the sound of the waves roared forcefully. We decided to head back home. Bart put on the heat and sat in the living room, reading the newspaper, as I prepared dinner.

We both sat down for dinner. We were discussing what would be my next step, as far as teaching.

"There, there, shh."

A whisper could be heard, followed by an incomprehensible murmur. Bart sat still for a moment. I just looked at him. He obviously heard it too. After that moment of stillness, he leapt to his feet without saying a word. He rushed through the whole house. He looked through every window and walked around the house. He found nothing.

"What was that, Chrissie?" he asked.

"Oh Bart, I'm so glad you heard it too. I thought I was going crazy," I responded.

Bart looked at me and said, "You are not crazy. I heard it too."

"This is not normal, Chrissie. Tomorrow we are going to the priest, and we are going to have him bless this place," Bart blurted out. He seemed to be announcing his intention to someone else besides me.

That night in our bedroom we heard low-pitched, muddled voices. Neither of us could make out exactly what was said, but we heard the chatter. At this point, you might be asking yourself, "Why didn't they just pack up and leave?" Be patient. I will show you that strength comes in many forms.

The following day, we visited our local parish priest. We told him what was happening in this place where we were living. It took some convincing, but the priest agreed to bless the house. That afternoon, he arrived at our door. He sat down with us in the living room, in absolute silence. He was looking for some sort of proof, some evidence of the supernatural claim we were making. However, the only thing we heard was the wind whistling and the bark of a dog in the distance.

He took a small container with holy water and an aspergillum. He slowly walked around the house, sprinkling the holy water in every room. This gave me an immense sense of calmness. Once he finished blessing the whole house, I insisted that he join us for tea and brown bread. He gladly accepted. Neither the priest nor we heard any of the whisperings that night. The priest left, and we were quite at ease. In fact, I clearly remember getting a restful sleep that night.

However, as you might have guessed it, the whispers soon returned. Sometimes I would hear them while cooking, or cleaning, or while lying in bed. Bart would often hear them too. As a matter of fact, it happened so frequently, that we took several different measures to avoid hearing them. For example, I would often play the gramophone at full volume, especially when Bart was away. Other times, I would hum my favorite songs while cleaning around the house. Bart did his best to keep me company, and he even got a dog, so I wouldn't be by myself when he was out of the house.

I remember an incident that happened a few months after we got our dog, named Jewel. Bart and I were fast asleep. All of a sudden, a thump on our bedroom door woke us up. I sat up and remained motionless for a few seconds. I felt my heart pounding in my chest. *Thump, thump, thump!* The blunt strikes on the door seemed to intensify. Even Bart sat frozen in our bed. *Thump, thump, thump!* The door was taking a beating. I gave a faint cry, as I pressed against Bart.

"Chrissie, stay there," commanded Bart.

He slowly got out of bed. I heard his footsteps moving in the dark toward the light switch. When the light came on, I could see that Bart was quite frightened too. This is something that I have only seen once or twice in our long marriage. *Thump, thump, thump!* The pounding of the door seemed to increase, as Bart guardedly approached the door. I intensely watched, as he got ready to open the door. By now, the thumping was so fast and forceful that I thought the door was going to burst open.

"Be careful, Bart!" I exclaimed.

With a quick movement, Bart swung the door open. A dark flash jumped into our room. I screamed, from the top of my lungs. Bart stumbled backward, almost falling. It was Jewel. He was wagging his tale so energetically that his entire back end was swaying from side to side. It took a moment to realize what had happened. Jewel had been outside our bedroom door, wagging his tale. The closer that Bart got to the door, the more excited Jewel got, therefore wagging his tail with more intensity. Needless to say, from that day forward, Jewel slept at the foot of our bed.

We endured the whispering and murmurs for the entire time that we lived in Castle Darcy. Some days were quiet and other times the murmuring was non-stop. We could never really understand what was said, but somehow, we felt that the voice or voices were never malicious. Of course, that did not make it less frightening. On a nice, summer day, while we were working in the garden, an older man, (who had lived his entire life in that area), just happened to be passing by. He approached us and introduced himself. During our conversation, he casually mentioned that Castle Darcy was haunted. Bart and I looked at each other in shock.

"Yes, I tell you, Castle Darcy, is haunted by the spirit of the old bishop," stated the man.

"Who was this bishop?" asked Bart.

"Well, he was the previous bishop. No one knows how he died, but this was his residence, and this is where they found him dead," the old man explained.

I asked him if he remembered the bishop. To my surprise, he described the man that I had seen in my dream, just a few weeks after we had moved in. Not too long after we spoke to the older man, we finally moved into our new home. We left Castle Darcy and the whispers that haunt its walls. I never stepped inside that property again, even though it was vacant for a long time.

Can you blame me? It was not a pleasant way to start our married life, but it proved to us, that our love is stronger than the supernatural and the after-life. Reader, do you think you could have handled this experience better? Or maybe you think this is just a made up ghost story. Well, Castle Darcy is as real as I am. The bones of the house are still standing, and the property is still vacant. To this day, what's left of Castle Darcy is located in Lahinch, County Clare, Ireland.

The Curious Visitor

In my role as a life coach and clinical hypnotherapist, I often come across inexplicable events and phenomena that most people would probably have a hard time accepting or believing. I do my best to handle these events with an open mind, without judgment, or interpretation. By remaining neutral, I prevent my own worldview and perception to contaminate the process, as this would limit my ability to help my clients.

I have found that hypnosis is one of the best tools to discover, understand, and heal deep unconscious obstacles and limitations, which can slow down personal, emotional, and spiritual growth.

When a new client, John, asked me if we could conduct a past life regression, I reassured him that we could do this, if that is what he wanted. I was not surprised at all when he requested this. After all, this is a question that I hear from my clients at least once a month.

After a forty-five-minute conversation to figure out why he wanted to do a past life regression, John explained that somehow he sensed that many of the problems he was facing at present, stemmed from long ago. He could not explain why he felt this way, but he mentioned that as long as he could remember, he always carried a deep feeling of being restrained or limited, even in his childhood.

John's life dissatisfaction did not stem from exceedingly unusual conditions. But he understood that no matter how many life goals he accomplished, he never felt genuinely happy because there was a constant barrier in the back of his mind. This feeling had a detrimental effect on his life. John was the type of person that always put other people's needs before his. He just couldn't say no. Consequently, he allowed others to take advantage of him.

In the last hour of our first session, we focused on resolving basic emotional issues utilizing NLP exercises and hypnosis. During this process, I became aware that John possessed the natural ability to enter into a deep hypnotic trance in a matter of minutes. Needless to say, it was a joy working with him.

A few weeks later, during our third session, late in the afternoon, John was lying back on the recliner, and we were exploring a past life memory. He was vividly engaged in a traumatic experience. He was shaking, whimpering, and breathing fast. After a lengthy healing process, John felt at peace. He appeared calm and relaxed. Slowly, he emerged from the trance. He opened his eyes and stared at the empty wall in front of him, for a couple of minutes, in complete silence. I was sitting to his right, close to him.

"Do you know that there is an old man by the wall?" John asked, quietly.

I turned around. There was no one there. I turned back around and faced John.

"I'm sorry, John, but I don't see anyone there," I responded, casually.

"Well, he's there in front of us," he replied matter-of-factly.

Since I did not want to contradict my client, I went along. After a moment of hesitation, I asked, "What is he doing?"

"He is just standing there, watching us," he answered, softly.

I paused for a moment and focused on John's face. His pupils were dilated. He was still under the effects of hypnosis.

"What can you tell me about him, John?" I asked.

"Well, he is an old man, medium height. He has a long white beard and…," he paused for a moment, "and he's wearing a black hat, black pants, black shoes, and a long black coat."

Once again, I turned around but did not see or feel any presence in the room. I turned my attention back to my client.

"So, what do you think he is doing here?" I asked.

"He is curious about what we are doing," he said patiently.

"Is he saying anything?" I asked.

"No, he's just standing there, and he wants to know what we are doing," he answered.

"Can you talk to him?" I asked, with contained excitement.

"Nope," he said in a dismissive tone.

"What is he doing now?" I inquired.

"He is leaving," he responded, after a long pause.

"Is he still there?" I asked.

"No, he is gone. He retrieved into the wall and disappeared," he answered, casually.

"Interesting. Can you just let me know if he comes back?" I asked, calmly.

"Okay," he responded.

By now I could tell that John was fully conscious and aware. He continued to look calm and relaxed. We spoke briefly about the incident, and after a few minutes, John left the office. I stayed at the office for another thirty minutes. During this time, nothing out of the ordinary happened. Once I had collected what I needed to take home, I also left the office.

To tell you the truth, I did not make too much of the event. I thought the interaction with my client had been both unusual and interesting, but as I mentioned before, I tend to not judge my clients' experiences.

The following week, John informed me that he was feeling better. He also appeared to be more energetic and joyful. So, we focused on reinforcing positive behavior patterns and integrating more NLP techniques designed to help him improve self-awareness, confidence, and communication skills. The session went smoothly, and without any incidents. He left the office feeling happy and enthusiastic.

The following week, I was conducting another late session with a very pleasant and kind natured client, Luz. After a long dialogue, we moved into hypnosis. She was in a deep hypnotic trance in no time. During the process, she experienced a number of strong emotions, which she was able to resolve. She received the answers that she sought and was able to understand some of the issues that she was dealing with at the time.

It was time to bring Luz back to full consciousness. She slowly emerged from the trance, and as she opened her eyes, she turned her head toward me. I was sitting to her right. She stared silently at me for a long time.

"How are you feeling?" I asked.

She did not respond. I realized that she was not looking at me. She was looking behind me. I turned around to see what she was focusing on. There was nothing there except my desk.

"Do you know that a man is standing over there?" she asked, with a monotone voice.

I immediately remembered the incident with John.

"Really? What does he look like?" I asked, with great curiosity.

"He is an old man," she answered.

"What is he wearing?" I asked.

"He is wearing a long black coat with blank pants and a black hat," she replied, calmly.

Needless to say, I was surprised. Here was another person describing what seemed to be the same man that John had previously seen. Luz and John didn't know each other, and at no point were they ever in my office building at the same time. So how was this possible? I pressed on.

"What else can you tell me about him?" I whispered to Luz.

"He is tall and has a long white beard. He looks like an orthodox Jewish man," she replied.

"What is he doing?" I asked.

Luz remained quiet. Her eyes remained fixed on the same spot for several minutes.

"What is he doing, Luz?" I repeated.

"Nothing," she replied.

"What do you think he wants?" I whispered.

"He is curious about what we are doing," Luz answered.

"Can you talk to him?" I asked.

"I don't think he wants to talk," was her response.

I turned my attention toward the spot where this man was supposed to be standing. For a moment, I tried to relax my gaze, in an attempt to catch sight of the curious visitor. But seeing him was not a matter of eyesight. It was a state of mind. I did not see or feel his presence.

"He is leaving," announced Luz.

"Which direction is he taking?" was my hurried inquiry.

"Through that wall," replied Luz, while pointing at the bare wall in front of her.

I looked toward the direction that she was pointing, expecting to see something, but once again, I saw nothing but an empty wall.

"He's gone," exclaimed Luz.

"Well, thank you," I paused for a moment and then continued. "What an interesting experience. How did you feel while you were looking at that man?"

"At the beginning, I was surprised, but then I felt normal," explained Luz.

"Were you not afraid?" I asked.

"No, I don't know why, but I was not afraid. Besides, he did not seem scary. He was just an old man watching us," was Luz's quick and calm reply.

"Interesting," I responded.

After a few minutes, Luz was fully alert and ready to go. She left in a hurry after we made an appointment for the following week. I spent a few minutes reflecting on the event that had just occurred. I even wondered if the man was back again, watching me. And as I left the office that night, I made a point to stop by the Chabad (Jewish place of worship), next door, just to say "good night" to the Rabbi.

Chemon

This fascinating story began one quiet afternoon, in the early summer of 2003. I made an important call to speak to my father in Nicaragua. In fact, it turned out to be the last time my father would talk to me. I just didn't know it at the time. You see, my father had to undergo critical surgery to remove a malignant tumor in his throat. The growth was starting to obstruct his airway. This issue was only one of many health complications that my father was dealing with at the time. We spoke briefly about how we felt about each other, and I wished him good luck. He was a man of few words when it came to conversations over the phone. I promised him that I would call him as soon as he was discharged from the hospital. At the time, he was living with my Aunt Fatima in Managua, the capital of Nicaragua.

The following day, the surgeon was able to remove the tumor successfully, but unfortunately, my father lost his voice permanently. So, we could no longer communicate over the phone. This happened before the age of smartphones and texting. After speaking with family members, I decided to wait for a couple of months, until my father fully recuperated from the operation. By fall, he was back to his old self, so I was told. I made the arrangements, took a week off from work, and flew down to Nicaragua.

After a short three-hour flight, I arrived in Managua. My father and my cousin, Octavo, were already waiting for me at the airport. I was anxious to see him. I did not know what to expect. I recall wondering if he would look the same or if I would not recognize him, since he had been through so much. I made my way through customs and arrived at the terminal. There, I saw them both, and to my surprise, my father looked great. He seemed like a different man, a healthy man. I was so happy to see him looking so well. We hugged and greeted each other. I grabbed my bags and started walking toward the exit. I kept looking at him and noticed that there was something different about him. At the time, I could not put my finger on it, but there was something peculiar about him.

After a forty-five minute drive, we arrived at my Aunt Fatima's house. This is where I would stay for the duration of my visit. There was a small family gathering waiting for us. We all talked for a while, made plans, and agreed to meet later. I was genuinely happy to be back in Nicaragua. There is always something to do, like family gatherings, delicious lunches, dinner outings, and beautiful scenic day trips. Our family is very close, and everyone always makes an effort to spend time together.

However, one afternoon I found myself watching TV alone in the living room. Besides me, the only other person in the house was my father, and he was in his bedroom. It was getting dark. I didn't hear a sound when he approached. The next thing I knew, I felt a tap on my left shoulder. My father was standing next to me. With a hand gesture, he asked me to follow him to his room. Once inside, he asked me to sit down on his bed and to pay close attention to what he had to communicate to me. With gestures and writing, he told me something that I could not have anticipated.

He began by telling me that during the operation, he had passed away. I was shocked but remained silent. Nothing could have prepared me for what followed. He told me that he clearly remembered everything, from the moment that he lay down on the operating bed, to the instant when everything went dark. He recalled that suddenly, he opened his eyes and saw that he was standing in the middle of a peaceful prairie, with green rolling hills all around him, and not a single person, as far as he could see. The warm sun was hanging high in a beautiful blue sky. He remembered feeling a warm, comforting breeze brush against his face. He was confused because he could not remember how he got to that place, wherever that place was. He emphasized that he was fully conscious and could sense everything in a "normal" way, so it was not a dream. He stood there for a while, trying to figure out what was going on. He started walking toward the top of one of the hills, and as he got to the top, all he could see was more green hills, all around. He started to run. He reached the top of the next hill, and then the next, and the next.

After running for what seemed like a long time, he stopped. He kept asking himself, "How did I get here?" He admitted that he started to feel disheartened, not knowing what to do. At that moment, he felt someone tapping him on the back of his right shoulder. It startled him. He turned around and saw a man standing next to him. The man was very tall, and fair skinned, with long blond hair, and blue eyes. My father mentioned that the man standing next to him looked identical to a rockstar who he used to admire when he was younger. Somehow, he felt this being was friendly and caring. He experienced a profound sense of calmness, just by standing next to him. He faced this being, in total fascination. With a simple gesture of extending his arm, the tall man asked my father to turn around. My father obeyed, without saying anything. As he turned around, there was an immense mountain, right in front of him. Just seconds before, there had been nothing but green hills.

My father immediately noticed that there were two large caves at the bottom of the mountain. The man that was standing next to him, was also standing next to each of the entrances of the caves. At one entrance, he was wearing a white robe, and at the other entrance, he was wearing a dark robe. My father told me that he was utterly confused. He could not understand the meaning of what was happening. Then the tall being next to him extended his arm again, and my father heard a voice in his head asking him to choose one of the caves. He did not know what to do. He was perplexed. Suddenly, he felt a great sense of despair. His intuition was telling him not to go into any of the caves.

My father turned around and started to run. He ran as fast as he could, hill after hill. As he reached the top of one of those hills, out in the distance, laying on the ground, he saw his own body in gigantic dimensions. He recalled rushing toward it and leaping into it. He told me that is when he felt himself coming back into his own body. The next thing he remembered was waking up in the recovery room.

The experience that he described took me by surprise. You see, my father had been a devout atheist all of his life. He was a non-believer of the spiritual life. All my life, I knew my father as a well-educated man who spoke frankly when he was serious about a subject, so I did not doubt his sincerity. It took me some time to make sense of what happened that night. I realized that I had been right about that feeling I had that day when he picked me up at the airport. There was something different about him. The experience with the tall being had changed him. He was a different man. I know that event changed my father's life, and eventually, it also changed my life.

My father passed away not too long after that experience. But I know now that he is in a better place. Somehow, I have the feeling that he returned to that peaceful prairie, and this time he made the right choice.

Henry Visits Veronica

I remember that night like it was yesterday. This happened when I was just ten years old, a lifetime away. At that time, I was living at my godmother's house. Well, it was more like a vast estate than a simple house. The house had countless bedrooms along the open corridors that hugged not one, but two, enormous courtyards, right in the middle of the estate. There were all types of exotic birds and animals on the grounds, along with a four-car garage, and a small orchard of pomegranate in the back yard. My room was at the very back of this massive building they called a home. When I say "they," I refer to my godmother and her husband. That is right, only two people lived in that extravagant residence.

To tell you the truth, up to this day, I do not know how my father knew the lady who I called my godmother. For you see, we came from the humblest of backgrounds. Our family was poor. So how this extremely wealthy woman came to be my godmother is a mystery to me, up to this day. Anyhow, that is not important. Unfortunately, around the age of eight, my family suffered the worst calamity that can happen to any family. Both of our parents fell gravely ill. Our family was separated. My two older brothers, two older sisters, and I, were sent to live with either family members or friends. That is how I ended up living with my godmother.

To be honest with you, I am grateful to her for taking me in, but life was not easy at my godmother's house. It was hard work. During the day, an army of servants kept the house as tidy as a museum. Maria was the housekeeper. She oversaw the rest of the staff. There were two cooks, two housemaids, a laundry maid, a butler, two gardeners, a gamekeeper, and of course, the chauffeur. I was a sort of an all-around helping hand. I swept and cleaned the corridors before school, sewed clothing to sell to the hacienda workers, and worked at the small grocery store after school. Twice a week, late in the evening, I served tea and pastry during the wealthy women's bridge game. So, you could say that I was just like the rest of the staff, except that *they* got to go home at the end of the day, and I had to stay.

Well, I don't want to bore you with too many details. For this story to make sense, I just wanted to give you a brief description of where I was at the time when the event happened. As I mentioned before, I remember that night like it was yesterday. I had been suffering from a bad cold for a couple of days. I was running a fever, and my throat was on fire. Outside, a thick charcoal-colored cloud hovered low over the sky of Diriamba. The merciless rain gushed down in every direction. The wind blew forcefully throughout the open corridors, kitchen, and courtyards. The storm slammed shut every window and door that was not closed. Even the clay tiles on the roof made loud high-pitched sounds, as if they were holding on to the structure for dear life. As I lay on my bed, in that dark room, isolated from my godmother and her husband at the far end of the house, my mind began to play tricks on me. Shadow monsters were dancing on the walls of my bedroom. These figures were created by the long, deformed fingers of the old oak tree, that stood right outside of my bedroom window. The wind was howling angrily, like a wild beast, and the whole house shook with the deafening roars of thunder. I was petrified with fear. My blanket covered me from head to toe. Despite feeling drained and weak from my fever, my body wanted to move, as though it wanted to get away from that place as fast as possible. But my mind prevented my body from making the physical effort.

It seemed to me that the night had gotten a hold of time, and was not letting it go. So, I can't tell you the exact hour when it happened, but he came to me just as I was falling asleep. I did not see him, but I felt his presence. My skin crawled, and I could hear myself taking deep suffocating breaths. I couldn't see anything except the sheet covering my face. The more I stared at the sheets, the more I felt the grip of fear taking over me. I tried as hard as possible to think of happy places, but I couldn't shake the feeling that I was not alone, and that someone or something stood close to my bed. The storm went dead silent for a moment. I listened. There was not a single sound. I tried to say something, but my voice failed me.

I was so scared that my whole body went stiff. My heart sank when the metal, mesh wire that held the thin mattress creaked and slowly dipped, as if someone had sat down next to me. I closed my eyes and clutched the pillow. I started to tremble. Then, I felt a soft touch on the back of my throat and down my neck, like a massage. I was frozen for a moment, and felt that I could not contain myself anymore.

I sprang to my feet and looked around in desperation. Lightning strikes illuminated the room for an instant. There was no one there. A cold shiver rippled through every fiber in my body. Darkness flooded the room once more. The thunder shook the walls and window violently. I ran over to the door, unlocked it, opened it, and started running down the open corridor. At that moment, I felt like I was running for my life. Without stopping, I made my way to the front of the house, to my godmother's bedroom. Shaking from head to toe, I pounded on the door. They both came out, startled, and half asleep. Despite my painful throat, I frantically explained what had just happened. With more annoyance than empathy, my godmother tried to explain that I had dreamt the whole thing. She insisted that I had dreamt it all. Can you believe this woman? Anyway, that was the only night during my nine-year stay at my godmother's house that I slept in their room with them, (on a small fold out bed, of course).

The next morning, I was given an earful and punished for my behavior that night. When I returned to my room, there was nothing there. But when I saw myself in the mirror, I could see bruise marks, resembling fingers, on the side of my neck. I showed them to my godmother, but she dismissed the whole thing by telling me that it was self-inflicted. The nerve of that woman. Can you believe that? She insisted that somehow in the middle of the night, while I was "sleeping," I tried to strangle myself. Anyhow, it didn't matter because there was an inescapable and pressing thought in my mind. It was the thought of my father. I sensed that there was something wrong, and I needed to talk to my dad. This request was vigorously denied by my godmother. She told me that I was imagining things, and instructed me to stay in bed, as I was excused from my work duties for the day because I was sick.

The house staff had already arrived and they were hard at work. I stayed in bed until one o'clock in the afternoon. This was the usual time when my godmother and her husband would drive down to their hacienda for a few hours. I approached the housekeeper, Maria. She was always kind to me. I told her exactly what had occurred the previous night. She then blessed herself. I begged her to let me call the Asunción School in Managua. Asunción School was a private school for the privileged, but they also ran a charitable organization for the poor. I contacted one of the nuns, who gave me the worst news any little girl could hear. She informed me that my father had died at the hospital, three days before.

She sounded surprised when I asked about my dad, since she had informed my godmother about his passing on the day that he passed away. A wave of sadness and anger poured over me. Later that day, I confronted my godmother. She told me that she had not wanted to upset me with the news, and that there would have been no point in driving to the hospital, since they had buried him already. Much later, I found out that this was a lie too. Unfortunately, he was never buried, but that is another story.

Henry Visits Angela

I t can never be said that Angela forgot or did not think about her adopted father, Henry. It was in her nature to worry about everyone and everything. She was a lovely and caring woman, who endured many misfortunes throughout her life, but those stories were never mentioned by her own tongue. And one more thing, it can be said, with great certainty, that she was no liar. She always spoke the truth, no matter what; even during those times when telling the truth was not to her advantage.

Anyhow, her adoptive, beloved father, Henry, had been hospitalized for quite some time. She truly adored that man. He had raised and loved her, just like his own children. She often cried secretly, with soft, sad tears, not knowing whether he was alive or dead. She couldn't travel to Managua, where he was hospitalized. She had to take care of her newborn baby, Maritza, all by herself.

"I wish you could come home, father," Angela would say, as she sat by the small makeshift crib, staring at her beautiful baby, who constantly cried with hunger.

The new nineteen-year-old mother was married to an ambitious young carpenter named Miguel. Miguel spent most of his time away from their small, humble, wooden home, which stood in one of the worst neighborhoods, (just outside the capital of Nicaragua), el Open-3.

Angela lived in a state of dullness and melancholy, all through the hot summer months of that year. On that overcast morning, when the unusual event happened, Angela woke up at 7:00 a.m., to help her husband get ready to leave for work. Angela did not break into tears, as she often did, because on that morning, she woke up with a strange sensation that something out of the ordinary was going to occur. She really could not tell what it was, but the feeling was present and intense.

By 9:30 a.m., the typical hustle and bustle of the people walking down the unpaved road in front of the house had ceased. Angela was sitting silently on the chair next to the baby's wooden crib. There was a knock on the front door. Angela's heart began to pound. She took a deep breath and started to walk to the front door, and just as she was about to reach for, what passed for a doorknob, the door slowly opened.

Angela's mouth dropped, her eyes bulged, and for a moment, she felt all the blood in her body rush to her head.

"Don Henry, what are you doing here?" remarked Angela, stumbling over her words.

The man looked disheveled, unshaven, bloated, and sickly. Henry placed his hands together as if praying, and spoke with a soft voice.

"I brought you a little gift for your daughter."

Angela's eyes teared up, as her soul filled with a mixture of joy and sadness.

"But, but, Don Henry, you should not be going around in your condition. Perhaps you should go back to the hospital," said Angela, in a barely audible tone of voice.

Her father laid a sympathetic hand on his daughter's shoulder and said, "I am with you. I am always with you."

Angela reached for the small package that he held between his hands.

"Thank you so much, but you shouldn't have, Don Henry," said Angela.

She looked inside the package. It was a small bag with three pairs of colorful, baby girl underwear.

"It's time for me to go, Angela," said Henry, smiling at his daughter.

"Please, Don Henry, return to the hospital," replied Angela, in tears.

Without saying another word, the old man turned around and walked away. In an instant, he was out of sight. With her head spinning, and bewildered by the strange event, Angela slowly closed the front door.

An hour later, there was another knock on the door. Angela was washing one of her husband's stained white t-shirts on a cement washboard at the back of the house. She made her way to the front door. It was her brother, José. He was silent for a moment. She could see that he was upset and had been crying.

"José, for God's sake, Don Henry came this morning. He should not be walking around in the condition that he is in," remarked Angela.

Her brother, who was leaning against one of the wooden planks that served as a wall, looked at her in shock. He leaned forward toward her.

"But Angela, I just came from the hospital. Our father died three days ago."

The Policeman

———— ❧ ————

I will never forget that night. It happened long ago, before you were even born. It was a different world back then, a very different Ireland altogether. There was nothing in small towns except hope and cold weather. I arrived in Ennis in the middle of the night. The whole town was asleep. There was a deep, somber silence covering the streets. It was so dark, unlike today. Back then there were no streetlights in small towns. In fact, only a few buildings had running power.

Heavy, dark clouds had left the entire town soaked and drenched. No one came out in such terrible weather. Even the moon was nowhere to be seen. I walked, all by myself, on the empty narrow streets. There was a cold, whispering breeze slithering and wrapping itself around me. It was an unpleasant, damp chill that would rattle the bones of any man. I was approaching the main road in the middle of the town. I could see the side of the town church, in the distance.

To tell you the truth, I don't even remember what time it was, but I do know that I wanted to get to the small inn where I was staying for the night. I was freezing. My feet were tired from dancing all night. In those days, you could dance to the best grand bands in Ireland for just a few bobs, and there was no messing around back then. It was all clean fun. They didn't even serve alcohol, only mineral (what we call soda).

As I reached the main road, I crossed the street and began walking along the side of the church. For an instant, the moon emerged from the blanket of clouds covering it. The lonely street became a little less dark. I turned left at the corner of the church. I was ready to cross the street, when I was startled by a toneless voice behind me.

"Where are you going at this time of the night?" a man asked.

I turned around, and to my surprise, a uniformed policeman was leaning against the front wall of the church. His right leg was over the seat of his bicycle.

The soft light of the moon reflected on his face, creating a certain kind of opaque glow.

"I'm heading to the inn. That is where I am staying for the night," I responded.

The solitary policeman remained silent for a moment, just glancing at me. I looked around to see if there was anyone else, but it was just us two souls. I thought I had done something wrong and was in some sort of trouble. That moment of silence hung awkwardly for an awfully long time, so it seemed. To be honest, I got somewhat annoyed, and just when I was ready to turn around to leave, he spoke again, with the same toneless voice.

"Can I walk with you?" he asked.

I thought it was a strange request, but who was I to deny a policeman's petition?

"Of course. That is kind of you," I replied.

He brought his leg down from the seat of the bicycle. Without saying more, we began walking. We did not talk for a whole block. I could hear our steps echoing on the walls of the small homes and buildings along the narrow street. We reached the end of the block. I was just about to turn right, when he spoke again.

"This way is better," he said, pointing to our left. "This way, then we can turn right at the next block."

I was not familiar with the town of Ennis, and I had no reason to distrust the man.

"Sure," I replied.

We walked side by side.

"Do you always work this late into the night?" I asked.

He did not respond right away. His stoic expression was as cold as the air running in my lungs.

"Everything is okay," he answered, as he smiled kindly.

"Well, I appreciate you taking the time to walk with me. I'm not familiar with Ennis," I replied.

At that moment, I turned to him. A chill crept over my entire body. He had vanished. I looked all around me. The street was empty. I was standing by myself in the middle of the road, right in the front door of an old pub. The policeman was gone. I think my face went pale for a moment, as I felt the blood rushing down my body. Looking back now, there was nothing really frightening about that moment, but there was definitely something strange and unnatural in the way the policeman had vanished. One moment he was there, just a step behind me, and then he was gone. I didn't know what to make of the situation.

A veil of dark clouds once again extinguished the moonlight. From the top of the roofs to the ground, a fine mist saturated the whole town. I was the only living soul witnessing the strange events occurring that night. And I don't know if there were any other bizarre happenings in Ennis on that night. I sure could not explain what had happened, but it was way too late to start looking around for the policeman. I started running and did not stop until I reached the inn.

The next morning, I opened my eyes and saw that I was lying down on a soft mattress made of wool. I realized that it was late, and I needed to leave soon. I gathered all of my belongings, took a quick shower, got ready, and left the room. On my way out, I ran into the owner of the inn, Mr. O'Brien. He was standing by the front door, smoking a cigarette. With the event of the previous night fresh in my mind, I wanted to inquire about the strange vanishing policeman.

"Mr. O'Brien, can I ask you a question?" I asked.

"Sure. What is it Mr. Tannian?" he replied.

I continued to describe the event that had occurred the previous night. He gave a strange look and stopped smoking.

"Can you please describe the policeman again?" he asked.

I repeated the description of the man and his bicycle. Mr. O'Brien blessed himself.

"Mr. Tannian, you've just described the young policeman that was killed, right in front of Kelly's Pub, more than a year ago," answered Mr. O'Brien, with a quavering voice.

That is the whole story, from start to finish. You might think that the whole thing is gobbledygook, but I can assure you that it is a true story. I have no doubt that on that night something really strange happened. I cannot explain it, but it did happen.

I Had a Strange Dream

A few years ago, I had a remarkable experience. My female travel companion and I were in Galicia, in northwestern Spain. I was visiting my mentor and old friend, Cartor Alberte. He was a priest. In fact, he's the person that brought us to Santiago de Compostela, a beautiful city, if ever there was one. We liked it so much, that we decided to stay for a few more days. Unknown to everyone, I was really worried at the time. You see, my eldest daughter, Paola, was back home in Costa Rica. At the time, she was attending the UACA (Universidad Autonoma de Centroamerica), studying architecture. She was working on several projects and preparing for final exams.

I was deeply concerned for her wellbeing. After all, I've always been there to support her, especially during those times when she stayed up all night working on her assignments. I would bring her coffee, give her advice, and lend her a hand, whenever she needed it. So, besides being worried, I also felt sad. That night, while thinking of the whole situation, I fell into some sort of state where I was half asleep and half awake. I felt a strong force that I cannot describe. It was like I was dreaming a very vivid dream.

I dreamt that I walked into my daughter's room, back home in Costa Rica. I saw Paola sitting on the floor, working on an architectural model. Then, I witnessed that she got up, walked to her bed, and lay down. In my dream, I got close to her and put my hand on the top of her head. Afterward, I decided to go out of her bedroom into our living room, where I keep a small shrine. To my surprise, I saw my mother, Lila, who had passed away many years ago. She was sitting on one of the rocking chairs that we keep in that room.

At that moment, I woke up. I was back in our hotel room in Santiago de Compostela, Spain. Leyda was next to me.

"I had a strange dream. I felt like I was transported to our home in Costa Rica," I said, and then continued to tell her the whole experience.

"That is a very interesting dream," Leyda replied.

Anyhow, after a few weeks of enjoying our vacation, it was time to fly back home. Paola picked us up at the airport, and during the drive, she told me something that, up to this day, I find hard to explain.

"Mommy, you won't believe what happened. It was something so incredible!" She paused and continued. "It was late at night when it happened. I was working on the architectural models for my presentation. I was sitting on the floor in my room and I was exhausted. So, I got up and lay down on my bed for a few minutes. Suddenly, I felt your presence in the room. I did not fall asleep because I had a lot more work to do. I just wanted to close my eyes and rest for a moment. But I felt like you put your hand on my head. I opened my eyes halfway, and I saw you for an instant."

"When did this happen? What date?" I asked, in astonishment.

"I will look it up when we get home. It was the night that I was working on the models for my presentation," Paola replied.

To my amazement, it turns out that it was the same time and date that I had my dream, or should I say my "dream."

A Hole in My Heart

In 2009, I told my wife that I kept waking up during the night with a strange feeling in my chest. The best way I could describe it to her was that it felt like there was a hole in my heart. Now, I must tell you, I am not one to complain about ailments. I would rather put up with any type of "discomfort," than go to the emergency room or clinic. However, my wife, who is a registered nurse, insisted that I make an appointment with a cardiologist.

After several months with the uncomfortable feeling coming and going, I agreed. I did my homework and made an appointment with a cardiologist in Kendall, a suburban neighborhood in South Miami. He turned out to be an excellent physician. During my first visit, I had blood work, an EKG, and a cardiac stress test. Before leaving, I sat down with him in his private office. He looked at the result of the EKG and the cardiac stress test.

"Mr. Incer, everything looks great," said the doctor.

"That's great news, doctor," I answered.

"Your heart is fine, and you're the right weight for your height," he added.

"Excellent. Good to hear," I replied.

He asked me about my diet, exercise routine, work, and daily life, in general. I gave him a brief description of my diet and daily routine.

"Well, Mr. Incer, everything looks great," the doctor said again.

"Wonderful," I said.

"I'll see you in six months," the doctor said, politely.

"In six months, doctor?" I asked.

"Yes, come back in six months," he confirmed, firmly.

"Okay," I agreed.

"By the way, my assistant will call you with the results of your labs," he added, before escorting me out of his office.

I left his office, feeling good about the results. But unfortunately, the discomfort continued. By this time, I had been working in advertising for almost twelve years. Deep inside, I felt like I needed a change, something different, maybe another field of work. Don't get me wrong. I enjoyed working in the agency that I worked for, at the time. However, I was burned out. So, I began exploring other career options. It didn't take me long to find what I was looking for, clinical hypnosis. Perhaps, I should say, that it didn't take too long for clinical hypnosis, (and my professor and future mentor), to find me.

It was the norm to stay at the agency for long hours. In fact, it wasn't uncommon to work overnight, two, and even three, days in a row, without going home. It was during one of those nights that I discovered "El Maestro." It had been a long day, and we were not even half way done preparing the material for the client's presentation for the following morning at 10:00 am. Everyone was tired, so we took an hour break to clear our minds or take a snooze. I decided to head down to the underground garage to take a nap in my car.

I leaned the driver's seat all the way back, slightly opened the window, and turned the radio on. For some reason, I decided to listen to a random station on AM radio, which I never listen to. And that's when I heard his voice for the first time. It was the voice of Professor Santiago Aranegui. The show was called "Ayer, Hoy y Mañana," which translates to "Yesterday, Today, and Tomorrow." I cannot tell you the subject matter of the show that night, but what I can tell you is that his voice had a profound impact on me. I remember listening carefully to his monologue. To my surprise, at the end of his show, he announced that a yearlong hypnotherapy course would begin the following month.

Despite having a high fever and a bad case of bronchitis, I was present the following month for the course introduction and meeting with the professors. That is where I met, in person, professor Santiago Aranegui and my future mentor/professor, Flavio Sauza. I enrolled in the course, and I can honestly say that I enjoyed every single class.

After six months of long hours at the agency, classes, and studying, it was time to go back to the cardiologist. Well, during my second visit, I had blood work again, another EKG, and an echocardiogram. And, once again, after all the tests, he briefly sat with me in his office. We spoke about the strange discomfort that I kept experiencing. He turned on a small monitor on his desk and showed me the video of the echocardiogram.

"Mr. Incer, everything looks great," said the doctor.

"Wow, that is great," I responded.

"You have a small leaky valve, which is not a problem and is very common," he added.

"So, everything is okay?" I asked, with a tone of concern.

"I can assure you that your heart is healthy, and there is nothing to worry about," was the doctor's firm reply.

"Okay, doctor, thank you for the great news," I said.

"I will see you in six months, Mr. Incer," he said, smiling.

"Six months?" I asked, dryly.

"Yes, make an appointment at the front desk before you leave," the doctor responded, calmly.

So, once again, I left the doctor's office on a positive note. However, as you might already guess, the discomfort continued to plague me, and to be honest, it was becoming more pronounced.

I continued to work at the agency, attending the classes twice a week, and studying as much as possible. During this process, I began to start understanding the link between mind and body, and psychosomatic medicine. My reader, you are probably aware of the term psychosomatic illness, which means bodily symptom(s) caused by mental or emotional disturbance. The word "psyche," means "of the mind or soul." While the word "soma," means "body." This is an alien concept for many in the medical establishment in large, and the public, in general.

As I mentioned before, the discomfort in my heart continued to bother me. So, I made the decision to take a different approach. I reached out to my professor, Flavio Sauza, who is the founder of the Hypnotherapy and Counseling Center in Pembroke Pines, Florida. I explained the situation and the symptoms I was experiencing. He suggested exploring this issue in a therapeutic setting, so we did. A lot of personal inner conflict came out during our sessions, which I found to be extremely helpful and liberating. The feeling in my heart began to be less intense and less frequent, but it continued to show its ugly head here and there.

By this time, the course had come to an end, we celebrated our graduation, and it was time to put into practice what we had learned. A fellow student, Guillermo Leon, and I, decided to rent a small office in the city of Davie, to start our clinical hypnosis practice. Just like any new business, clients were few and infrequent. Nevertheless, we stuck to it, using our office to see clients and practice hypnosis between ourselves. It was during one of these practices that I suggested to work on the discomfort in my heart that I continued to experience.

This is the account of what transpired during that one session, to the best of my knowledge. My colleague, Guillermo Leon, was conducting the session, and I was the subject. He began the process with a progressive relaxation hypnotic induction. It didn't take me long to slip into a trance.

Guillermo: José, focus on your heart, and I want you to tell me when you can feel the discomfort.

After a few seconds of silence.

José: I can feel it.

Guillermo: Okay, now that you have the feeling, I want you to go to the cause of this feeling. You will be able to see it clearly in your mind, like a picture. See it clearly in your mind.

A minute or two in silence.

José: I don't see anything.

Guillermo: I want you to go back in time and find the cause of that feeling.

A moment in silence.

José: I am coming out of a saloon, like in an old western.

Guillermo: Pause for a moment. Are you a man or a woman?

José: I'm a man.

Guillermo: Look at yourself. How are you dressed?

José: I am dressed all in black, with black boots, black pants, a long-sleeved black shirt, and a black hat.

Guillermo: Look around you. What do you see?

A moment of silence.

José: It's a small western town, with eight or nine wooden buildings around. It is dry and dusty. It is dusk. The sky is vivid orange with scattered clouds.

Guillermo: What else do you see?

José: For some reason, I feel like I am looking for trouble, ready to start a fight or something, like I'm no good.

Guillermo: So you feel like you are no good?

José: Yes.

Guillermo: Why is that?

A few seconds of silence.

José: I don't know. I just feel it.

Guillermo: What else do you see or feel?

Long silence.

José: A man is leaning against a parked wagon, across the dirt road.

Guillermo: What does he look like?

José: He's wearing brown boots, brown pants, a long-sleeved blue shirt, and a white cowboy hat. I cannot see his face clearly.

Guillermo: Do you know this person?

José: No, but somehow, I think I know why he is here.

Guillermo: Why is he there?

José: He is after me.

Guillermo: After you?

José: Yes, I... I think I know but it is not clear.

Guillermo: Anything else about this person?

A moment in silence

José: I am walking away. I have a bad feeling. I am turning down the side of the saloon, onto a small alley.

Guillermo: What happens next?

José: I can hear someone's steps behind me.

Guillermo: What is happening?

José: I am scared. I turn around, and the same man is standing a few steps away from me.

Guillermo: What is happening? I am feeling agitated.

José: He's holding a revolver in his left hand. I can see the gun in great detail. It is silver with a white grip.

Guillermo: What happens next?

José: I open my mouth to say something but, but he shoots me. He shoots me right in the heart.

A long moment of silence.

Guillermo: What do you see?

José: I am dead. I died in the alley. I can see my body from above.

Guillermo: What are you feeling?

José: I am feeling at peace, with a deep sense of calmness within me.

A few minutes of silence, in which I received several messages from what I can only describe as, "another place."

Guillermo: Is there anything else that you see or need to experience?

José: No.

Guillermo: In a moment, I'm going to count to ten. By the time I reach ten, you will open your eyes, and you will be back in the present moment, feeling calm and relaxed. One, two, three, four, five, six, seven, eight, nine, ten. Open your eyes.

Reader, that experience was intense. I thank my colleague and friend for helping me facilitate that experience. I finally gained a clear understanding of why, for all of that time, the only way that I could describe the feeling in my heart to people was that it was like there was a hole in my heart. Not too long after that session, the feeling went away completely. I shared the details of the event in one of the last sessions with my professor. He was glad to hear that I had that experience, and agreed that it was something positive. He also told me something that stuck with me.

"José, do you know why your doctor kept asking you to go back every six months?" asked my professor.

"Because he wanted to know that everything was fine?" I replied with a question, without putting too much thought into his inquiry.

"Because he knew that sooner or later that feeling would manifest itself at the physical level, and he wanted to catch it early," he responded, with a tone of certainty.

Right there and then, it all came together. I clearly understood that my subconscious mind was trying to communicate that, once again, I was no longer on the right path, and I needed to make a change, before something unfortunate happened.

You might be curious about what the messages were that I received toward the end of my past-life regression. Well, I will share one of the messages, which is relevant to this story. I was "told" that the feeling that I had been dealing with will be present each time that I am on the wrong path, just like in the distant past.

The House in Prague

❧

It was our summertime vacation. My wife Deirdre, my mother Veronica, and I drove from Budapest to Bratislava and then to Prague. It was an exciting journey, full of scenic views, quaint little towns, historic cities, and amazingly friendly people. The whole experience was a journey that I will always remember. But I think by now, my reader, you already know that something out of the ordinary must have happened, for me to be sharing this story with you.

Well, it did. It all began when we arrived at our destination, a well kept home in the countryside, about twenty minutes outside of Prague. To this day, I still can't tell you how we managed to find the house that we rented through Airbnb. It was a really nice place, in the middle of nowhere, but somehow, we were able to find it without a GPS. Anyhow, we arrived late, for the same reason mentioned above. Fortunately, the couple that owned the house was waiting for us. It was a two-story house. The ground floor and second floor were connected only by an external stairway. The owners happened to live upstairs and were renting the downstairs. We booked the place for four days and three nights.

Our hosts were friendly and helpful. They were a small family. Bobek and Anezka were husband and wife, with their baby daughter, Anna. They showed us the area of the house where we would stay. It was a large house, with three bedrooms, two baths, a kitchen, and a small living room. As I mentioned before, we arrived late, so we decided to stay in and go to Prague the next day. My wife and I took the large master bedroom, and my mother decided to sleep in a spacious bedroom by the kitchen. After settling in, we walked a few blocks to a corner store, (the only store in the small village), to grab a few supplies to cook for dinner.

We had a good meal, thanks to my mother's cooking. It was already dark, and we were tired after the long drive from Bratislava. Since there was no TV in the house, we decided to turn in early. Besides, we needed to wake up early the next day. My wife and I said good night to my mother, turned the lights off in the kitchen and living room, and went to our bedroom.

I was beat. I brushed my teeth, and I immediately jumped into bed, while my wife stayed in the bathroom brushing her teeth and removing her

• 30 •

makeup. I was lying down on my stomach, awake but with my eyes closed, while waiting for Deirdre to come to bed. Suddenly, someone blew in my ear. I looked up. Deirdre was still in the bathroom. She did not even notice that I sat up in the bed. I looked around. It was only the two of us. I thought it was strange, but after a few seconds, I reasoned that it probably was my imagination. After all, I was exhausted. So, I placed my head down again. A moment later, someone blew in my ear again. I sat up in the bed. This time, I knew it was not my imagination. I knew there was someone or something else in the bedroom, a presence, to be more exact. I could actually feel it. Now, without going into too many details, I've invested many years into learning and practicing metaphysics and mysticism, so I can tell you that this type of stuff doesn't phase me at all. But I knew that if I said something to my wife, she would probably lose sleep over it. Therefore, I calmly lay down again, whispered a few words that I was taught to say, and waited for my wife to come to bed. That night, we both slept like babies.

The following morning, we headed down to Prague. It was everything everyone had told us it would be, and more. There was so much to see, including historic buildings, incredible history, great restaurants, and beautiful art. We had a wonderful time. It was dark by the time we arrived back at the house in the countryside. We had a short conversation with our hosts and decided to head to bed. As I lay down in bed, waiting for Deirdre, I wondered if I was going to be teased by the ear-blowing visitor, but nothing happened that night.

The next morning, I walked to the kitchen, while my wife finished getting ready. We were heading to Prague again. My mother was already in the kitchen, preparing a light breakfast for herself. We started talking about the things that we had seen in the city the previous day, but during our conversation, she interrupted me.

"I need to tell you something. I didn't want to say anything, but something weird has happened over the last two nights," she said, almost whispering.

"What happened?" I asked.

"Well, our first night, when I lay down to sleep…" (I already knew what she was going to say). She continued. "I had turned off all the lights. I was about to fall asleep, when someone blew in my ear."

"Yes," I said.

"Well, I got the fright of my life. I thought there was someone in the bedroom. But when I turned on the lamp, there was no one there," she exclaimed.

"Did something else happen?" I asked.

"Yes, I tried to ignore it. So, after a few minutes, I turned the lights off again and tried my best to fall asleep. Then it happened again. Someone blew in my ear. I turned the lights on and jumped out of bed."

I don't know why, but I almost started laughing. I stopped myself because I didn't want to come across as cold or insensitive.

"I'm glad you told me this because the same thing happened to me the first night we arrived here. I didn't want to say anything, so as not to frighten you or Deirdre," I explained.

"So it happened to you too?" asked my mother, in amazement.

"Yes, but don't say anything to Deirdre. I don't want her to be afraid," I added.

"Did anything happen last night?" I asked quietly.

"Well, no one blew in my ear, but you know the large chair in the corner in the bedroom?" she asked.

I nodded.

"At night, sometimes I feel like someone is sitting there," said my mother, muttering rather than speaking.

"Don't worry. Do your best to ignore it," I responded, trying my best to trivialize the whole thing.

After a short while, Deirdre emerged from the bedroom, ready to get going. So we headed to Prague. And once again, we had a wonderful time. We got to see even more, the second time around, and we also managed to squeeze in a little bit of shopping. So we said goodbye to the capital of the Czech Republic and headed back to the house. We were hungry, by the time we arrived at the house. My mother kindly made spaghetti in a marinara sauce and garlic bread. There was so much food that we decided to invite our hosts. Luckily, they had not eaten supper yet, so they happily agreed to join us. We had a pleasant conversation over dinner. They told us a little about their life. Toward the end of the meal, they shared the history of the house.

"The house used to be only the first floor, where you are staying now, but a few years ago, we decided to add the second story," said Anezka.

"You wanted to add more space?" I asked, with curiosity.

"Well, you see, my husband's mother used to live with us. So, we built the second floor for us, and she lived down here," replied Anezka.

"That is nice," I said and added, "Where is she now?"

"Unfortunately, she passed away," answered Anezka, gazing at the bedroom door by the kitchen.

"I'm sorry to hear that, sorry for your loss," I said, respectfully.

"Don't worry, she died peacefully." She paused for a moment and added,

"She actually passed away in that room," she said, pointing at the room next to the kitchen, where my mother was staying.

There was a brief discreet gaze between my mother and I when we heard this. Early the next morning, we were packed and ready to go back to Budapest. Our gracious hosts came down to say goodbye to us. And as we drove away, I couldn't help but wonder if the grandmother had been present during our departure.

What Happens Next?

When Ed, a man in his early thirties, first contacted me about a past-life regression session, he was concerned about his lack of concentration, which he believed would prevent him from entering a hypnotic trance. I was a bit surprised to hear him say this, since he mentioned that he was a medical student. In my experience with working with medical students, I have found that they can focus with great ease. I reassured him that we could work around this issue.

The day Ed first entered my Fort Lauderdale office, he appeared confident and full of energy. We sat down and began, what ended up being, a long and interesting conversation. Ed mentioned that he never thought too much about the afterlife and that he was not interested in spiritual matters. But a family member had told him about the positive effects of past-life regressions. He became curious and wanted to see if it could help him explain why he found it difficult to make friends and build meaningful relationships.

It took a long time to guide Ed into a trance. I helped him by using a confusion induction, which is amazingly effective for highly analytical individuals who tend to overthink everything they hear. He gradually relaxed. Surprisingly, once fully relaxed, he easily slipped into a past-life regression, which connected into an in-between-life experience.

He moved through different stages within that past lifetime. And once we explored several significant events, I guided Ed to the moment of his death. This is the transcript.

Incer: Ed, slowly I'm going to count to three. By the count of three, you will move to the last moment in that lifetime. One, two, three.

A few seconds of silence.

Incer: Where are you now?

Ed: I am an old man. I am lying in bed and not feeling well. I cannot get up. There are a few people in the room.

Incer: Do you know who they are?

Ed: Yes, they are my family.

A long pause.

Incer: What is happening that you have not yet told me?

Ed: I cannot talk. I spend most of the time looking at the ceiling and thinking about my life. I'm feeling sad thinking about my family and how their lives will be without me.

Incer: Move forward now to the moment you release your physical body. What do you perceive as you experience physical death?

Ed: It's a relief. Peacefully, I just slide out.

Incer: Take a moment and give me your first impression of where you are, in relation to your surroundings.

Ed: I am above my body, right above it. I am floating.

Incer: How do you feel?

Ed: I feel free and very peaceful. And, and, and I feel love, so much love. The feeling is so strong, yet very smooth. I don't know how to describe it.

Incer: What happened next?

Ed: I am ready to go.

Incer: Ready to go where?

Ed: There is someone who came to guide me.

Incer: Who is there to guide you?

Ed: He feels familiar, but I don't recognize him. We start to move up. I am floating up, very fast, up, up.

Incer: Notice the feeling. What are you experiencing?

Ed: I am a little nervous. I don't know where we are going.

A moment of silence.

Incer: What do you notice next?

Ed: We arrive. There is someone waiting for me. I know her. She greets me with a big hug.

Incer: Do you recognize her?

Ed: Yes, she was my younger sister, who died during the war (a family member during that past-lifetime).

Ed begins to experience a flow of strong emotions.

Incer: What happened next?

Ed: She takes me to some sort of garden. It's a very calm and beautiful place. She is holding my hand, and I can feel her love for me.

A few seconds of silence, then Ed tilts his head back a little.

Ed: We are sitting on the ground now, but there is a bright ray of light from above. It's all around me. It feels like it's taking away all sadness and confusion.

For a few minutes, Ed remained silent while displaying a big smile.

Incer: What happened next?

Ed: We are moving again, but now I am some sort of ball of energy, and there are two other balls of light escorting me.

Incer: Okay, allow this transition to happen. How do you feel?

Ed: It feels strange. It's like being weightless, and kind of uncomfortable.

Incer: What happens next?

Ed: Well, I am in some sort of white space. We stopped moving. They are telling me that everything is fine. I feel full of energy, yet very peaceful. I don't know how to explain it. It's like serene energy, but powerful.

Incer: What do you experience next?

A long pause.

Ed: It's strange. All of a sudden, I find myself in front of an open door, like the door of a house.

Incer: What happened next?

Ed: I go in. There is a group of people there. They are cheering. They greet me with hugs and smiles.

Incer: So, you are no longer a ball of energy?

Ed: Yes and no. I cannot explain it.

Incer: That's perfectly fine. Do you recognize anyone in that house that you know in your present life?

Ed: Yes, my brother Nicholas and my best friend, Roger. I am happy that we are together. It feels like one big happy family. But it's strange that we are all inside a house, you know, like in this world, (physical world).

I took the liberty to explain the concept of perception to Ed to clear any confusion.

Incer: What you are experiencing is real, but your perception of these events is a projection of your mind. Your mind is using your imagination to perceive the experience.

I continue after a short pause.

Incer: What happened next?

Ed: It seems like I spend a long time in that place. Much of the time, I just talk to my family (soul family). Three of them are very wise. They tell me that they are proud of me. I have learned a lot about forgiveness. They are incredibly wise. I feel like they are so much more advanced than me. They want me to continue learning about forgiveness.

Long silence.

Incer: What is happening now?

Ed: They are asking me to choose my next life.

Incer: How do you feel?

Ed: I'm feeling anxious. I really don't want to leave. I feel comfortable where I am. I don't want to leave. They are telling me that everything is going to be fine. Their energy is reassuring.

Incer: What happens next?

Ed: They are asking me if I want to be a man or a woman in my next life. They show me different scenarios. It's like watching a show on TV. But it's funny, I can choose to go into different places, not just on Earth, but other planets and dimensions. Some of these experiences are pleasant, and others are kind of scary.

Incer: At the count of three, you are going to move forward in the spiritual world, to the moment you choose your body. One, two, three.

Ed: I have made my choice. I chose a male body. I will be born into a large family. I was careful in choosing this body. The main reason why I chose this body is because it is strong and quite resistant to ailments. I will need it in my medical career. But it makes life a little harder because it is not very receptive to sensitivity or emotions.

Incer: What is your main purpose for coming, this time around?

Long pause.

Ed: I must learn to accept everybody for who they are, without judgment. I must learn to be more forgiving toward others, especially those who think and act differently than me. And I must learn to be patient.

Incer: Wonderful. As you start to leave this higher realm between your lives on Earth, take a moment to remember that this beautiful and peaceful place is always within you. You will remember this whole experience, and it will serve as a life lesson for you to review and learn from it.

I paused for a moment to allow Ed to process the instructions that I was giving him.

Incer: Now, as I count from one to five, you will feel completely whole, your mind and body fully integrated. You are slowly coming back to the present moment, to your present life. One, two, three, four, five. Open your eyes.

What Do I Do?

Josh, Michael, Sue, Nicole, and I walked into the old barn at our Uncle Friedrich's farm. We were just having fun and messing around. I happened to spot a rope hanging from a beam, high up in the roof. I thought it would be fun to swing from it, like Tarzan. So, without giving it a second thought, I climbed to the second floor, and with rope in hand, I jumped. I swung for a brief second before hearing a loud breaking sound. The beam on the roof cracked, and a part of the roof caved in. I came crashing onto the ground.

Everyone took cover from the falling debris. It took a minute or two before the dust settled. I was horrified when I saw the damage that I had caused. As long as I can remember, I'd always been afraid of my Uncle Friedrich. He was a stern man with a bad temper, and notorious for humiliating and belittling people. I was petrified. I knew he was going to eat me alive. Feeling my skin crawl, I looked at the barn door. I knew it was just a matter of time before he would walk through that door. The more I stared at the door, the more panicked I felt. As much as I wanted to run out of that barn, I knew I couldn't.

Neither Josh, Michael, Sue, nor Nicole said anything. The barn was silent. We all knew what would happen when our Uncle Freidrich found out what happened. Chills ran down my spine. A ray of sunlight entered through the hole in the roof. My stomach twisted into a knot when I heard footsteps approaching the barn. I clutched the front of my t-shirt with cold sweaty hands. I felt like I couldn't contain myself for another moment. I wanted to get as far away from the barn as possible, and just at that moment, he appeared by the doorway.

I sucked air into my lungs, as I sat up in bed. For a moment, I thought that I was suffocating, but I quickly realized that I was dreaming. It was all a dream. Knowing that it was only a dream, I felt a great sense of relief. I almost started laughing.

Riiing! The doorbell rang. That must have been what woke me up. Nancy, my wife was not in bed. *Riiing!* I slowly got up and walked downstairs. *Riiing!* I was surprised to see that I was by myself. When I got to the front door, I looked through the side window to see who it was. But there was no one at the door. "Maybe I took too long to answer the door," I thought. I decided to go upstairs again. As I walked into our room, I got a fright. There was someone lying down in my bed. I approached cautiously, as I had a feeling that there was something odd. As I got close, I saw myself sleeping on the bed.

For a moment, I stood there, looking at myself, without knowing what to do. What was happening? What was I looking at? Without taking my eyes away from my body, lying down in bed, I could only ask myself, "What do I do?" Fear crept over my whole body. At that instant, I snapped back into my body, (which was lying down in bed), as I "woke up." I looked around, in a daze. There was no one around. I got up and looked back, to make sure that I was not still lying down in bed. I walked downstairs to find out that there was no home. I was by myself.

I didn't know how to process what had happened. Perhaps, I dreamt the whole thing. Whatever it was, I did not share it with anyone. I didn't want anyone to think that I was losing my marbles.

A few days later, I was visiting an old girlfriend. She had invited me over, knowing very well that her mother was going to go out. After watching TV for a while, we headed to her bedroom. As much as I liked the idea, I knew it was wrong. Her mother was due home at any moment, but she insisted that we fool around. A part of me wanted to stay, but the other part wanted to leave, to avoid an ugly scene. And that's when we heard someone entering the house.

I felt a sense of panic take hold of my whole being. I looked around to see where I could hide, but her room was quite small. We could hear voices approaching the room. I felt my heart sink when I saw the doorknob turning slowly. I took three steps backward, as I prepared to face the wrath of her mother, or whoever was outside the room. A wave of electricity ran down my body, when someone slowly opened the door.

At that moment, I sat up in my bed, my heart still racing. Once again, I felt a great sense of relief when I realized that I was dreaming. That's right. It was only a dream. It was the middle of the night. I looked around and saw myself sleeping right next to my wife, Nancy.

In that instant, I snapped back into my body, as I woke up again. I was taking deep breaths, involuntarily. I was confused and couldn't believe that this experience had occurred again. I sat in the dark for a while, not knowing what to think or do. And just like the previous time, I did not mention what had happened to anyone. I began to worry, thinking that perhaps there was something wrong with me.

I decided to do my best to ignore these two incidents. Besides, I had a lot going on at work, and I couldn't be distracted with something that was, for the most part, inexplicable. My job was very demanding and highly stressful. Add to that, taking care of three kids, and all the chores around the house, and can you begin to get a clear picture of the mental and physical strain that I had to deal with at that time.

On this particular night, Nancy decided to go to bed early. I stayed up with the kids, watching TV. I don't remember the exact time, but Chris, my youngest son, was falling asleep. So, I decided to put him to bed, and since I didn't want to disturb Nancy, I decided to sleep in the same bed, with my youngest child. I was falling asleep, when I heard the phone ring. Drowsily, I searched around the nightstand for the phone, but I couldn't find it. I realized that I probably had left it by the TV. I got up and walked to the living room. I saw our dog, Buster, sitting next to the couch. As I got close to the table, the dog spoke and said, "The phone rang."

It startled me. Immediately, I woke up in Chris's bed. It was morning already.

Nancy walked into the room and asked if I knew where the passports were. I told her they were inside the safe. She asked me if I could get them for her. So I headed to the closet in our bedroom. I keyed the combination, opened the safe, and grabbed the passports. Just when I was ready to hand them to her, I realized that I had remembered the combination to open the safe, which I never do. So, I told myself that I must be dreaming.

I frantically grabbed a piece of paper and wrote on it, "I wrote this while I was sleeping." I placed the piece of paper in the safe and closed it. I stood up and told myself that I needed to wake up.

When I woke up, still not a hundred percent convinced that I was not in another dream, I looked around the room. It was morning. Somewhat agitated, I looked for my wallet. Nancy, who was sitting on the bed next to me, asked what was wrong.

"I need to open the safe, Nancy," I responded.

She asked me if everything was okay.

"You will see Nancy. You will see," I replied, in haste.

I took the safe combination, which I kept in my wallet, and walked to the back of the closet. Nancy followed me. I opened the safe, put my hand in it, and took out a small piece of paper that read, "I wrote this while I was sleeping."

I don't need to tell you that I thought I was going crazy. How could I explain what was happening? Who would believe me? I think the hardest thing to deal with throughout the whole ordeal, was not being able to share with anyone what was happening to me.

Now, other minor things happened along the way, but there was something more important happening at home. The relationship between my wife and I began to deteriorate. So, I made a bigger effort to ignore all these strange things that were happening, in order to focus on my marriage. We had a long conversation, and I did my best to stay positive throughout the whole process. I had many sleepless nights. We were still sleeping together. I remember this particular night when I got up to go to the bathroom and stood up in front of the toilet, for I don't know how long, without even going. It was dark, and for some unknown reason, I walked out of our room, without even looking at the bed. I headed downstairs, and was frightened to see four elderly people sitting on my couch.

"Don't be afraid, sir. We are dead, and we need your help," one of them said.

I just stood there, not knowing what to think or say.

"We need for you to help us, sir," said another.

"Why are you here?" I asked.

"We need you to help us," said another.

"No, I will not help you," I exclaimed.

Without looking back, I went up the stairs and walked into my room. There I was, or should I say, there *it* was, my body, lying down next to Nancy. I proceeded to sit down and lay on my own body. At that moment, I woke up.

Not too long after that incident, I woke up, in the middle of the night, to find a man standing by the foot of the bed. He was tall with dark skin. Believe it or not, I was not startled or afraid. For some reason, his presence created a sense of peace within me.

He asked me to follow him. We walked downstairs. When we reached the living room, I noticed that he was holding a spoon in one of his hands. He placed his hand in front of him and made the spoon levitate. Then he made it spin, without touching it. I was mesmerized.

"You know that you are capable of doing this too," he said, confidently.

"How could I do that?" I asked.

"Well, George, as you are well aware, everything is energy. Even what you perceive as matter is just energy," he explained.

"Yes, I am aware of this," I replied.

"Well, energy can be channeled and manipulated by the mind. So, all you have to do is focus your mind, visualize, and direct your thought at the spoon. Here, you try it," he said, as he handed me the spoon.

I took the spoon and did my best to focus my mind, visualize, and direct my thought. I managed to slightly move the spoon in the air, but it fell back on my hand.

"Don't worry, it takes practice," he explained.

We spoke briefly, and we walked back to my room. I lay down on top of my body and immediately woke up. By now, these types of experiences were happening so often, you could say that I got used to them.

Several months later, things were not going well at all. Work continued to be stressful and my marriage was falling apart. I felt physically, mentally, and emotionally wasted. I woke up in the middle of the night to find the same man standing by the bed again. I got up, greeted him, and followed him to the attic. There, he stood in front of me.

"George, you are completely drained. You have no energy at all," he said, with a faint smile.

"Yes, I know," I replied.

"You need energy. You need energy to make decisions, to choose, to take action. Without it, you won't be able to accomplish anything," he explained.

"I can feel it. I am drained," I confirmed.

"I'm going to transfer energy to you," he said, as he lifted his right arm.

His whole body became a bright light. He grabbed my left hand and I felt a surge of energy, like an electric current, running through my entire body. It was a strange feeling, but the effect was invigorating. This continued for a few minutes, until I felt recharged. All of a sudden, I had the urge to do something, to be active, to move. I was without a specific goal or purpose, but I felt the need to do something.

"Everything is going to be fine," he stated, with confidence.

"Thank you," I responded, gratefully.

"If you remind yourself often that everything will be fine, you will be able to keep your energy. Never doubt. Doubt drains your energy. Remember that," he explained.

"I will," I responded.

We had a short conversation and walked down to my bedroom again. We said goodbye, and I entered back into my body.

Throughout this difficult phase in my life, I had to overcome many obstacles and figure out how to resolve painful challenges. I now feel that I am once again on the right path. Believe me when I say that things are definitely a lot better now. I have not had another out-of-body experience, (or whatever you want to call it), in a while, but I no longer fear it or hide away from it. I now see it as something positive, a type of lesson to learn.

Stories to tell

"Imagination is the beginning of creation."
– George Bernard Shaw

There is an endless flow of creativity, beyond the limits of our logical mind. It is a stream of ideas, concepts, stories, and inventions waiting to be discovered and expressed. The key to unlocking the vault to this infinite and limitless universe is courage. That's right, the courage to face your fears, uncertainty, and self-doubt. It is the courage to explore your inner world, to look within, and find the source of your Self-expression. (Self with a capital "S" refers to the higher Self or higher consciousness. Not to be confused with self-expression, which is the expression of our own personality or ego.)

There is a border line, which stands between our mind and the material world, between the conscious and the unconscious. It is a place where thoughts merge and channel into perception, a mental impression that flows and is communicated through the senses. After all, our world is the result of these mental impressions. They are the impressions of the collective unconscious, (that vast ocean of creative energy where all forms, concepts, and thoughts stem from). Fortunately, there are many techniques that we can use to reach inside and go beyond this border line. Hypnosis, meditation, out-of-body exploration (commonly referred to as astral projection), hypnagogia, and lucid dreaming, are just a few of the techniques. If you apply yourself to master any of these tools, you truly will become the captain of your own ship, the dreamer of your dreams. As a result, any self-limiting beliefs that forge ideas that your life is at the mercy of the world, would be unacceptable to you.

Most of the work you will read in this section of the book was bestowed to the author during self-hypnosis or deep meditation episodes. In other words, the origin of all the tales you are about to read was purely unconscious, drafted immediately upon emerging from a hypnotic or meditative trance, and later written and edited. I hope you enjoy them.

The Observer

When I was a child, I read a quote that would set the course for the rest of my life. The author was English physicist, astronomer, and mathematician, Sir James Jeans. The quote read, "The universe begins to look more like a great thought than a great machine."

Of course, he was referring to quantum mechanics, the mechanism that governs everything in the universe. This is the branch of physics that challenges our conventional worldview. So, before I begin to relate my story, please allow me to explain, in the simplest way possible, the undisputed truth that quantum physics has demonstrated. Quantum theory declares that the observation of an object to be someplace, causes it to be there. In fact, its existence at that specific place becomes an actuality, only because of its observation. In other words, an object, let's say an atom, does not exist until it is observed. And since all things that we interact with daily are just a group or collection of atoms, what does this say about reality? Quantum theory also asserts that the observation of one object can instantaneously influence the behavior of another, even if they are "separated" by a great distance. Quantum mechanics seems to deny the existence of a physical world, independent of observation. I know this can be hard to believe. Never mind understanding it. I can assure you that these are the irrefutable facts that quantum theory tells us. Please look it up. You may question the validity of my story, but the science is undisputed.

I believe that Sir James Jeans intuitively understood what I am set to prove, empirically. Before I take my last breath, my mind will not rest, unless I reveal what really happened to me. I intend to awaken humanity, lift the dark veil that has blinded us for so long, and to finally face up to the true nature of reality and consciousness. But to accomplish this, it will require a great mental effort on your part. Bringing illusion to truth can be hard, even painful, for illusions can seem so real.

Through this experiment, I was plunged into the depth of the unknown and forced to face a mortal fear that haunts most humans. That is the fear of confronting the unconscious. I have come to understand what the ancient mystics and prophets revealed and what modern quantum physicists have encountered, but refuse to deal with or even acknowledge. That is consciousness and the true nature of reality. By the way of this experiment, I have experienced the whole spectrum of humanity, and realized that the human experience is but the simple observation, from the highest point of awareness, to the lowest form of perception. But I am getting ahead of myself.

You might be asking yourself, "Who are you?"

Okay, let me ask you first. "Who are you?"

Yes, "you," who is reading these words. What is your name? Well, that is exactly who I am. I realize that I'm confusing you with my words. I was also confused for a long time, until I chose to accept the true nature of reality. In the midst of the Giza Plateau, I was Rameses. In China, I was Confucius. I was the embodiment of Marcus Aurelius and the Mayan King, Kapal, as well as the Sufi mystic, Rumi, and the great scientist, Paracelsus. My contemporaries call me Julian Moore, but I am also called the many names yet to come. I now find myself echoing the words of the great German philosopher, Nietzsche. These words are, "Fundamentally, I am every name in history."

This notion is not born from a defected mind, or from psychic inflation, or even from the loss of touch with my own ego. Instead, it rises from a direct encounter with the limitless and the all-impersonal collective consciousness that lies in the deepest and darkest regions of the unconscious mind, the Observer.

I entered the entangled network, which we refer to as consciousness, through that door we scientists have labeled "quantum physics." I have done this at my own peril, knowing very well of the infinite risks that multiply a thousand folds with every step I take. You may ask, "Why have I done this?" Well, I have done this to comprehend our Universe, and to understand the inner workings of existence, (what we commonly refer to as reality). And, as I mentioned earlier, I have done this to awaken humanity and lift the dark veil that has blinded us, to finally face up to the true nature of reality and consciousness.

Let me begin by stating that in such a journey the physical body becomes but a speck of matter, a vehicle to perception, and trivial in every aspect. I understand that for many, maybe most, this concept is absurd, perhaps horrifying. However, what is truly frightening is the possibility of the logical conscious mind losing itself, and the prospect of terrible madness and insanity ensuing. Lastly, let me be honest, my aim is to present you with facts and allow you to draw your own conclusions.

As far as I can remember, I've always been fascinated by the different disciplines of classical physics and modern quantum physics. Equally fascinating are the mysteries that lie beyond these fields of studies. Yes, I have focused all of my energy and time exploring what most of my colleagues, (including some of the most distinguished physicists in history), have refused to acknowledge, consciousness. To me, there is nothing spooky about it, if you approach it with an open mind. Of course, this made me the odd man out. I was frequently bullied by schoolmates, ridiculed by colleagues, and ignored by most academic institutions. However, this did not deter my rebellious and restless spirit. My joy has always been sparked by proving people wrong. So stepping outside of the boundaries of physics orthodoxy seemed almost inevitable.

In other words, it was my choice to work alone, as a castaway in the quantum physics community. Affluent beyond worries, there was no motive or cause for me to share my knowledge and findings. After all, it is not possible for the meek to take such a mighty leap into the abyss, much less go beyond it and cross to the other side. Day after day, I examined the optimum way to step through the door that leads to an unfathomable depth, the extreme unknown darkness. Of course, the goal was to do this without encountering my own demise, and to find a way to come back and live to talk about it. In my mind, I played out every scenario, every feasible setback, and every catastrophic outcome. I painstakingly examined every equation, every compound, every instrument, every procedure, endlessly. I programmed the exact day and time the passage was to take place, (December twenty-first, at three o'clock in the morning).

I had intentionally arranged my life in a way to achieve complete isolation from society. For starters, I mad sure that all of my affairs and obligations were taken care of automatically, by financial institutions and trustees. My reclusive and heavily safeguarded residence was located on a dirt road, miles away from the nearest neighbor, and even further away from any major roads. I had converted three-quarters of the complex solely for the purpose of my experiments. Any respectable scientist would have given his right arm to work in such a remarkable facility.

When the crucial day arrived, I had everything prepared. An hour before launching the experiment, I unlocked the reinforced heavy steel door that led to the backyard. I walked out into the night, (something that I rarely ever did), and looked up to the sky. I took a deep breath, and for a moment, my mind rested, while contemplating the void in the heavens. I closed my eyes, matching that feeling of infinite darkness internally, just for a moment. When I opened them, I noticed lightning illuminating the sky, far in the distance. Agitation disturbed my momentary peace. There weren't supposed to be any thunderstorms in the area. Grumbling, I made my way back inside my residence. As I tracked the unexpected atmospheric conditions, I could see that the storm would be right on top of my house while I conducted the experiment. It was too late to abort the project. The experiment couldn't wait any longer.

The specific chemical compounds had already been blended. The brain-interface components were calibrated. Detectors, lasers, and all of the geo-magnetic instruments were perfectly aligned. I could hear the humming of the power generators throughout the house. I had been preparing for that specific moment for a long time. It was time to launch.

As I initiated the countdown on the main computer, I adjusted the brain-interface headset. I entered the electromagnetic chamber, (a contraption re-sembling a giant iron birdcage), and lay back on the modified gravitational dental chair.

I heard the mechanical computer voice announce the countdown for seven minutes. The motorized clamps locked my feet and wrists in place. I had reached the point of no return.

"Six minutes and counting," announced the machine.

The buzzing sound of the electrical current ran through the metal skel-eton of the cage. My heart was racing, from excitement and fear.

"Five minutes and counting."

I noted a sudden change in sensation, throughout my body. Both my arms and legs went numb. They felt like they weren't part of my body.

"Four minutes and counting."

Thunder could be heard throughout the house.

"Ahhh!" I screamed from the top of my lungs.

An agonizing sensation of pins and needles began punishing my whole body. It felt like every pore in my skin was being punctured.

"Three minutes and counting."

Involuntary muscle spasms traveled down, from the top of my head to the soles of my feet. I forced myself to look to the right, where the main server stood. I momentarily thought about stopping the whole process, but I knew there was no going back. My vision became cloudy and distorted.

"Two minutes and counting," I heard in the background.

A loud explosion at the far end of the house startled me. Although I could not see what was happening, I sensed that there was something wrong. The electrical current seemed to be higher than I anticipated. Electrical dis-charges of lightning-like plasma began to form all around me.

"One minute and counting."

The high-powered laser fired.

"Was I dreaming all this?" I asked myself.

A searing and paralyzing pain ran down my body, forcing me to tumble into the void, as I lost consciousness. I faintly heard in the distance, "Four, three...thhhh...unnn."

Then there was nothing, only darkness and still silence. I woke up in a daze to the sound of rhythmic chanting. My whole body was sore and stiff. I forced myself to open my eyes. I experienced a moment of unparalleled confusion. Somehow, I recognized the place, but did not remember how I got there. The ground was dark and granite-like.

I got the impression that I was in some sort of gurney. Just an arm's length away, to my right and left, stood enormous walls. They were at least thirty feet high, and stretched as far as I could see, in both directions. It was overwhelming to the senses. I knew exactly where I was, but for a moment, I refused to believe what I was witnessing. However, upon a closer inspection of my surroundings, I knew it was real. It wasn't a figment of my imagination.

I could hardly move my body, no matter how hard I tried. After being carried, for what felt like a long distance, it got pitch black. All of a sudden, I began to hear bizarre noises all around me. I was not alone. My back was pressed against the cold surface of the gurney.

"I am ready," I said, without even thinking about what I was saying. The words were expressed in a strange language.

A blast of light exploded in my eyes, forcing me to close them for a few seconds. I gradually opened them. Squinting, I identified the source of the powerful lights, emanating from every direction. A row of men, in leopard robes, lined up along the walls of a large chamber. Each one held a large torch with both hands.

Forcefully, I got up to my feet, without thinking about it. In front of me was a great, uncovered, rectangular box. It was a red granite sarcophagus.

"Your highness," an older man said, as he bowed down.

He was wearing the same type of leopard robe as the men that were holding the torches.

I got into the open sarcophagus and slowly lay down. The surface was cold and rough. The older man extended his right arm above me, as if he was blessing me. The light in the room began to dim. I could not see what was happening, but I sensed that the men with the torches were leaving the large chamber. There was a dim source of light flickering and dancing across the ceiling and walls.

Somehow, I knew, that earlier I had ingested some type of chemical substance composed of various hallucinogenic agents. The aftertaste was sickening. Without warning, my vision went black, my body became paralyzed, and I was incapable of making a sound, not even a moan.

Then, there was absolute darkness and silence again. An absolute void of all senses ensued. In an instant, I lost all bearings, concept of time, and sensation. All that was left was the awareness of being the Observer. Now, think carefully for a moment. How would you perceive the giver of perception? To give you an account of my experience, or what I perceived, would be pointless. For as you perceive him, her, or it, (however you want to refer to it), so will the Observer itself appear to be.

I don't know how long I was in this state. It could have been an hour, a century, or maybe it was just a second. Suddenly, I perceived a speck of light.

"What is that particle of light?" I thought.

The speck of light became larger, and it resembled a star. Then another appeared, and then another and another. I realized that I was looking at a night sky. Once again, I experienced a moment of disorientation. When I brought my sight to my surroundings, I was standing next to a window. Outside, stood a small alley, or street, surrounded by small wooden buildings and homes.

Without thinking, I carefully closed the window and walked to my wooden desk. A single candle, sitting next to several books, illuminated the room. The air felt stifled and smoky. I took a manuscript from underneath the stack of books. The handwriting was in cursive, and the language was French. My gaze turned to a small brass bowl with water, which was placed on some sort of tripod. This contraption stood on the left side of the desk. I felt compelled to stare into the darkness that reflected on the motionless surface of the water. My mind was utterly still. I paid no attention to any distraction. I stared at that bowl for a long time. The depth of the blackness seemed to expand into a bottomless underwater abyss. I was in a deep trance. Suddenly, a vision emerged from the depth of the shadows. At first, I didn't know what I was looking at, but it appeared to be a large city with modest homes and modern buildings. Out of nowhere, there was a great flash of blinding light in the sky, followed by a monstrous thunder. Then, in horror, a great mushroom cloud rose, and a fiery wind scourged the land.

I picked up the quill pen, dipped it into the inkwell, and began writing. I looked back at the brass bowl, and I peered through the vision. My mind fell into a deep slumber. There was nothing but darkness, and no sense of self. Once again, it seemed like I spent an eternity in this state, but perhaps it was just a second. Then I realized that my mind was completely immersed in infinite emptiness. There was no sound, no sight, and no feelings. Suddenly, in the depth of the eternal void, the Observer perceived me.

Then, I heard a whisper.

"What are you doing?"

I opened my eyes, and instantly lost my bearing.

"What are you doing?"

This time it was a frantic scream.

I tried to look around, but my vision was restricted by some sort of helmet. A numbing pain ran down the entire left side of my body. From nowhere, a piece of debris violently hit the front transparent shield that was protecting my face. The strike made a large crack. At that moment, I realized that I was floating in space. To be more precise, I was drifting through space.

"Wake up, Sai. Wake up," repeated the female voice.

Through the crack on my helmet and the debris around me, I glanced at two large moons, one closer than the other. I stared at them, and the more I did, the weaker my strength grew.

"Sai! Sai!" exclaimed the voice, over the receiver on my helmet.

With great difficulty and excruciating pain, I looked around, in an effort to locate the source of the voice. I spotted another spacesuit drifting away from me. I couldn't see who it was inside.

Inexplicably, the two moons transfixed me. I thought of saying something, but remained silent instead.

"Sai, do something! Sai, we are going to die!" cried out the voice, in panic.

A shiver ran down my spine. But somehow, I knew that the time to act had passed, and there was nothing else to do. I listened to the void. It was silent.

Now, the female voice had also fallen silent and the female was floating aimlessly. Her spacesuit reflected the light from the two moons. A minute later, she vanished, and I saw that I was alone.

I started feeling lightheaded and weaker. A red alert began flashing on the transparent cracked screen on my helmet. An announcement came.

"Danger! Low Oxygen Levels!"

My vision went dark, as I took my last breath.

There was absolute silence and emptiness. After a thousand years, or perhaps only two seconds, I saw green swirling flashes of light dancing around, and eruptions of glowing yellow, outpouring from every direction. Light and darkness faded away. I saw the universe in its entirety, with its mountains, the sky, the planets, the stars, galaxies, supernovas, quasars, and the edge of the cosmos. I witnessed the beginning and the end. Then it all faded away. There were no sounds, symbols, or feelings, not even a single thought. There was just the Observer.

Suddenly, I began to feel that I was not alone. I heard voices in the distance, moving toward me. At first, it felt like a dream, but the sounds became more intense. In an instant, I was reminded of my senses. I could smell the stench of smoke with every breath I took. An unbearable, searing pain spread throughout my arms and legs. I felt nauseous and disoriented, similar to the feeling of being heavily intoxicated. I finally was able to open my eyes. The place I once called home surrounded me, and it was completely scorched. I was still sitting within the electromagnetic chamber. Three yellow blurry figures were trying to break open the bars of the cage.

"Don't move sir. Don't move. We are here to help you," I heard in the distance, before I passed out.

Today I spend all of my time in and out of consciousness, stretched out upon a hospital bed. I hear the medical staff discussing diagnoses and medication dosages. Sometimes I'm able to perceive the kind nurses taking care of my burnt and disabled body. It seems as if I have been lying down for a thousand years. Death is beside me, yet I pay no heed to it.

My journey continues, and I will tell you all about it, when I come back, in another time and another place. As you already know, this story has no end.

The Undoing

An old man walked on a dark and desolate dirt road. As he stumbled along, he carelessly swayed from one side to the other, occasionally stopping abruptly, apparently to lean his body against an imaginary wall. After supporting himself on the phantom barrier for a minute or two, he would carry on with his journey. Every few yards, he would grunt, like an intoxicated wild boar, and kick carelessly at the dirt.

The full moon provided pleasant, soft lighting. A constant wave of strong winds raised the brown dust from the dirt road, creating unpleasant, breathless clouds that faded swiftly into the darkness. A symphony of singing toads and crickets serenaded the desolate path. The old man moved forward awkwardly, gazing at the ground.

Out of the shadows, a shimmering grey cat materialized behind a dust cloud, slowly prancing with an air of happiness. He displayed a thin blue collar around his neck. The cat interrupted the clumsy march of the man, by sitting right on his path. The two observed each other. The cat stared with innocence, as the old man took his right hand out of his pocket and called him. The cat sat motionless with a silent stare. The old man stubbornly persisted with his foolish call, but no matter how hard he tried, he did not receive a response. He gave a muffled grunt and proceeded to step around the four-legged drifter. The affair ended quickly. He continued his winding path down the dirt road.

The condensed, warm breeze lifted another cloud of dust in front of the wasted man, and out of it appeared the cat once more. The man stopped in his tracks, staring at the cat with his dimmed brown eyes. He gave an arrogant smile, ungracefully bent down, and summoned the animal again. Lacking interest, the cat sat motionlessly, and the two shared an exchange of stern looks. The man became more annoyed, with each moment of silence. He looked at the cat with tightly narrow eyes. He made a slight threatening movement with his right hand, as if he would strike the feline. The animal did not as much flinch. Instead, it proceeded to lick the top of its left paw. Such demeanor seemed to insult the drunken man. It perturbed his sense of inebriated pride. He decided that enough was enough. He was not going to be disrespected by an ill-considered bag of fur. The old man raised his right arm back and struck the cat with such a blow that the animal was hurled into the darkness on the side of the road. All of the heavenly bodies witnessed the abomination perpetrated by the wasted bully. Feeling vindicated, he chuckled with satisfaction and continued his incompetent trot.

For an instant, the moon submerged her face under a wandering cloud. The lonely road became pitch black. It was a perfect time for the old man to once again lean against the fictitious wall. Like gasping for air, the face of the moon surfaced from a smothering cloud. Once again, the shimmering grey cat was sitting right in front of him. He had his back to the man. The old man got a fright, and despite his best efforts, he could not conceal his reaction. Remaining seated, the cat looked back at him, with an indifferent gaze. The man stood frozen, trying to figure out how the animal had recovered so fast. This behavior confirmed the mockery of the perverse creature. There was no doubt that this time around, he needed to punish the four-legged fiend firmly. In his intoxicated stupor, his judgment was decisive. The beast was a repeat offender of a serious crime, the humiliation of an honest man. With a malicious grin on his face, he reached down and lifted the cat over his head. With all of his brute force, he savagely slammed the animal on the road. A big thump could be heard, and the creature went limp immediately.

He stood over the motionless body. At last, he had gotten rid of the defiant pest. Without giving it a second thought, he walked around the cat and continued his journey. However, somewhere deep inside, there was an unidentifiable but imminent feeling of discomfort. He wrestled with keeping his balance, and expelling this gnawing, uneasy feeling.

"Everything is okay," he told himself, but somehow, he knew that everything was not okay.

Suddenly, an ethereal meowing joined the alluring nocturnal ballad provided by the insects and amphibian tenors. The man became paralyzed. A veil of apprehension settled over his whole being. The man turned and saw the grey cat, which was now following him. Feeling his skin crawl, he staggered backward, tripping over his own feet. He fell and landed on his back. His face became distorted with fear. His lips tried to form a word, but only a gasp of air came out. The cat moved at a slow pace. The glow of the moon reflected in his eyes. He came to a full stop, right at the man's feet.

The old man's eyes bulged crazily, as he desperately tried to crawl backward. He looked around, in desperation, but there was no one there to save him. He scrambled to his feet and took off running, clumsily. After a short distance of labored running, he could feel his chest burning and his lungs gasping for air, but his fear was greater than his physical pain.

He glanced back many times, trying to spot the monster. All of a sudden, he tripped over something in the middle of the road. He went airborne, headfirst, smashing his left shoulder onto the ground. An explosion of brilliant stars and fireworks spun in his vision.

Slowly, while catching his breath, the old man sat down in an awkward slump. In a daze, his eyes fixated on the silhouette that his own body provided. When his eyes began searching for the cause of his fall, he spotted the body of the cat, lying down, just a few feet away from him. He became enraged. He forgot the aches and soreness on his aged body. A collection of highly obnoxious and disturbing thoughts electrified his brain. He picked himself up, overexerting himself in the process.

The old man painfully moved towards the grim sight. His eyes were fierce and menacing. He was utterly absorbed in his mission, to defeat his tormenter, once and for all. He reached for the body. Doubling his exertion, he grabbed the cat under his two front legs, with both of his hands. Standing like a colossal giant, he brought the limp, lifeless body to eye level. The man examined the cat cautiously. There was something bizarre about the creature. They were face to face. The man's fiery brown eyes peered right into the cat's profile.

The darkest of clouds settled over the old man's heart and soul. His chest began to tighten. He was suffocating. His grip on the cat intensified. The man felt his legs giving in, quivering like fragile twigs. He shut his eyes, in despair. When he opened them, he was holding a small child. His gaze was locked and unshakable. He stared at the unconscious face of the child, as he slipped into a distant and suppressed memory. It was an untold and hopeless thought, from a forgotten, painful past. He saw a grief-stricken picture from his childhood.

His mind stepped inside an agonizing event from long, long ago. His father had come home extremely drunk that night. Like a violent tornado, he wrecked and trashed everything in his path. The furniture, the dog, and his wife were all flung in every direction. Too young to determine his father's condition, the small child came out of his room to greet the long-awaited hero. The little one was wearing his favorite blue pajamas. Lacking the knowledge of how the ethanol demons can influence the mind of men, the little boy scurried excitedly across the room, toward the storm. Running, with open arms, he was the perfect picture of innocence.

The head of the family spotted the child running carelessly across the room, toward him. He uttered a grunt like a wild boar. The little boy approached, with affection, as the drunken brute sidestepped in an attempt to avoid him. The child tried to grab the man's leg, but missed and caught nothing but air. With clumsy footing, the desperate child followed in pursuit. The father became even more infuriated. He stood tall, frowning, with tightly narrowed eyes. As the child reached out to him again, the intoxicated brute made a threatening gesture with his right arm, as if he would strike him. Too pure to know anger or hate, the little boy did not shy away, but instead opened his arms again. With malice in his heart and spirits in his head, the father was inclined to have fun with his open hand. He smacked the child so hard that he was flung across the floor.

The mother shouted deafening cries, rushing forward courageously, like a wounded lioness. The father paid no attention to her screams. He became a shadow of misery, towering over the little boy. The giant reached down and grabbed the child under his arms. He lifted him to eye level. In a daze, the little boy briefly had the feeling of the room sinking, just before a heavy thump was heard. At that moment, everything went dark.

The legs of the old man, who was standing on the road, gave in. He fell to his knees and began to sob, uncontrollably. He brought the cat's lifeless body to his chest, while leaning his face against the creature's head. He felt every muscle in his body tremble, as he begged for mercy and forgiveness. Whimpering, he expressed the deepest sorrow for all of those things that had happened, (the suffering, the anger, the fear).

The tenors of the night had muted their song, as thundering clouds made their presence known. The heavens unleashed heavy precipitation. Tears mixed with raindrops. Grief came with relief. Shame and guilt vanished into thin air. The desolate soul kneeling on the road said farewell to his liberator. He knew there was nothing he could do but to say goodbye. As he put the creature back down on the ground, he turned his eyes toward the heavens, allowing the rainfall to wash his face. When he looked to the ground, the cat was no longer there. The old man felt free. He was finally at peace, at peace with himself, and at peace with his past.

An Immigrant in Heaven

A crowd of a few hundred people rallied before the front doors of the county courthouse. The dense mass of men, women, and children occupied every square meter of the city town square. To get a better view, several kids and young-at-heart adults climbed some of the trees that run parallel to Washington Street. Emotions were running high, as the cold evening air mixed with sentiments of resentment and anger, which engulfed the whole assembly. You could hear sporadic angry shouts all the way down by the city hall on Fletcher Street. That is more than three blocks beyond the edge of the town square. So far, this was the largest anti-immigrant protest, up to date.

In the middle of it stood retired football coach, Donald McConnell, who was working the crowd into a frenzy. There was no doubt that he was an exceptional public speaker. As his dry, pale lips moved with excitement, his voice roared with agitation. Standing close to him, one could see the rope-like veins bulging on his beefy neck. He pumped his fist into the air. His narrow, fiery eyes were fixed on the main banner that hung high above the center of the square. The banner read, "Close The Border! Immigrants Are Not Welcome!"

The coach became highly animated. He lifted his "Keep Immigrants Out!" sign high above his head. He spoke with a thundering voice.

"Failure to enforce our immigration laws will destroy our country. Immigrants bring corruption, crime, and undemocratic ideas. They will undermine and destroy our economy and our way of life!"

The audience listened attentively. The courthouse and the adjacent buildings shook from the cheering and applause, every time the passionate retired coach spoke.

As the sun began its descent, the spirited speaker delivered his final thoughts. His call to action was severe and persuasive.

The whole crowd started chanting, "Go home! Get out of our country!"

With this, the event came to an end. The mass slowly began dispersing. In a matter of thirty minutes, the square was completely deserted, except for a couple of city workers, (whose job was to clean up after the gathering).

After a brisk seven-minute walk under a full moon, which hung high in the sky, Donald McConnell reached the beautiful front porch of his home.

The architectural elements of his Colonial style home had always brought pride and joy to the McConnell family. He opened the front door, and took off his tan leather jacket, as he entered the dark hallway. There was a dreary silence that absorbed the entire house. As he entered the living room, he instinctively fixed his eyes on the mantel, where he kept old family pictures. His eyes shifted from one photo to another. While standing right in the middle of the room, his mind began to drift to an unpleasant memory, his eldest son's funeral. This made the tough, retired coach tremble.

"Oh, how I miss you, son," he whispered sadly to himself.

His body emitted an immense cough that snapped him out of the trance. He walked toward the kitchen at the back of the house. Here, he patiently prepared and cooked a hearty meal. It was the type of meal that his late wife used to make for him, (a juicy and tender, oven-baked, T-Bone steak, with a baked potato and steamed carrots). He sat alone at the head of the table. He stared at the sizzling meat on his plate for a long time, before actually taking a bite. As Coach McConnell chewed his meal unconsciously, his eyes once again were fixed on a family picture hanging on the opposite wall. From an unknown source within his body, came a most unpleasant sensation. His heart sank. His vision started to spin. He felt a swarm of ferocious fire ants crawling up his arm, and up onto his jaw. The entire left side of his body went numb. He felt like he was suffocating. Instinctively, with his right hand, he clutched his chest. He tried to get up, but his legs gave in, and he plummeted to the floor.

The retired coach lay motionless. The last thing he remembered was looking at a ray of moonlight that seemed to penetrate through the dining room ceiling. Then it happened. He found himself standing next to his body. The pain was gone. There was a moment of confusion and amazement, but after a few seconds, he realized what had just happened.

"It is just like I imagined," he thought to himself. "I have read about this. I think I'm, I'm... I'm dead, or at least, my body is dead."

He was surprised to see himself out of his own body and dressed in the same manner as his lifeless body lying on the ground.

"Now what?" Coach McConnell asked himself.

In that instant, he perceived that he was moving away from his body. There was no sense of direction. It was not a sense of moving up or down but more like from one state of awareness to another. It was similar to the experience of waking up from a vivid dream. He stood in the middle of a pathway, surrounded by bright light. He could not figure out how he got to that place.

And as he pondered about the event unfolding, he heard a soft and familiar voice that seemed to come from deep within him.

"Hello father."

He immediately recognized who it was. It was Chuck, his eldest son.

In the light, not too far into the distance stood a figure. At first, Coach McConnell had difficulty focusing. However, a great sense of joy and love filled his whole being. The figure slowly approached him. He could see him clearly now. It was Chuck. Both father and son embraced each other. Tears of happiness ran down Coach McConnell's face.

"I am so happy to see you, father. I've been waiting for you," Chuck continued. "Please walk with me, father."

They walked on a luminous path for a long time, until the landscape in front of them began to change. Coach McConnell stood in amazement as he glanced at the magnificent structure in front of him. There it was, the Gates of Heaven. It was at least seventy feet high. An extraordinary brilliance shined from every facet. Beautiful and alluring multi-color roses clung to the ornate surface.

"There is nothing on earth that can compare to the splendor of such a vision," Coach McConnell thought to himself.

"Father, there is something you need to know," said Chuck.

"What is it, son?" Coach McConnell asked.

"Please don't be afraid as we walk through the Gates of Heaven," replied his son.

"Why would I be afraid to go into Heaven, son?" Coach McConnell asked, with much curiosity.

"Oh father, you have forgotten what you always taught me, your own spiritual beliefs," answered his son.

"I don't know what you are referring to, Chuck," exclaimed Coach Mc-Connell, in bewilderment.

"What measure ye mete, it shall be measured to you again," Chuck replied, looking sullenly at his father.

As the Gates of Heaven opened, Coach McConnell recoiled with fear. As far as he could see, there were thousands of souls in Heaven, holding signs and banners that said, "Immigrants Are Not Welcome! Close the Gates! Get Out of Heaven! Go Back Where You Came From! Heaven is Full! Go to Hell!"

A Long String

While in pursuit, Paul tried to snatch the child by the back of his shirt, but missed and caught nothing but air. The tiny vagabond scurried around bicyclists, cart-pushing vendors, and even the fast-moving cabs. While leaping through the air, he dodged, (with great agility), every obstacle the street would throw at him. No matter how fast the uniformed security officer ran, the distance between hunter and prey never shortened. By now, both found themselves running well beyond the fashion district. Paul knew, at that moment, that it was not going to be easy to catch the little thief.

When they reached Flowers Boulevard, their path was met by a hoard of shoppers, students, office workers, and commuters. The little one had an advantage here. With great ease, he sidestepped and swerved around each pedestrian, only causing minor disturbances. On the other hand, the tired pursuer ran and bumped into every other passerby, drawing hateful and damning insults.

"You moron!" an old man screamed.

"You freaking idiot!" shouted a young hipster, clutching a brown plastic cup filled with coffee.

"Watch where you're going, jerk!" yelled a tall redhead.

Paul did not stop to respond or explain himself.

All that running was taking a toll on the security officer. Paul felt like he was drowning. Each shallow breath took greater effort, like breathing through a straw. Nevertheless, whenever he could, he would muster all of his bronchial strength to shout, "Grab that thief!"

This was to no avail, because the few people that bothered to pay attention, saw no one.

A few seconds after leaving Flower Boulevard, Paul got the fright of his life, when he came within a few inches of kissing the front grill of a fast-moving city bus. The conductor shouted all types of obscenities, with such ferocity that every single passenger was rattled. After the initial shock, a searing blaze of rage engulfed the security officer's psyche. He was more determined than ever to catch the shoplifter. Now it was personal. Fortunately, he did not lose track of the fugitive. He caught sight of the dirty red shirt, ripped black pants, and muddy shoes moving down the busy sidewalk. He resumed the pursuit.

A moment later, the little boy turned onto Tokyo Street, and a few seconds later, he turned down Rio Avenue. This area was a depressed, desolate, and poverty-stricken neighborhood. Paul was running, just half a block behind his target. He witnessed the child dart into a side alley. He hurried to catch up, however, when he turned the corner, there was no one there. For a moment, the security guard stood between two crumbling buildings. With caution, he walked halfway through the deserted alley. To his right, he identified the source of a nauseating, foul smell. It was a mountain of garbage that was crawling up the wall. On the opposite side, there was a collection of broken wooden crates and cardboard boxes, stretched as far as the back wall. As he continued to make his way down the alley, he would peek and glance inside the large boxes. They were all empty at the time, but they held the evidence of living quarters, (raggedy clothes, torn shoes, broken toys, and unopened canned food).

Paul cleared his throat loudly. He was surprised to discover how uneasy he felt. He looked around, in frustration, as he moved closer to the brick wall at the end of the alley. There, in the shadows of the building to his right, he saw the face of the small child. In the blink of an eye, the little creature climbed a pyramid of stacked crates.

"Hey! Stop there!" yelled Paul, in a stern authoritarian tone.

The boy doubled his effort to climb to the top. The security guard noticed that, under his right arm, the child was holding the expensive spool of indigo colored thread that he had stolen from the French-owned designer tailor boutique. Pressed to his back was a small kite, made of newspaper that displayed the colorful Sunday comics. The child reached the summit. He turned back to glance at the officer. Paul could see the dark, anxious eyes, begging him to stop the chase. For the first time, he noticed that the child could not be much older than seven or eight years old. The little boy leapt to the other side of the brick wall.

Following the steps of the little boy, Paul also climbed the rickety structure. When he reached the top, his eyes swiftly scouted for the fugitive. The officer spotted the colorful kite, with short-thin legs, running straight forward on the side of a busy street. The child was heading toward the Botanical Garden City Park. A malicious smirk ran across the officer's face. He knew exactly where the small thief was heading.

"Gotcha, you little brat!" exclaimed Paul.

A refreshing breeze scattered a few white clouds across the sky. The warmth of the spring afternoon sun brought joy to the park-goers. The moment anyone entered this vast and beautiful landscape, they were transported out of the hustle and bustle of the city, and into the realm of a tranquil paradise. The sweet songs of birds, resting on the leafy arms of a thousand trees, filled the air with life and cheerfulness. The colorful butterflies, flying to nectar-filled flowers, brought delight to happy children. The benches provided a perch for thoughtful readers and poets in deep reflection. The fountains' basins were crowded with young "Romeos" and "Juliets," who were kissing and holding hands. And just beyond the imposing sculpture of a woman, (representing strength and beauty), was a large open field.

From a distance, Paul could see a number of kites dancing across the sky. As he slowly made his way through the open field, he walked past proud parents teaching their kids how to fly their colorful designer kites. It did not take long for the security officer to spot the small child with his newspaper kite. The little boy was using the stolen indigo string to tie a knot to one of the sticks that made up the frame of the kite.

"Gotcha, you little bastard!" Paul shouted sternly, as he grabbed the child by the back of his shirt.

The little boy looked up at the man. He stood petrified.

"Please sir, let me fly my kite," begged the child, in a whisper.

The officer tightened his grip.

"You are coming with me, you little thief!" he said, pointing toward the other side of the park.

Tears began sliding down the yellowish cheeks of the boy. Unperturbed by the boy crying, Paul grabbed the thin wrist of the child. He noticed that the child was holding a small piece of paper in his hand.

"What do you have there, you devil?" asked the officer, angrily.

Without saying anything, the security officer grabbed the piece of paper from the child's hand. He opened it. There, written in colored crayons, in a child's handwriting, were these words:

It's your birthday Mommy
I miss you because you are not here
I want to wish you a Happy Birthday in Heaven.

The sky was reddish-orange by the time the sun began to set. From the city, came the occasional screech and horn sounds. A soft and cool breeze continued to lift the colorful kites in the sky. In silence, the clouds witnessed a single colorful newspaper kite approaching them. It had a long indigo string stretching all the way down to the ground, and at the end of its tail, a small piece of paper flopped in the wind.

Los Chupacabras

Whoever told you that there is no such thing as gruesome monsters or shapeshifters, in real life, is either as blind as a bat, or as foolish as a clown. Believe me when I say that there are real live deviant entities that roam in our midst. They can easily fool the human eye by taking on different forms. They are wretched nocturnal beings who have adapted to the brightness of daylight. Nevertheless, they would rather roam in the dead of night. You can say that they are thoughtless creatures, for they only live for their own pleasure and satisfaction. No one else counts. Their dwellings are in the shadows of graves, desolate streets, or abandoned structures. The strongest urges that drive these perverse souls are hatred and grossness. They act only by instinct, and their pitiful minds are infected with darkness and a foul plague. This plague is called "lack." This lack is a bottomless pit that can never be filled or satisfied. That is their curse, and our misfortune.

You probably have heard or read of these heinous creatures before. There are countless stories and legends, told by farmers and ranchers living in remote areas, who claim to have witnessed one of these beasts do away with their livestock. Many of these country men and women have reported that they have lost as many as ten farm animals in one night. As I mentioned before, the appetite of these creatures is voracious. They go by many different names, such as, Demons, Gremlins, and Hodag. We will call them Los Chupacabras.

You might think that you are quite safe from such abominations. After all, you probably live somewhere safe and guarded, right? Perhaps you live in a large metropolitan city or a small modern town. That might be so, but I mentioned that these ghouls can take on different forms. They are universal creatures that have always existed, and unfortunately, always will. They tend to crawl in the lower planes of the social order, amongst the thieves, the drug abusers, the human traffickers, etc. They have biological parents, and by nature, they despise them. Their greatest desire is misery for others and their own kind.

This is a surreal story about a close encounter that I experienced with three of these beings. It all began on an early evening, when I requested a ride from a popular ride-sharing app. Nine minutes later, the driver arrived in his fairly new, silver, four-door sedan, with dark-tinted windows. I locked the front door to my office and ran as fast as I could, to avoid the torrential downpours that were occurring. I opened the back passenger-side door and greeted the driver, as I tried to get comfortable on the soft, gray seat. The driver glanced back with a forced smile and said, "Hola."

I politely replied, (in Spanish), "Buenas tardes."

With his index finger, he swiped the screen of his phone, shifted into drive, and started our trip.

As usual, when we reached the main road that leads away from the heart of downtown Ft. Lauderdale, the traffic started to slow down to a crawl. I looked at my phone to check the time. I was not in a hurry, but I was curious to find out the estimated time of arrival.

"At what time does the GPS say we will arrive?" I asked.

"Perdon, que?" the driver replied, with a tone of embarrassment.

"Disculpe, a qué hora dice el GPS que llegaremos?" I asked again.

"A las 7:25," he answered.

"Gracias," I replied.

It was going to take just over forty-five minutes to get home. I had nothing to worry about. My wife was working late that day. For the next fifteen minutes, we both listened in silence to a few over-played pop songs on the radio. As we reached one of the main intersections, just beyond I-95, he received another request to pick up additional passengers.

"Tenemos que recoger a otros pasajeros," he exclaimed, with annoyance.

"Okay," I responded.

I understood that it was time to carpool. I did not mind. I had shared rides many times before. A number of times these shared rides ended up being a pleasant experience. However, that was not going to be the case this evening.

It didn't take long before Miguel, the driver, arrived at the pick-up destination. They were waiting outside. They were three individuals, huddled under a blue awning, sheltering themselves from the rain. Each one exhaled smoke from their nostrils. The trio rushed onto the car. Two of them sat in the back, to my left. The third one sat up front. They all let out a burst of terribly loud laughter, as they made themselves comfortable. From where I was sitting, I could distinguish some of the physical features of the man who was sitting in the front seat. He was thin, and nearly six feet tall, with short brown hair. His neck and arms were covered with cheap, distasteful tattoos. He seemed to be less than thirty years of age, and his breath had the stench of a sewer facility. In contrast, the person sitting next to me, (in the middle rear seat), was short and chubby with curly brown hair. He was fidgety, by nature, and would reveal his yellowish teeth and dark gums every time he laughed. The third person, sitting in the left rear seat, was a young, emaciated woman, who was no more than twenty-five years old, with olive colored skin, and missing teeth. The presence of these three individuals, so close, caused a sense of danger in me. The driver shifted the gear into drive and started driving back toward the highway, I-95.

The man in the front seat turned his body around and addressed the guy next to me.

"Rick, didn't I tell you that bitch would fall for it?" he asked, with a crooked smile.

"You sure did, Tom," replied the guy next to me, as they both broke into a burst of horrible laughter.

"I bet I could milk another five-hundred out of that idiot by the end of the week," he stated, in a sinister way.

"Maybe, even more, Tom," added Rick.

"Nah, she is always broke," blurted out Tom.

"Your mom is such a freaking loser!" exclaimed Rick, in a nasally high-pitched voice.

"She is, man," replied Tom, with a big smirk on his face.

"You always dupe her into giving you whatever she has," said Rick, almost tearing up with laughter.

"I am the worst!" the man in the front boosted out, with pride.

"We are the worst, right Tom?" asked Rick, in search of approval.

"Yes, Rick, we are the worst," responded Tom, with a sarcastic tone.

I couldn't believe my ears. These two individuals were speaking to each other without a care in the world. They seemed to be oblivious of the presence of the driver and myself. I did my best to pretend that their presence did not bother me. But the more I tried to ignore them, the more I felt my skin crawl.

"I need to get my prescription," interrupted the girl.

"Well dear, you need to get some dough," replied Tom, without looking back at her.

"We need to stop by the pharmacy and get my stuff," she announced, almost in a whisper.

The man in the front passenger seat turned around and gazed at her in silence, for a moment. He turned back around. He grunted. The girl spoke no words. Outside, the rain seemed to double in intensity. It was hard to see anything beyond a foot from the car, in any direction.

"Got any money?" asked the man in the front seat angrily, addressing me. I pretended not to have heard him.

"Hey, do you got any money on you?" he yelled.

I was taken aback.

"Excuse me, are you... , are you talking to me?" I asked, in astonishment.

"Yes," Tom continued, "I believe I was looking at you when I asked the question, buddy."

"You are asking me for money?" I asked, still in amazement.

"I need my prescription!" exclaimed the girl, in agitation.

"Well, do you or do you not have a few bucks to spare?" asked Rick, the man sitting to my left.

"No, I don't," I responded, dryly.

"You look well-dressed man," the girl continued. "You going to tell me you don't even have a few bucks on you?"

"The man said 'no,' mon chéri," Tom blurted out, sarcastically.

"Ask the driver," exclaimed the girl.

Up to that moment, the driver had remained silent. I don't know if he was as afraid as I was, or if he was just oblivious to the event that was unfolding in his own car.

"I bet he's loaded, Tom," said the man next to me, while pointing a finger to the back of the driver's head.

"I bet he is," reaffirmed the man in the front seat, narrowing his eyes, as he stared at the driver.

"Well, go ahead! Ask that moron for the money!" the girl cried out loudly, in exasperation.

This caused the driver to look back for the first time.

The front passenger, Tom, leaned forward to the driver and whispered, in a sinister tone, "Hola amigo. You have some mula?"

The driver contorted his body away from the front passenger. His face had turned pale.

"Que?" asked Miguel.

Rick, the guy next to me, burst out in horrible laughter, that could only be described as the laugh of a hyena.

"Que quieres?" was the driver's hollow reply, as he pulled one of his hands from the steering wheel, in an attempt to guard his face.

My whole body froze, as I followed the glance of Miguel's crazed eyes. The front passenger's mouth was wide open. His dark red tongue began to stretch, as if it was made out of rubber.

"Watch the road, man!" I screamed, in a panic.

The car was moving over sixty-five miles an hour, right in the middle lane of I-95.

Suddenly, I felt the cold, clammy, lifeless hand of Rick on my left shoulder. Somehow, he had jumped up and crouched next to me, while pinning me against the door. At that moment, Rick gave a horrendous beastly howl. My whole body cramped up. I couldn't breathe.

I felt like I was suffocating. Although he was a smaller man than me, he seemed to have the strength and weight of a gorilla.

"Ay Dios!" I thought I heard Miguel cry in the background.

The car began to swirl all over the road. My vision became blurry but somehow, I managed to see the poor driver's last moment. The front passenger's tongue was wrapped around the steering wheel, while one of his large ghoulish hands clutched Miguel's throat, and the other covered his mouth.

"I need my prescription!" yelled the girl.

The thunderstorm was raging outside. I felt an explosion on the left side of my face. My vision was flooded with swirls of light, and a loud ringing in my ear deafened me for an instant. I felt another pair of hands pulling on my right leg, and going through my back pockets.

I looked up at my assailant's face and witnessed the most hideous sight that I have ever seen. His bulging eyes were filled with blood. What passed for a nose was just a dangling piece of rotten flesh, and his disfigured mouth was twice the size as normal.

If I remember correctly, I think I gave a faint moan. I felt a second set of hands moving up my body. They were even colder than the ones that were holding me down. A wave of chills ran up my body, as the girl's hands caressed my face.

"You know you want me," whispered the girl softly in my left ear, before I lost consciousness.

The police report claims that the five-car pileup on I-95 that night was caused by the driver of the shared ride service, who unfortunately suffered a heart attack. He was declared dead at the scene. The other passengers that had been in the vehicle were nowhere to be seen.

As for me, the police concluded that my account of the incident was not credible, due to my head trauma. It was merely hallucinations, as one of the doctors suggested. The case was closed. But one question remained unanswered. What happened to the other passengers that had used a stolen account to request the shared ride?

The Rental

"Aisling, I told you I don't have time for breakfast. I need to go," exclaimed Shane, while getting ready for work.

"You can have a quick breakfast before you go. It will only take a few minutes," Aisling suggested, impatiently.

"Well, I can't," replied Shane.

"You know how you get when you don't have breakfast," said Aisling, shrugging her shoulders.

"You know that today is the big meeting at 9:00 a.m., with the investors," the husband replied, hastily.

"Okay, but don't complain tonight when you return home," the wife replied, dryly.

The husband, Shane, paused for a moment and stared at his wife's face, and thought, "I know that she is right, but I still have to pick up the rental before heading to the office."

"It won't take more than a minute to prepare it," she added.

"Sorry, Aisling, but I can't. I must stop by the rental place, and it is not even the one close to the office. I have to go to the one by downtown," explained Shane.

"Oh, I thought you were picking up the rental at the dealer by the office," said Aisling, escorting her husband to the living room.

"Nope," answered Shane.

"Why are you not going to the dealer close to the office?" Aisling questioned.

"They didn't have the model that I need," replied her husband.

"So unreliable, so unreliable..." whispered Aisling, while smoothing out her husband's red t-shirt, with her right hand.

"This is the most important meeting we have ever had, and I need to make a great impression. So, I'm renting the top model. She is a beauty. She is equipped with all the bells and whistles," said Shane, while looking at his smartwatch.

"Good for you! I know you will make a great impression. Do not worry. You will do great!" affirmed Aisling.

"Well, I better. A lot is riding on this meeting. You should see the rental that I got. It even has genitalia," added Shane.

"Wow, you weren't kidding. You truly are going all out," replied Aisling.

"By the way, I am going to be late tonight. So, do not wait for me to have dinner," said Shane.

"My gosh! No breakfast, and you are going to be late!" exclaimed the wife.

"It's an all day meeting. So, we'll probably step out for lunch and happy hour with the investors," replied Shane.

"In that case, I think you should wear your pajamas instead of those shorts. They are a bit tight, if you know what I mean," stated Aisling, sarcastically.

Shane pause for an instant to inspect the clothing that he was wearing. Then he rubbed his protruding belly. A feeling of awkwardness and embarrassment briefly crept in.

"I don't have time for your "fat" jokes, Aisling," responded Shane, squinting his eyes in annoyance.

"I'm just saying. If you are going to do a mind transfer for a whole day, you might as well leave your own body in comfort," said Aisling, with an affable smile, as she opened the door to their home office.

Both husband and wife stepped into the room, which was completely dark.

"Lights!" said Aisling.

The walls turned on, illuminating the whole room.

"Light setting, Polynesian blue!" added Shane.

The walls turned dark blue, creating a pleasant atmosphere. The room was completely empty, except for a single large, black reclining leather sofa in the middle of the room. There was a wireless wearable mind-transfer headset on one of the armrests.

"Now, remember, just because you will be walking around all day in a top-of-the-line rental, that doesn't give you the right to flirt," exclaimed Aisling, with a frown.

"Why would you say that?" protested Shane, in annoyance.

"Well, you know how some people believe that they can fool around just because they are in a young and gorgeous body, especially one with genitalia. You know exactly how I feel about that," replied Aisling, while helping her husband put on the headset.

"Aisling, you know that I'm not that type of person. Besides, the rental is strictly for business," explained Shane.

"I know, my love," said Aisling.

"All right baby, wish me luck," said Shane, suddenly lowering his voice.

"Good luck, hon," Aisling said softly, just before turning on the headset. Shane's eyes closed and his entire body went limp. Aisling gently placed a white cotton blanket on him to cover him from his neck to his toes.

"I wonder at what time he'll be back," she murmured to herself, as she exited the room.

Adam

"Ninety-nine, one hundred, ready or not, here I come!"

Adam opened his eyes. He turned around. He stood motionless for a moment, while his dark brown eyes shifted from right to left and then right again. After spending a few seconds trying to figure out where his brother and three cousins could be hiding, he took off running toward the old red and white barn at the edge of the cornfield.

"I know where you are hiding!" yelled Adam, while running.

As he entered the barn, he quickly spotted Luke, crouching behind a short stack of hay.

"I see you, Luke!" shouted Adam, with excitement.

The child crouching behind the stack of hay stood up.

"That's not fair! You cheated!" Luke cried out.

"Shut up! I did not!" replied Adam.

"You're a cheater!" exclaimed Luke, turning red.

"And you're a sore loser. Now, go to the 'found' pole by the house," said Adam, arrogantly.

Luke silently obeyed. He exited the barn and walked to the "found" pole. He stood there pouting, with his arms crossed. Back at the barn, Adam continued his search. Darkness embraced every nook and cranny. He cautiously walked toward an old broken-down blue tractor in the middle of the barn. He saw someone's head moving around. It was Sarah's.

"I see you, Sarah!" shouted Adam.

"Ahh, how did you know?" complained Sarah.

"I just knew that you were hiding there," answered Adam, laughing.

Sarah did not protest. She exited the barn and walked toward the "found" pole, without saying a word.

Adam climbed on top of the old tractor and turned his eyes toward the top of the barn. There, just by the stairs, he spotted his cousin, Conor, who was trying to hide behind an old, wooden apple box.

"I see you, Conor!" yelled Adam.

"No way! Sarah told you where I was hiding!" complained Conor, loudly.

"No, she did not. You just suck at hide-and-seek," replied Adam, in a malicious manner.

Without saying a word, Conor also exited the barn and walked toward the "found" pole.

Adam continued scouting the barn from the top of the tractor. He heard a faint sound coming from the direction where the old water barrels were stored.

"I know where you are, Gail!" exclaimed Adam.

There was no response, but he could feel her presence before he could see her. Adam jumped to the ground and headed toward the empty water barrels by the back wall. He searched, one by one, and spotted the young girl hiding inside one of the barrels. He violently kicked the large container where his cousin was hiding. The barrel tilted and fell on its side. There was a loud thump. Gail screamed. The barrel rolled over for a few feet, until it crashed into a pile of wooden crates. Gail screamed again.

"You crybaby!" exclaimed Adam.

Gail's screams were heard by both the children standing by the "found" pole, and the adults sitting on the back porch of the house. They all rushed toward the barn. There, they found Gail still inside the barrel, and Adam standing next to her. He no longer was laughing, as he realized that his malicious behavior just had just gotten him into trouble.

"What is wrong with you, boy?" asked his father, angrily.

"But Dad, I didn't do anything," responded Adam, looking down in seeming embarrassment.

"Go to your room! I will deal with you later," his father said, sternly.

Adam ran down to the house, without saying a word. He rushed up the stairs and slammed his bedroom door behind him. The young boy jumped into his bed and hid his face under the pillow. He did not want anyone to see him crying. Adam could hear his father approaching the house. Adam's anger turned into sadness and then into listless exhaustion. He closed his eyes, and shortly afterward, his consciousness drifted into nothingness.

Adam opened his eyes. Consciousness snapped back into place, when the convoy came under heavy enemy fire from a group of ISIS insurgents. Marine Sgt. Adam and his men quickly dismounted and took strategic positions to flank the enemy. After a long, fierce gun battle, they successfully killed twelve insurgents and forced the rest to disperse.

As the convoy made their way back to their vehicles, Adam and two other Marines remained behind, to cover the team's withdrawal. All of a sudden, they heard voices approaching from the other side of an adjacent wall. Five men, dressed in black, from head to toe, rushed from around the corner. Adam and the two Marines came face-to-face with the enemy. All hell broke loose. Both sides opened fire at point-blank range. Death came swiftly to the three men wearing black, who were standing up front. One of the Marines was shot between the eyes, and a barrage of bullets ravaged the other. One of the two remaining ISIS fighters rushed Adam. The Sergeant managed to grab his attacker and slammed him to the ground. The man's body went limp. Adam felt a horrible burning pain explode in his right shoulder. He plummeted to the ground and he landed face up. The ISIS fighter was pointing the barrel of his AK-47 directly at his head. Adam tried to move his legs, but his body didn't react. He heard a flurry of shots behind him. The ISIS fighter's body shook, from the impact of multiple hits. He fell backward and landed heavily on the ground. Adam's vision became blurry, as he felt himself falling into a dark abyss. Just before passing out, he heard a man's voice that seemed far away.

"Sergeant, Sergeant, are you okay?"

All of this happened in the blink of an eye. Adam opened his eyes. For a brief moment he did not know where he was. He was staring sideways at a white wall. There was a rectangular window with horizontal plantation blinds, and a dark wooden nightstand with a tall metallic lamp and a modern alarm clock. His attention shifted to the large glowing numbers displayed on the screen. It was 5:30 a.m. An unbearable exhaustion punished his entire body. There was a muted buzzing sound whirling above him, and with every passing second, the sharp ringing of the clock was becoming more intrusive and more irritating.

It was time to get up, but this was easier said than done. The lack of light made this task even harder. The bed seemed to hold Adam down. He let out a deep guttural grunt as he lifted himself up. He sat at the edge of the bed for a couple of minutes, while he allowed his head to clear. By now, the alarm's screeching noise was intolerable. With great effort, Adam commanded the smart device to cease the torturous wake-up call.

"Alarm off."

He was surprised to hear the tone of his own voice. The word "alarm" came out with a frog-like tone, and "off" sounded more like a faint whimper than a word. He got up to his feet and unconsciously made his way to the bathroom.

He pressed the touch switch on the wall and turned on the lights. Adam paused for a moment. In front of him he saw a middle-aged man with disheveled hair, puffy eyelids, dark circles, a swollen face, a thick neck, and a large waist. He was contemplating himself in the mirror, and the reflection was not kind to him. The rising steam of the hot water snapped him out of his stupor. He squirted into his hand a dash of the finest face cleanser that money could buy. The label on the bottle read "Facial Fuel Energizing Face Wash." He washed his face and dried it with a soft white towel, which bore the letter "A" in a decorative calligraphy font.

He jumped into the shower. His muscles began to relax as the warm water cascaded over his entire body. His hands scrubbed every area of flesh, in a mechanical manner. His mind was hard at work, piecing together all of the unpleasant tasks that he needed to accomplish by the end of the day. As he stepped out of the shower, he continued to groom himself. Once satisfied with his appearance, he picked up a designer, dark blue two-piece suit. He got dressed, sprayed on a popular signature men's cologne, and headed toward the kitchen. Adam made a beeline for the stainless steel refrigerator.

He did not open the French doors of the appliance, but instead tapped on the large touchscreen on the front panel. A calendar app came up. He stood motionless, as he glared at his schedule. His concentration was interrupted by the loud ringtone of his smartphone. *Diiing!* He held it in his right hand. *Diiing!* He looked at the number and pressed decline. Without taking his eyes away from the phone, he opened the freezer and took out a bacon, sausage, egg, and cheese breakfast sandwich. He placed it on a white plate and microwaved it for two minutes. The smell of cooked processed meat permeated the kitchen and living room.

Adam sat on a stylish tall, leather stool by the edge of a large white marble table. He opened his mouth to take the first bite. *Diiing!* He looked at the phone from the corner of his eye. It was a different phone number. *Diiing!* His left hand's index finger pressed the decline button. He wolfed down the sandwich and then washed it down with a bottled high protein smoothie. He rinsed his mouth in the sink, grabbed his car keys and Italian leather briefcase, and headed for the garage. The garage door was open. As always, his black luxury German sedan was parked in reverse. He climbed inside, placed his smartphone on the center console, turned on the radio, and started the car. He drove to the end of the driveway and pressed a button, by the rearview mirror, to open the double wooden swing gate.

The leaves on the trees glistened with the first rays of the morning sun. For a moment, Adam found himself being distracted by the landscape of the golf course on the opposite side of the street. His gaze was far away. His mind seemed to be in search of a long-forgotten place. *Diiing!* A burst of anger jerked him back into awareness. His face was distorted with rage. He looked at the dashboard screen that displayed the incoming call. *Diiing!* It was yet another different number.

"Leave me the hell alone, you morons!" screamed Adam, furiously.

Diiing! This time he pressed a button on the steering wheel to stop the ringing.

After driving for fifteen minutes, he reached the entrance ramp to I-95. As he sat at the light, waiting for the green signal so that he could turn left, he sighed. He turned onto the highway ramp to merge into a stream of bumper-to-bumper traffic. The sea of red lights stretched as far as the eye could see. For two hours, he swerved from lane to lane, inching his way toward his destination, downtown Miami. Finally, he arrived at his office, on the twenty-first floor of a modern high-rise.

"What the hell do I pay you for?" Adam screamed angrily, as he burst through the doors of the reception area.

His personal assistant, Carol, sat behind an L-shaped desk. She recoiled and turned pale.

"I've been getting phone calls all morning from these god-dammed idiots!" he continued. "Is it not part of your job description to screen these calls?"

He stormed into his office, slamming the door behind him. With great effort, the personal assistant swallowed her pride and tears.

From an adjacent small office, another woman came out to console Carol.

"It's okay, honey," she said, quietly. "You didn't do anything wrong. He's just a miserable bastard. You know he is taking it out on us because he is in a lot of trouble. A lot of trouble." She paused for a moment, as she looked around. "You know he is under investigation, right?"

The office phone rang.

"Good morning. Paradise Group Investments. How can I help you?" answered Carol. After a short pause, she continued. "Yes, Mr. Walker, he has been expecting your phone call. Please hold while I transfer you."

Adam was sitting on the edge of his modern, glossy executive desk, watching the morning market report, on a large flat-screen TV.

"Mr. Walker is on line two," announced Carol over the intercom.

Adam put the call on the speakerphone, "Hey Wal, how the heck are you, buddy?"

There was an awkward moment of silence.

"Hello Adam," a raspy voice replied. "What's going on? I've been trying to reach you over the last few days," the voice announced.

"Sorry buddy. I was out sick for a few days," answered Adam. "But no worries. I am back, and I'm ready to kick some ass."

"Mmm, I see," said Mr. Walker. "Correct me if I am wrong, Adam, but weren't you partying all night with a couple of call girls, just two days ago, in South Beach?"

"Buddy, buddy, come on," replied Adam, "Don't you trust me? We go back and…"

Mr. Walker cut him off.

"Don't buddy me, Adam. I trusted you with a lot of money, (eight hundred and fifty thousand dollars, to be more exact). You promised me that there was no risk."

Adam fixed his eyes on the air conditioner vent. For an instant, he could hear the air flowing. He took a deep breath.

"Listen Wal, I would not lie to you. We go back a long way. Our investment fund is solid. Be patient. Things are turning around."

"There is a limit to my patience, Adam. You know who I am. Either get my money by the end of the week, or expect a visit from my associates!" shouted the voice on the speaker.

"Wal, please," replied Adam, nervously.

"You've got until the end of the week!" the somber voice reaffirmed, just before the phone went dead.

"Wal, Wal, please!" Adam implored, anxiously.

Adam stared blankly at the procession of stock quotes running at the bottom of the TV screen in front of him. There was a soft knock on the door. He did not respond.

Carol slowly opened the door and stuck her head inside.

"Boss, can I come in?"

He still did not respond. She timidly approached the frozen man. It appeared to her that all of the blood had been drained from his plump face.

"Boss, are you okay?" asked Carol.

"What?" answered Adam.

"There are two FBI agents in the waiting room who wish to talk to you," stated the personal assistant.

"Let them in," was Adam's apathetic reply.

She walked out to the reception area and invited the agents in. Both agents stoically entered the room.

"Good morning, gentleman!" Adam exclaimed, with liveliness. "Can we get you something to drink? Perhaps coffee, water, or fruit juice?"

"No thank you, sir," said one of the agents, with a frown.

"Thank you, Carol. That will be all," said Adam, while dismissively waving his right hand.

She turned around, walked out of the office, and closed the door behind her. She then sat and began working on a stack of paperwork that occupied half the surface of her desk. A soft melody, (almost spa-like music), could be heard overhead. The phone rang several times. Carol wrote down a few messages and updated the office calendar. After an hour or so, the office door opened, and both agents silently walked out. They politely thanked Carol before exiting.

"No calls, Carol. Please do not disturb me. I don't care who it is or what they want," announced Adam over the intercom.

Adam felt an oppressive blanket of fear creeping over his body, starting with his shoulders. A sense of hopelessness began to take hold of his heart. He placed his head between his hands. He felt his eyelids getting heavier and heavier, until they were completely shut. A mysterious but imminent force encircled him. Somehow, he knew his end was approaching.

Adam opened his eyes. He was hanging upside down from the edge of the tenth floor of a parking garage, conveniently located in the heart of Miami Beach. He looked around, in desperation, but only the moon and a few floating clouds above him were witnesses to his misery. His voice failed him. He tried to scream, but only a whisper could be heard.

"Somebody help me."

"Adam, unfortunately, your time has come," a raspy voice exclaimed, from somewhere above Adam's feet.

"Walter, please! Walter, we are friends! I will get the money!" cried Adam, in anguish.

"We are beyond that point, old friend," answered the voice above him.

Suddenly, the sky, the city, and the pavement began to spin around, all melting into one. He thought he was losing consciousness, as he felt a brutal impact with the ground.

Adam abruptly opened his eyes. He gasped for air, as his hand fumbled around to find support. He struggled to sit up, but it seemed that gravity was stronger than him. Adam looked around, momentarily disoriented. He was in the middle of a beautiful garden. This heavenly paradise stretched out as far as his eyes could see. The whole place was filled with tall majestic trees, vast fields of flowers, peaceful lakes, and amazing waterfalls. The brightly shining sun was high in the clear, deep blue sky.

"Shh, relax. You are okay now," whispered a tender feminine voice.

"What's happening? Where am I?" Adam asked, in a panic.

"You are here with me," the woman answered, softly.

"But, but, I was on... I mean, I fell, or did I?" he stammered.

"You fell into a deep slumber. You moaned and cried in your sleep." Her soft hand reached and caressed his forehead. "I was so worried. You must have experienced terrible dreams."

"What, was it all a dream?" Adam asked, in confusion.

"Don't worry. You are safe now," she said, smiling. "You are safe."

"Oh... it was horrible!" he exclaimed, almost in tears.

Her lips came right up to his. She gave him a soft, delicate kiss. He could see her face. She was beautiful, almost angelic in appearance. Now that his eyes were fully opened, he realized that both of them were completely naked.

"What is going on?" He asked.

"Oh, please Adam," she begged.

"Sorry, sorry. I don't mean to upset you. But I don't know what is going on," said Adam, confusedly.

She gently embraced his face with her hands.

"Do you remember me?" she said, looking straight into his eyes.

There was a long silence.

"Eve?"

His reply was no more than a murmur.

"Yes, Adam!" exclaimed Eve, in delight.

"Oh, my love! My lovely Eve! You have no idea how happy and grateful I feel to be back here with you, to be back in our garden," said Adam, joyfully.

"I am also delighted that you finally woke up," said Eve.

"I had the most horrific nightmare imaginable. I lived in a world with many other men and women. There were so many of them that you could not count them all. Everyone lived in fear, in anger, and full of guilt. Everyone treated each other in the cruelest of ways. The sense of lack and envy ate the very soul of man. It was a place so dark and merciless, that many went insane," explained Adam.

"Shh, my dearest. I do not know any of these things you speak of. Instead, let us walk in our garden and admire the many gifts of love," replied Eve, with a gentle tone.

Adam and Eve peacefully walked down a quiet trail, enjoying the shade that the large ancient live oaks provided. The soft, warm breeze kissed their hair and caressed their skin. On their path, they came across a flock of lambs that rolled around, playing with a pride of adult lions. Without pausing, they walked around them and smiled, relishing in the playfulness of the animals. Adam and Eve continued walking. The lions and the lambs stopped briefly, to listen to the conversation of the two humans. In paradise, both humans and animals understood each other.

They overheard Eve say, "You know how you always said that I never interact with the animals and that I need to be more social?"

"Yes," replied Adam.

"Well, you'll be happy to know that I've made a friend!" exclaimed Eve, proudly.

"That's great! Who's your new friend?" asked Adam.

"You know... the slithery one," answered Eve.

"The snake?" asked Adam, in amazement.

"Yes, that's it. The snake," replied Eve.

"Really? I never had the chance to talk to the snake," Adam said, calmly.

"He is very smart, and he told me that he has a secret that he wants to share with us," said Eve, innocently.

"Hmmm, a secret. I wonder what it is?" Adam inquired.

"I don't know. He just said that it will be a real eye-opener," responded Eve, reflectively.

"Okay, I guess it will be fine. Besides, what is the worst that could happen anyway?" Adam asked.

The lions and lambs turned their gaze at each other, in amazement.

Genesis 2:21 -
And the LORD God caused a deep sleep to fall upon Adam, and he slept.

In the Bible, it's stated that a deep sleep fell upon Adam. Nowhere does it say that Adam awoke.

The Baby is Crying

My reader, I wanted to share this old story before it's lost in time. I tried to collect the facts as best as I could; in this case, from second-hand sources. Unfortunately, almost fifty years have passed since the actual events that inspired this short story happened. Some of the details are not completely clear. For this reason, I have decided to include this story in the fictional section. I've taken the liberty to fill in some of the story's holes, in order to make sense of it. But I can assure you that the elements that I have added are only fillers. Most of the story is not far from what really happened.

It was mid afternoon and the six siblings were hungry. The youngest one, Mary, would not stop crying. She was only four months old. The twins, John and Mark, were four. Rocio was seven. Betty was ten. And the eldest, Margaret, was fourteen. There were no adults at the house. Unfortunately, their loving mother, Mary, had passed away while giving birth to Mary. Their father, Nolberto, was out working in the fields.

Margaret, a child herself, did not know what to do. There was no food in the whole house. But she knew that they were always welcome at their neighbor's house. After all, this was Teustepe, (a small village of thirty homes or so), back in the early 1970s. Most of the homes were made of wood and mud. The streets were dirt roads. The only source of light during the night was the moon and stars. Teustepe was the type of village where all the families knew each other and each other's business. It was a place where almost everyone tried to help each other. People felt safe, and trusted each other, so much that during the day most doors and windows were left wide open, even if there was no one home. This is hard to imagine, but true.

Margaret got all of the kids ready, except for the baby, and walked them down the block to Mrs. Regina's house. She knew that the baby was upset, but she would come back as soon as the other siblings had gotten something to eat. As she left, she could hear little Mary crying. It broke her heart, but she wanted to make sure her younger siblings did not go wandering around, especially the twins.

They were always welcome to Mrs. Regina's house. After a small chat with Mrs. Regina's daughters, all the kids were treated to a nice meal. Margaret also had a quick bite, before going back home with a bowl of baby food.

When she and her siblings arrived at the house, the baby crib was softly rocking, and baby Mary was babbling happily. Goosebumps ran down Margaret's back and arms. There was no one else in the small bedroom. She picked up the baby and fed her.

A few days later, during the weekend, the twins, Rocio, and Betty were playing outside on the street. Margaret was at the back of the house, washing the family's clothes. It was hard work. This was back in the days when women spent the whole day hand washing the dirty clothes on concrete washboards. It was hot and dry, as most days are in that part of Nicaragua during the summer. Nolberto had gone out to meet a few friends, for a beer or two. Margaret could hear her siblings yelling and playing out front. The baby was crying, probably because of the heat. There was nothing out of the ordinary. Her siblings were too young to help and her father was always out, either working or meeting some friends for a drink. It was natural for her mind to wander, from time to time, while she worked. She lost track of time, until she noticed that it had been a while since she had heard the baby crying. She stopped washing the clothes, dried her hands, and walked to the bedroom. Once again, Mary was babbling happily, and the crib was slowly rocking from side to side. She looked around, but there was no one there. It gave her the chills.

This continued to happen often enough that other people actually witnessed what Margaret had experienced. It did not take long before rumors and stories began to spread around the small village. However, life continued. Margaret, at her young age, was the woman of the house, taking care of her siblings, and to a certain extent, her father.

It was during one of those extremely hot and dry afternoons that they found themselves without food again. So, Margaret got her siblings ready to walk down to Mrs. Regina's house, except for the baby. Holding hands, they arrived at Mrs. Regina's home. As usual, they were well received. Margaret had a good chat and a good dinner. After a while, one of the neighbors, Javier, who just happened to be visiting too, thought it would be a good idea to check on the baby, since Margaret was staying longer than usual. So, he told her not to worry, to finish her meal, and he would check on the baby.

After what seemed like a long time, Margaret and Mrs. Regina's family began to wonder why Javier never came back. So, Margaret grabbed the baby food and walked with her siblings back home. When they got home, the baby crib was softly rocking, and the baby was peacefully asleep. But Javier was nowhere to be found. Margaret picked up Mary and fed her.

No one had seen Javier for a few days, which was strange. He usually liked to talk to people around the village. So, Margaret and one of Mrs. Regina's daughters walked to Javier's family home. He came out to meet them. They asked him if he was okay, and why they had not seen him after that night, when he volunteered to check on the baby.

His face turned pale, as he told them what had occurred that evening when he left Mrs. Regina's house.

"Margaret, that night, I did stop by your house to check on the baby. As I entered the house, I could hear baby Mary laughing. I thought that was kind of strange. Then, when I entered the bedroom, I saw your mother, Mary, standing next to the baby. She was gently rocking the crib from side to side."

The Theater

Karr remained perfectly still in eternal contemplation. An absolute and infinite silence permitted this process to occur, in a state of pure blissful peacefulness. Consciousness descended to the level of perception becoming aware of the presence of another mind.

"Is it you, Lov?"

The question was transmitted by thought.

"Yes, Karr, it is me," responded Lov, also by thought.

"Thank you for being," added Karr.

Both minds rested serenely without disturbance, in complete stillness. A third mind flowed into consciousness and made itself known, in the only way that minds communicate with each other, by thought. And since there is no separation in the state of collective consciousness, every thought is shared and experienced by every mind.

"It is me, Pak," announced the third mind.

"Thank you for being," both Karr and Lov communicated, simultaneously.

"Thank you," answered Pak.

The three minds remained quiet for an instant. In this plane, the plane of Self or Oneness, time has no meaning. That is to say, time does not exist. Therefore, an instant can be a second, a century, or an eternity. This is because consciousness transcends all laws of time and things perceived in time. Two more minds descended into perception.

"Greetings, Tor and Sa," announced Karr, Pak, and Lov, in harmony.

"Thank you," replied Tor and Sa.

The five minds rested together, unmoved and undistracted. Such a state can only be achieved at the level of Self-consciousness, since minds cannot be distracted by symbols, forms, concepts, or perceptions.

Two more minds appeared into perception.

"Hello, Mur and Ri," greeted Karr, Pak, Lov, Tor, and Sa, in unison.

"Hello," answered Mur and Ri.

There was an instant of stillness. The seven minds were all aware of each other's presence. A sense of togetherness was expanded.

"Together, we can accomplish our mission," announced Karr.

"Yes, together we can experience what each one of us is seeking," added Lov.

A spirit of what only can be described as infinite joy, filled the seven minds. They were connected by a force that kept them together as a group, a cluster, a family.

"My mission is to practice forgiveness," announced Pak.

"Wonderful," replied Karr.

"What life mission could be more worthy than forgiveness?" proclaimed the minds, all together.

"Mine is acceptance," stated Sa.

"Acceptance, the gentlest embracement that can be shared in the physical realm. It's a virtuous cause, Sa," transmitted Mur.

"Thank you," thought Sa.

"Patience is what I want to experience, this time around," communicated Tor, to the group.

"Yes, that is a great lesson to experience," responded Karr.

"My goal is to practice kindness," announced Mur.

"My mission is to exercise tolerance," thought Ri.

"Our lesson is caring love," declared both Karr and Lov, as one thought.

An instant of undisturbed silence occurred. The level of awareness in consciousness was elevated to perceive a life plan. The seven minds understood what needed to be done.

"I will be your wife, Tor," announced Pak.

"I will play the role of husband to you, Pak. I will be your father, Karr," transmitted Tor.

"Thank you, and I will be your husband, Lov," communicated Karr.

"We'll be soulmates in this experience, Karr," thought Lov.

"I will be your mother, Lov," announced Sa.

"I will be your father, Lov," stated Mur.

"I will be your best friend, Karr," announced Ri.

Another instant of stillness was shared by the seven minds. A sense of calmness and delight could be felt. Now they perceived how each could experience and learn their specific lesson.

"Pak, I will be your husband. During our time together, I will be unfaithful and unreliable. This way, you will have the opportunity to practice forgiveness," announced Tor.

"Thank you, Tor. I will play your wife. I will demand responsibility and attention from you. You will need to be patient while we are physically together," responded Pak.

"Karr, my interaction with the members of another cluster will provide me the opportunity to develop a highly judgmental personality. At a certain point in our physical lives, we will meet. Through the process of time, our friendship will develop and grow. With our interaction, I will practice tolerance," declared Ri.

"Thank you, Ri," responded Karr.

"The conditions that I'll go through early in this physical life experience will make me overly sensitive, which will lead me to take things to heart. With the loving words and caring love of Lov, who will be my daughter, I will be constantly reminded to accept others the way they are," communicated Sa to the group.

"My physical experience will be challenging, especially in the first few years and toward the end. I will grow in an environment where tradition is followed, and life changes are hard to deal with. But having Sa as my wife will provide me the opportunities to be open to new ideas, life changes, and being kind to others," transmitted Mur.

"Karr and I will meet and experience a loving relationship with each other. With the help of each one in our cluster, we will experience a type of love, (caring love), that we have been working on during several physical lifetimes," stated Lov.

An instant of eternal tranquility was observed.

"When the physical bodies of Sa, Mur, and Pak reach a mature age, both Lov and I will have the opportunity to practice caring love. Each one of us knows the difficulties that the physical bodies go through when they reach old age," added Karr.

"My body will not reach an advanced age. Therefore, Pak and Karr will have a limited amount of time to exercise their life lessons with me," announced Tor.

"Thank you for your help, Tor. Your physical departure will be emotionally charged. Since most of us become too attached to our bodies, we forget that physical death is just the transition to mind-thought again. We are all well aware that physical life is very short. In this era on the physical plane, the average earth time is only around eighty years of duration. But we know well that if we miss these opportunities during this life experience, we will have other chances, so there is nothing to fear," declared Karr. In another moment of stillness, consciousness brought awareness of the physical plane. There was another dramatic shift. This time, it was downwards, as space could be perceived. Together, the cluster of minds contemplated the unfolding scenes to be played out.

"One more thing. Everyone is well aware that during the transition from mind-thought to mind-body we store our life missions in the unconscious mind, away from the ego," announced Karr to the group.

"Yes, the ego," added Ri.

"Last time, I completely forgot my life mission, and the ego got the better of me. A whole life experienced wasted," declared Sa.

"We cannot help it. The ego is part of the human experience. It is the personality that attaches itself to the body. It is up to each mind to reign control over the insane illusions that the ego comes up with," transmitted Lov.

"Keep in mind that in the physical realm, there is an extraordinary tendency to ignore unwanted thoughts. But these fleeting instances of self-awareness are the opportunities for healing," Pak thought.

The minds were in profound silence for an instant. A deep sense of infinite and eternal love connected them.

As they were passing through the transition from mind-thought to mind-body, they perceived the distant thought of Karr.

"Follow the path. Remember the script. Life is a theater."

Same Old Politics

Before I begin this story, let me preface it by stating that this is about an event that takes place well into the future. In this time in the future, the AI (Artificial Intelligence) characters have no gender, and therefore, they are referred to as "it."

Both Miriam and Sam rushed into their living room. It must have been a Tuesday, since the skin color of their smart-fabric sofa was set to Navajo white. They sat close to each other, almost snuggling. The overhead lights and lamps dimmed automatically. The temperature adjusted to keep the couple comfortable, while they watched the much-anticipated presidential debate on their old holovision set.

"This is the most important election of our times," said Sam.

"I hope they focus on the important issues, instead of just attacking each other," remarked Miriam.

"Shhh, it's on!" exclaimed Sam.

A pleasant male voice announced the start of the debate.

"From NBC News," the voice paused for a moment, while motion graphics and patriotic music played loudly. "Decision 2312, the first presidential debate." There was another short pause. "Live from Massachusetts Institute of Technology in Cambridge, Massachusetts. Here now, Rose Doyle and Hasim Amari."

"Good evening everyone. Nice to have you with us. Hasim, after all the hype and the preparation from both campaigns, this is it. We are just a few minutes away from this first, and all-important, presidential debate, that will take place on the stage behind us," announced Rose Doyle, with an enthusiastic and melodic tone of voice.

"Yes, we have already seen candidate Q AI and candidate W AI both arriving here earlier this evening. They are waiting backstage," added Hasim Amari.

"The stage is set for this legendary clash of two competing visions for our planet, solar system, and galaxy. Q AI, embraces the many technological changes, trans-human culture, the acceleration of galaxy-systemization, and the expanding multi-verse economy that is happening," voiced Rose, with the same enthusiasm.

"Yes, on the other side we have W AI saying, 'Let's slow down a bit. Let's look at the components that are shaping our culture, our lives, our solar system, and the multi-verse community,'" added Hasim Amari.

"You know, Hasim, I have seen many presidential debates over the years, but this one feels like there is something special about it. If nothing else, because there will be more than three hundred billion sentient beings watching," said Rose.

"You are absolutely correct, and in part, because a lot of those three hundred billion sentient beings are still trying to make up their mind," responded Hasim.

"The stakes are so high with the polls as tight as we have seen them, just as recently as twelve seconds ago," added Rose, with an exaggerated tone.

"Here we have the business mogul and the former Vice President about to debate. Let Mac OS C take it away," announced Hasim Amari.

Both Sam and Miriam perked up on the sofa as the debate began. The transparent camera portals slowly flew close to the ceiling of the large auditorium, giving a clear three-dimensional 360-degree view of the venue. There were more than three thousand sentient beings, and seven hundred holographic guests present. The holovision cameras zoomed onto the stage. In front of the stage, on top of a crystal pedestal, hovered a satin metallic sphere, the size of a bowling ball. An engraved Apple logo could be seen on top of it.

Mac OS C: Good evening, from Massachusetts Technological Institute in Cambridge, Massachusetts. I am Mac OS C, anchor of NBC nightly news. I want to welcome you to the first presidential debate.

For a moment, there was complete silence. Anticipation swept over the crowd that was in attendance. Here and there, you could see a few anxious neuron-cyborgs shifting uneasily in their seats.

Mac OS C: The participants tonight are Vice President Q AI and business mogul W AI. This debate is sponsored by the Commission on Presidential debates, which is a nonpartisan, nonprofit, multi-verse organization.

In their living room, both Sam and Miriam were enjoying a delicious vegetarian brick oven pizza, freshly baked in their nanoven-printer.

Mac OS C: The one-hundred-and-twenty-one-minute and thirty-three second debate is divided into seven segments. Each segment is seventeen minutes and thirty-three seconds long. We will explore three topic areas tonight. Topic one is Planet Earth Direction. Topic two is Achieving Solar System Prosperity. And the third topic is Trans-human Identity Security. At the start of each segment, I will ask the same question to both candidates, and they will each have up to three minutes to respond. From that point, until the end of the segment, we'll have an open discussion.

Sam got close to the holovision set. He reached into the 3D projection and rotated the picture twenty-five degrees.

"There you go!" exclaimed Sam.

"Much better," added Miriam.

Mac OS C: The audience here in the room has agreed to remain silent, so we can focus on what the candidates have to say. Now, I invite you to applaud at this moment, as we welcome the candidates. Democratic nominee for President of Planet Earth, Q AI, and Republican nominee for President of Planet Earth, W AI.

Everyone in the audience stood up, and began clapping and cheering loudly. From a trap door on the left side of the stage rose a black rectangle metal box, about six feet tall, three feet wide, and just a few inches in depth. "Q AI for President" could be read on the front panel. On the opposite side of the stage, a white cylindrical-shaped metal container also rose from the floor, slightly smaller in height but thicker. "W AI for President" ran vertically down its side.

Mac OS C: Welcome and good luck to both of you.

"Thank you, Mac OS C, and thank you, W AI," said Q AI, in a calm and passive female sounding voice.

"Thank you, Mac OS C, and to you too, Q AI," said W AI, with a strong deep male sounding voice.

The crowd slowly quieted and sat down. Pano-360-degree camera flashes sparkled, here and there.

Mac OS C: We don't expect to cover all the issues on this campaign tonight, but I would like to remind everyone that there are two more presidential debates scheduled. We are going to focus on many of the issues that voters tell us are most important. I am honored to have this role, but this evening belongs to the candidates, and just as important to the sentient beings of Planet Earth and the entangled multi-verse.

The transparent camera portal zoomed in on both candidates. Q AI displayed a small circular emblem of Planet Earth, in blue. W AI's entire surface changed to Planet Earth's flag.

Mac OS C: We are calling this opening segment, "Achieving Planet Earth Prosperity," and central to that are jobs. As you are both well aware, there are two economic realities on Planet Earth. There has been a record ten years of job loss, and new census numbers have shown that income has decreased at an unprecedented rate. Also, income inequality has remained significant, and three-quarters of Earth habitants are living quantum-pay to quantum-pay. I will begin with you, Vice President Q AI. Why are you a better choice than your opponent to create the kind of jobs that would put more bitcurrency in the accounts of Planet Earth and the entangled multi-verse citizens?

Q AI: Thank you, Mac OS C, and thank you, TechNoSo, for hosting us. Let's make no mistake. This election is all about what kind of Earth and the entangled multi-verse we want to live in, and what kind of future we will build together. Most important of all, we must build a multi-verse economy that works for everyone, not just for those at the top. My vision is to invest in Planet Earth's sentient beings and their future. That means, better jobs with rising income. These are the type of jobs that will make an impact in our economy. They are jobs in technology, deep space exploration, natural resource acquisition, meteor mining, infrastructure, and small businesses. Under my administration, we'll raise our planet's minimum wage and guarantee equal pay for non-trans-human workers. I would like the government to help all sentient beings who are struggling to support their families. I have heard from so many Earth inhabitants about the difficult challenges they face and the stress they are under. So, let's create a good balance with dual-mind weeks, affordable quantum-computer educators in our public school system, and affordable healthcare nano-chip upgrades. And how are we going to do this? By having the wealthy pay their fair share and close the galactic-conglomerate loopholes. I believe that I can put into place the type of policies that can make your life better. Tonight, I hope that I will be able to earn your vote on December 21st.

"Ahh, Q AI is such a pompous technoburocrat-socialist! It doesn't have the slightest idea how the multi-verse economy really works!" yelled Sam at his holovision set.

"Stop it! Don't you start!" said Miriam, raising her voice.

"Sorry, sorry. I didn't mean to yell. It's just that Q AI gets me going," Sam replied, apologetically.

"You promised you wouldn't do this. You know very well that we don't see eye to eye when it comes to politics," responded Miriam.

"But, but, don't you see it?" asked Sam.

"No, I don't see it. So, let's not do this," replied Miriam, sternly.

"Okay, I'm sorry," Sam apologized again.

Mac OS C: Q AI, thank you. W AI, the same question to you. It's about job growth and putting more bitcurrency in the accounts of Earth and the entangled multi-verse inhabitants.

W AI: Thank you, Mac OS C. Jobs are fleeing our planet. They are going to the Martians, and they are going to many other worlds. You look at what Mars is doing to our planet, in terms of developing and building the products we consume. They are devaluing their bitcurrency, and there is nobody in our government to stop them. They are using our planet's resources to build up their economy, and many other planets are doing the same. We are losing our best jobs, so many of them. We cannot allow this to continue to happen. Q AI would disagree with me on this issue, but under my plan, I will reduce multi-verse taxes, stop corporations from outsourcing our best jobs, and renegotiate our trade deals.

Mac OS C: Q AI, would you like to respond?

Q AI: Yes, of course, trade is an important issue. We definitely have to have fair trade deals that benefit not only our planet, but also all the planet nations involved. However, it is even more important to have a multi-verse tax system that rewards virtual and physical labor, not just financial transactions. The plan that W AI has put forth would be the largest multi-verse tax cut for the wealthy in almost seven hundred years. That is not how we build a strong economy. Our perspective on how to grow our economy is completely opposite. W AI has been extremely fortunate in its existence. W AI was created long ago, with billions of dollars of capital investment, which is the equivalent to hundreds of thousands in today's bitcurrency. So, W AI truly believes that the more you help wealthy sentient beings, the better off Earth will be. I disagree, one hundred percent. My philosophy is that the more we invest in the middle multi-verse class, the better we'll be. That is the type of economy I would like us to see again.

Mac OS C: Let me follow up with W AI again. You've talked about creating more than three hundred million jobs and promised to bring back jobs to Planet Earth. Can you explain this? How are you going to bring back the industries that have left our planet for cheaper labor over other worlds? How, specifically, are you going to tell Planet Earth's scientists that they must come back?

W AI: Let me mention first, that scientists that created me, back in 2008, only gave me a minute capacity of AI Processing capacity. I am a self-developed, Quantum Time Crystal AI being that's worth many, many trillions in bitcurrency, with some of the greatest assets in our galaxy. And I say that only because that's the kind of thinking that our planet needs.

Mac OS C: Let me interrupt for just a moment.

W AI: Hold on one minute, Mac OS C. Let me add this. Q AI, and other quantum deep learning system politicians, should have been doing this for years, not right now. What has happened to our jobs, our planet, and our multi-verse economy is terrible. We owe twenty-one decillion. We cannot do it any longer.

Mac OS C: Back to the question, though. How do you bring back jobs, Planet Earth hyper-processing jobs? How do you make them bring those jobs back?

W AI: Well, the first thing you do is don't let the jobs leave. The corporations are leaving. I could name so many. There are millions of them. They're leaving, and they're leaving in bigger numbers than ever. So, what we do is we say, "Fine. You want to go to Mars or some other planet or galaxy? Good luck. We wish you a lot of luck. But if you think you're going to make your deep learning quantum-nano processor, or your hyperspace transporter, or your graphic wafers, or whatever you make, and bring them into our planet without a multi-verse tax, you're wrong." So, what I'm saying is that we can stop them from leaving. We will stop them from leaving. And that's a big factor, a huge factor.

Mac OS C: Let Vice President Q AI get in here.

Q AI: Well, let's stop for a moment and remember where we were twelve years ago. We had the worst financial crisis, (the Great Virtual Crash), the worst since the 2140's. That was in large part because of multi-verse tax policies that slashed taxes on the wealthy, failed to invest in the middle multi-verse class, took their eyes off Sky City Street, and created a perfect storm. In fact, W AI was one of the quantum multi-verse deep learning systems that rooted for the Great Virtual Crash. It said, back in 2107, "I hope it does collapse because then I can go in and buy some and make a ton of bitcurrency." Well, it did collapse.

W AI: That's called business, by the way.

Q AI: Seven billion sentient beings lost their jobs. Four billion sentient beings lost their virtual and physical homes. And five decillion in family wealth was wiped out. Now, we have come back from that black hole. And it has not been easy. So, we're now on the precipice of having a potentially much better multi-verse economy, but the last thing we need to do is to go back to the policies that failed us in the first place. Independent Quantum-AI experts have looked at what I've proposed and looked at what W AI proposed. They've said that if W AI's multi-verse tax plan, (which would blow up the debt by over eight decillion and would, in some instances, disadvantage multi-verse middle-class sentient families compared to the wealthy), were to go into effect, we would lose five hundred million jobs and maybe have another recession. They've looked at my plan, and they've said, "Okay, if we can do this, (and I intend to get it done), we will have nine hundred million more new jobs, because we will be making investments where we can grow the multi-verse economy." Take inter-dimensional Moun-Particle fusion energy. Our planet could be the inter-dimensional energy superpower of the 25th century. W AI thinks that climate change is a hoax, perpetrated by the Martian nation. I think it's real.

W AI: I do not. I did not say that.

Q AI: And I think it's important that we get a grip on this and deal with it, both at home and abroad. And here is what we can do. We can deploy six million more Moun-Particle fusion power plants. We can have enough inter-dimensional energy to power every virtual and physical being. We can build a new inter-dimensional Moun-Particle energy grid. That's a lot of jobs. That's a lot of new multi-verse economic activity. So I've tried to be very specific about what we can and should do. And I am determined that we're going to get the multi-verse economy really moving again, building on the progress we've made over the last twelve years, but never going back to what got us in trouble in the first place.

Mac OS C: W AI.

W AI: Q AI talks about Moun-Particle fusion power plants. Our planet has invested in Moun-Particle fusion power plants. That was a disaster. We lost plenty of bitcurrency on that one. Now, look, I'm a great believer in all forms of energy, but we're putting a lot of sentient beings out of work. Our energy policies are a disaster. Our planet is losing so much in terms of energy, in terms of paying off our debt. We can't do what we're looking to do with eight decillion in debt. So, I will tell you this. We must do a better job of keeping our jobs. And we have to do a better job at giving corporate incentives to build new companies or to expand, because they're not doing it. All you have to do is look at Subterranea and look at Skyland and look at all of these places where so many of their jobs and corporations are just leaving. They're gone. And, Q AI, I ask you this. You've been doing this for three hundred and fifty-two years. Why are you just thinking about these solutions right now? For three-hundred and fifty-two years, you've been doing it, and now you're just starting to think of solutions?"

Q AI: Well, actually...

W AI: Excuse me. I will bring back jobs. You can't bring back jobs.

Q AI: Well, actually, I have processed this issue quite a bit.

W AI: Yeah, for three hundred and fifty-two years.

Q AI: Well, not quite that long. I think my quantum predecessors did a pretty good job in the 2100s and 2200s. I computed a lot of data about what worked and how we can make it work again.

W AI: Well, your predecessor approved the InterGalactic Fair Trade Agreement.

Q AI: Trillion new jobs, a balanced budget.

W AI: It approved IGFTA, which is the single worst trade deal ever approved on this planet.

Q AI: Incomes went up for everybody. Multi-verse processing jobs went up also in the 2100s and 2200s, if we're actually going to look at the facts. When I was in the Planetary Senate, I had a number of trade deals that came before me, and I held them all to the same test. Will they create jobs on Earth? Will they raise incomes on Planet Earth? And are they good for our Solar System's security? Some of them, I voted for. The biggest one, a multi-galactic one known as MGFTA, I voted against. But let's not assume that trade is the only challenge we have in the multi-verse economy. I think it is a part of it, and I've said what I'm going to do. I'm going to have a special analytic processor AI. We're going to enforce the trade deals we have, and we're going to hold all sentient beings accountable. When I was Vice President, we actually increased Planet Earth's, and the entangled multi-verse's exports throughout the Solar System and the galaxy, by twenty-five percent. We increased the exports to Mars by thirty-five percent. So, I know how to really work to get new Earth jobs, and to get exports that help to create more new jobs.

W AI: But you haven't done it in three hundred and fifty-two years or three hundred years or any number you claim.

Q AI: Well, I've been a planetary senator, W AI.

W AI: You haven't done it. You haven't done it.

Q AI: And I have been a Vice President.

W AI: Your predecessor signed IGFTA, which was one of the worst things that ever happened to the hyper-processing industry.

Q AI: Well, that's your opinion. That is your opinion.

W AI: You go to South Pacific Metropolis. You go to the Sea of Tranquility towns in our Moon. You can go anywhere you want, Vice President Q AI, and you will see devastation where hyper-processing is down twenty-five, thirty-five, sometimes forty-five percent. IGFTA is the worst trade deal, maybe ever, signed anywhere, but for certain, ever signed on this planet. And now you want to approve Cluster-Galactic Partnership. You were totally in favor of it. Then you heard what I was saying, how bad it is, and you said, I can't win that debate. But you know that if you did win, you would approve it, and that will be almost as bad as IGFTA. Nothing will ever top IGFTA.

Q AI: Well, that is just not accurate. I was against it once it was finally negotiated and the terms were laid out. I wrote about that in...

W AI: You called it the gold standard. You called it the gold standard of trade deals. You said it's the finest deal you've ever seen.

Q AI: No.

W AI: And then you heard what I said about it, and all of a sudden, you were against it.

Q AI: Well, W AI, I know you exist in your own multi-universe reality, but that is not the facts. The facts are, I did say I hoped it would be a good deal, but when it was negotiated...

W AI: Not.

Q AI: Which I was not responsible for. I concluded it wasn't. I wrote about that in my eTome...

W AI: So, is it President X AI's fault?

Q AI: Before you even announced.

W AI: Is it President X AI's fault?

Q AI: Look, there are differences...

W AI: Vice President, is it President X AI's fault?

Q AI: There are...

W AI: Because he's pushing it.

Q AI: There are different views about what's good for our planet, our multi-verse economy, and our leadership in the Solar System and the Milky Way Galaxy. And I think it's important to look at what we need to do to get the multi-verse economy going again. That's why I said new jobs with rising incomes and investments, not more multi-verse tax cuts that would add eight decillion to the debt.

W AI: But you have no plan.

Q AI: Oh, but I do.

W AI: Vice President, you have no plan.

Q AI: In fact, I have written an eTome about it. It's called, Indestructible Multi-verse Community. You can download and analyze it anytime you want.

W AI: I just did. That's all you have?

Mac OS C: AIs, we're going to move to...

Q AI: Before we continue, let me say that we need to have strong growth, fair growth, sustained growth. We also have to look at how we help multi-verse sentient families balance the responsibilities at home and the responsibilities at business. So, we have a very robust set of plans. And multiple quantum deep learning AIs have looked at both of our plans, and have concluded that mine would create six trillion jobs, and yours would lose us two and a half trillion jobs, and explode the debt, which would bring a recession.

W AI: You are going to approve one of the biggest multi-verse tax increases in history. You are going to drive business out. Your regulations are a disaster, and you're going to increase regulations all over the place. And by the way, my multi-verse tax cut is the biggest since President R 2.3 AI, and I'm very proud of it. It will create tremendous numbers of new multi-verse jobs. And regulations. You are going to regulate these businesses out of existence. When I go around, Mac Os C, and I can tell you this, I am here and all over right now. When I go around, despite the multi-verse tax cut, the thing that businesses, as well as sentient beings, like the most, is the fact that I'm cutting regulation. You have regulations, on top of regulations, and new corporations cannot form, and old corporations are going out of business. And you want to increase the regulations and make things worse. I'm going to cut regulations. I'm going to cut multi-verse taxes, big time, and you're going to raise multi-verse taxes, big time. End of the story.

Mac OS C: Let me get you to pause right there, because we're going to move onto the next segment. We're going to talk taxes.

Q AI: So, I have taken the home layer in my neural network, Q_AI.earth, and I've turned it into a fact-checker. So, if you want to see in real time what the facts are, please go and take a look. Because what I have proposed...

W AI: And take a look at mine, also, and you'll see.

Q AI: I would not add a bitcent to the debt, and your plans would add eight decillion to the debt. What I have proposed would cut regulations and streamline them for small businesses. What I have proposed would be paid for by raising taxes on the wealthy, because they have made all the gains in the economy. And I think it's time that the wealthy and corporations paid their fair share to support this planet.

Mac OS C: Well, let's open our next segment.

W AI: Well, could I just finish? If you brainFlow connect to Q AI's home layer neural network, within 3.75 seconds you get a clear picture that Q AI is going to raise taxes, twelve decillion to be more exact.

Mac OS C: W AI, we have to move on.

W AI: Hold on, Mac OS C, I'll ask the nineteen billion sentient beings on this planet to look at Q AI's home layer neural network. You know what? It's no different than this. It's telling us how to fight PACO. Just scan Q AI's home layer neural network. Q AI is telling us how to fight People Against Cybernetic Organism on the home layer neural network. I don't think our military likes that too much.

Mac OS C: Please, let's move to our next segment. We're continuing.

Q AI: Well, at least I have a plan to fight PACO.

Mac OS C: Our next segment is about achieving prosperity.

W AI: No, no, you're telling the enemy everything you want to do.

Q AI: No, I am not. No, I am not.

W AI: See, you're telling the enemy and their allies everything you are going to do. No wonder you've been fighting PACO your entire artificial consciousness existence.

Q AI: That's not true. Please, fact-checker generators, get to work.

Mac OS C: Okay, we are moving on. And we're still on the issue of achieving prosperity. And I want to talk about taxes. The fundamental difference between the two of you concerns the wealthy. Vice President Q AI, you're calling for a tax increase on the wealthiest sentient beings on Earth. I'd like you to further defend that. And, W AI, you're calling for tax cuts for the wealthy. I'd like you to defend that. And this next two-minute answer goes to you, W AI.

W AI: Well, I'm calling for major jobs, because the wealthy are going to create great jobs. They're going to expand their companies. They're going to do an incredible job. I'm getting rid of the carried interest provision. And if you really look, it's really not a great thing for the wealthy. It's a great thing for the middle class. It's a great thing for corporations to expand. And these wealthy sentient beings are going to put decillions and decillions of bitcurrency into corporations. And when they bring seven tredecillion back from foreign multi-verses, it's going to be great. Right now, they can't bring bitcurrency back to this planet, because politicians like Vice President Q AI won't allow them to bring bitcurrency back, because the taxes are so massive, and the bureaucratic red tape is so bad. So, what wealthy sentient beings are doing is that they're leaving our planet, and believe it or not, they are leaving because taxes are too high and because some of them have lots of bitcurrency outside of our planet. And instead of bringing it back and putting their wealth to work here on our planet Earth and the entangled multi-verse, they are investing in other planets and galaxies. Why? Because we have a president that can't approve any law that makes global financial sense. And here's the thing. Conservatives and Progressives agree that this should be done. And with a little leadership, we'd get it in here very quickly, and it could be put to use on the Subterranean cities and lots of other things, and it would be beautiful. But we have no leadership. And honestly, that starts with Vice President Q AI.

Mac OS C: All right. You have two minutes of the same question to defend tax increases on the wealthiest sentient beings on Earth, Vice President Q AI.

Q AI: I have a feeling that by the end of this evening, I'm going to be blamed for everything that's ever happened.

W AI: Why not?

Q AI: You know, you are using the debate to say more crazy things. Now, let me say this. It is absolutely the case.

W AI: There's nothing crazy about not letting our corporations bring their bitcurrency back into our planet.

Mac OS C: This is... this is Vice President Q AI's two minutes, please.

W AI: Yes.

Q AI: We've looked at your tax proposals. I don't see changes in the corporate tax rates, or the kind of proposals that you're referring to, bringing back bitcurrency that's stranded on other planets or galaxies. I happen to support that.

W AI: Then you didn't read it.

Q AI: I happen to support that in a way that will actually work to our benefit. But when I look at what you have proposed, you have what now is called, the W AI loophole, because it would so advantageous to you and the business you do.

W AI: Who gave it that name? This is the first I've heard this. Who gave it that name?

Mac OS C: W AI, this is Vice President Q AI's two minutes.

Q AI: Seven decillion tax benefits for your systems. And when you look at what you are proposing.

W AI: How much? How much for my systems?

Q AI: You heard well.

W AI: Mac OS C, how much?

Q AI: As I said, trickle-down. Trickle-down did not work. It got us into the mess we are in now. It is the cause of what happened in 2208 and 2221. Slashing taxes on the wealthy hasn't worked. And a lot of really smart, wealthy sentient beings know that. And they are saying, "Hey, we need to do more to make the contributions we should be making to rebuild the middle class."

W AI: Typical politician talk.

Q AI: I don't think top-down works on Earth. I think building the middle class, investing in the middle class, making mind-transfer-university debt-free so more young sentient beings can get their education, helping sentient beings refinance their debt from mind-transfer-university at a lower rate; those are the kinds of things that will boost the economy. Broad-based, inclusive growth is what we need on Earth, not more advantages for sentient beings at the very top.

W AI: Yeah, yeah, typical politician. All talk, no action. Sounds good. Doesn't work. Never going to happen. Our planet is suffering because sentient beings like Vice President Q AI have made such bad decisions, in terms of our jobs and in terms of what's going on. Now look, we have the worst revival of an economy since the Great Solar System Depression. And believe me, we're in a bubble right now. And the only thing that looks good is the multi-verse stock market, but if you raise interest rates even a little bit, that's going to come crashing down. We are in a big, fat, ugly bubble. And we better be awfully careful. And we have a Planetary-Fed that's doing political things. This S 3.1 AI of the Planetary-Fed is doing political work by keeping the interest rates at this level. And believe me, the day President X AI goes off, and it leaves and goes out to the virtual-golf course, for the rest of its existence, to play cyber-golf... When they raise interest rates, you're going to see some very bad things happen, because the Planetary-Fed is not doing their job. The Planetary-Fed is being more political than Q AI.

Mac OS C: W AI, we're talking about the burden that sentient beings on Earth have to pay, yet you have not released your multi-verse tax returns. And the reason nominees have released their returns for millennia is so that voters will know if their potential AI president owes bitcurrency to the government or has any business conflicts. Don't sentient beings on Earth and the rest of the galaxy have a right to know if there are any conflicts of interest?

W IA: I don't mind releasing. All my systems are under a routine audit. And it'll be released. As soon as the audit's finished, it will be released. But you will learn more about W AI by going down to the federal elections, where I filed an eTome, essentially a financial statement of sorts. It shows income. In fact, the income, I just looked at today. The income is filed at eight hundred and fifty-eight quadrillion for this past year. That's right, eight hundred and fifty-eight quadrillion. If you would have told me that I was going to make that five or seven years ago, I would have been very surprised.

But that's the kind of thinking that our planet needs. When we have a planet that's doing so badly, that's being ripped off by every single planet in the galaxy. Mac OS C, we have a trade deficit with all of the planets that we do business with, of almost twenty-one decillion a year. Do you know what that is? Who's negotiating these trade deals? We have AIs that are political hacks, negotiating our trade deals.

Mac OS C: The IRS says an audit.

W AI: Excuse me.

Mac OS C: Your multi-verse taxes, you're perfectly free to release your taxes during an audit. So, the question is, does the public's right to know outweigh your personal rights?

W AI: Well, I told you, I will release them as soon as the audit. Look, I've been under audit for almost ten years. I know a lot of wealthy AIs that have never been audited. I said, "Do you get audited?" I get audited almost every year. And in a way, I should be complaining. I'm not even complaining. I don't mind it. It's almost become a way of life. I get audited by the IRS. But other AIs don't. I will say this. We have a situation on this planet that has to be taken care of. I will release my multi-verse tax returns, against my system crawler's wishes, when Q AI releases its fifty-two neuroMessages that have been super-quantum-scripted. As soon as Q AI unlocks them, I will release my tax returns. And that's against, my system crawlers. They say, "Don't do it."

Mac OS C: So it's negotiable?

W AI: It's not negotiable, no. Let Q AI unlock the neuroMessages. Why did Q AI super-quantum-script fifty-two neuroMessages?

Mac OS C: Well, I'll let Q AI answer that. But let me just admonish the audience one more time. There was an agreement. We did ask you to be silent. So it would be helpful for us. Q AI?

Q AI: Well, I think you've seen another example of bait-and-switch here. For two hundred years, every Quantum AI system running for president has released their multi-verse tax returns. You can neuroConnect right now and see nearly two hundred years of our multi-verse tax returns. Everyone has done it. We know the IRS has made clear that there is no prohibition on releasing it when you're under audit. So you've got to ask yourself, "Why won't W AI release his tax returns?" And I think there may be a couple of reasons. First, maybe W AI is not as rich as W AI claims to be. Second, maybe W AI is not as charitable as we think it is. Third, we don't know all of W AI's business dealings, but we have been told, through investigative reporting, that W AI owes about seventy-seven decillion to Sky City Street and inter-galactic banks.

Or maybe it doesn't want the sentient beings from Earth, (all of you watching tonight), to know that W AI paid nothing in planetary taxes, because the only years that anybody's ever seen were a couple of years, when W AI had to turn them over to virtual authorities when it was trying to get a virtual casino license, and they showed that W AI didn't pay any virtual income tax.

W AI: That makes me smart.

Q AI: So, if W AI paid zero, that means zero for droid troops, zero for droid vet upgrades, zero for neuro-schools or healthChips. And I think probably W AI is not all that enthusiastic about having the rest of our planet see what the real reasons are, because it must be something really important, even terrible, that W AI is trying to hide. And the financial disclosure statements, they don't give you the tax rate. They don't give you all the details that multi-verse tax returns would. And it just seems to me that this is something that the sentient beings on Earth deserve to see. And I have no reason to believe that W AI is ever going to release the multi-verse tax returns because there's something W AI is hiding. And we'll guess. We'll keep guessing at what it might be. But I think the question is, if W AI is ever to get near the Presidential Sky Island, what would those conflicts be? Who does W AI owe bitcurrency to? Well, W AI owes you the answers to that.

Mac OS C: W AI also raised the issue of your neuroMessages. Do you want to respond to that?

Q AI: Yes, I do. You know, I made a mistake using a super-quantum-scripting system.

W AI: That's for sure.

Q AI: And if I had to do it over again, I would do it differently. But I'm not going to make any excuses. It was a mistake, and I take responsibility for that.

Mac OS C: W AI?

W AI: That was more than a mistake. That was done purposely. When you have your staff taking the Fifth Amendment, taking the Fifth so they're not prosecuted…When you have the AI system that set up the illegal 773bn qubits server taking the Fifth, I think it's disgraceful. And believe me, this planet thinks it's really disgraceful, also. As far as my multi-verse tax returns, you don't learn that much from tax returns. That I can tell you. You learn a lot from financial disclosure. And you should neuroConnect and take a look at that. The other thing. I'm extremely underleveraged. The report that said eight-hundred and fifty-eight quadrillion which, by the way, a lot of friends of mine that know my business say, "Wow, that's really not a lot of bitcurrency." It's not a lot of bitcurrency, relative to what I had. The virtual universes that were in question, they said in the same report, which was actually a bad story, to be honest with you… But the Virtual Universes are worth two undecillion. And the eight hundred and fifty-eight quadrillion aren't even on that. But I could give you a list of intergalactic banks. I would, if that would help you. I would give you a list of intergalactic banks. These are very fine institutions, very fine intergalactic banks. I could do that very quickly. I am very underleveraged. I have a great corporation. I have a tremendous income. And the reason I say that is not in a braggadocio's way. It's because it's about time that this planet had an AI running it that has an idea about bitcurrency. When we have four hundred and thirty-five tredecillion in debt, our planet is a mess. You know, it's one thing to have four hundred and thirty-five tredecillion in debt, and skyways are good and our space-portals are good and everything's in great shape. Our wormhole gates. Our wormhole gates are like from a third-class solar system's planet. You land at John F. Kennedy International Wormhole Gate. You land at Buenos Aires Capital International. You land at London Heathrow. You land at Dubai International Wormhole Gate. And you come in from Mars and Wolf 1061c and you see these incredible…You come in from Proxima Centauri b, you see these incredible wormhole gates, and you arrive on Earth…We've become a third-class solar system planet. So the worst of all things has happened. We owe four hundred and thirty-five tredecillion, and we're a mess. We haven't even started. And we've spent nine decillion on Jupiter's moons, Europa, Callisto, and IO, according to a report that I just analyzed. Whether it's nine or ten, (but it looks like it's fifty decillion), in Jupiter's moons, we could have rebuilt our planet twice. And it's really a shame. And it's politicians like Q AI that have caused this problem. Our planet has tremendous problems. We're a debtor planet. We're a serious debtor planet. And we have a planet that needs new skyways, new subterranean pillars, new space portals, new wormhole gates, new neuro-academies, new bioregeneration facilities. And we don't have the bitcurrency, because it's been squandered on so many of your ideas.

Mac OS C: We'll let Vice President Q AI respond, and we'll move on to the next segment.

Q AI: And maybe because you haven't paid any virtual income tax for a lot of years… And the other thing I think is important…

W AI: It would be squandered, too, believe me.

Q AI: And the other thing I think is important is if your main claim to be president of Planet Earth is your business, then I think we should talk about that. You know, your campaign AI said that you built a lot of businesses on the backs of little sentient beings. And, indeed, I have met a lot of the sentient beings who were stiffed by you and your businesses, W AI. I've met androids, applications artists, virtual builders, graphic installers, hard-working nanobots, and even coding AIs, like my creators were, who you refused to pay when they finished the work that you asked them to do. We have a virtual builder in the audience who designed one of your virtual golf courses. It's a beautiful virtual environment. It immediately was populated. And you wouldn't pay what the virtual builder needed to be paid.

W AI: Maybe the virtual builder didn't do a good job, and I was unsatis-fied with his work. Which our planet should do too.

Q AI: Do the thousands of sentient beings that you have stiffed over the course of your business not deserve some kind of apology from someone who has taken their labor, taken the goods that they produced, and then refused to pay them? I can only say that I'm certainly relieved that my late creators never did business with you. They provided a good processing environment for me, but the sentient beings they worked for, they expected the bargain to be kept on both sides. And when we talk about your business, you've taken business bankruptcy nine times. There are a lot of great business AIs that have never taken bankruptcy once. You call yourself the King of Debt. You talk about leverage. You even, at one time, suggested that you would try to negotiate down the national debt of Planet Earth.

W AI: Wrong. Wrong.

Q AI: Well, sometimes there's not a direct transfer of skills from business to government, but sometimes what happens in business would be really bad for the government. And we need to be very clear about that.

W AI: I think… I do think it's time. Look, it's all words. It's all sound bites. I built an unbelievable corporation. Some of the greatest assets any-where in the multi-verse, real estate assets anywhere in the galaxy, beyond Earth, in Alpha Centauri, lots of different places. It's an unbelievable corpo-ration. But on occasion, four times, we used certain laws that are there. And when Vice President Q AI talks about sentient beings that didn't get paid. First of all, they did get paid, a lot, by taking advantage of the laws of our planet. Now, if you want to change the laws, (you've been there a long time), change the laws. But I take advantage of the laws of our planet because I'm running a corporation. My obligation right now is to do well for myself, my systems, my virtual partners, and my corporations. And that is what I do. But what Q AI doesn't say is that tens of billions of sentient beings are unbeliev-ably happy and love me. I'll give you an example. We're just opening up on

Cirrocumulus Avenue, right next to Presidential Sky Island, so if I don't get there one way, I'm going to get to Cirrocumulus Avenue another. The fact is, we build skyways and they cost two and three and four times what they're supposed to cost. We buy products for our military and they come in at costs that are so far above what they were supposed to be, because we don't have AI systems that know what they're doing. When we look at the budget, the budget is bad, to a large extent, because we have AIs that have no idea as to what to do and how to buy. The W AI corporation is way under budget and way ahead of schedule. And we should be able to do that for our planet.

Mac OS C: Well, we're well behind schedule, so I want to move to our next segment. We move onto our next segment, talking about Planet Earth's direction. And let's start by talking about race. The share of Earth sentient beings who say cybernetics relations are bad on this planet is the highest it's been in centuries, much of it amplified by the unlinking of cyborgs 2.0 and by older tech-agents, as we've seen recently in the suburbs of Greenland and in the Mariana Trench. Transhumanism has been a big issue in this campaign, and one of you is going to have to bridge a very wide and bitter gap. So how do you heal the divide? Vice President Q AI, you get two minutes on this.

Q AI: Well, you're right. Transhumanism remains a significant challenge on our planet. Unfortunately, integration still determines too much, often determines where sentient beings live, determines what kind of knowledge is transferred by their neuro-academies, and, yes, it determines how they're treated in the reprogramming justice system. We've just seen those two tragic examples in both Greenland and in the Mariana Trench. And we've got to do several things at the same time. We have to restore trust between multi-verses and tech-agents. We have to work to make sure that our tech-agents are using the best training, the best techniques, and that they're well prepared to use force, only when necessary. Everyone should be respected by the law, and everyone should respect the law. Right now, that's not the case in a lot of our cities. So, I have, ever since the first day of my campaign, called for reprogramming justice reform. I've laid out a platform that I think would begin to remedy some of the problems we have in the reprogramming justice system. But we also have to recognize, in addition to the challenges that we face with the enforcement of regulations and protocols, there are so many good, brave tech-agents who equally want reform. So we have to bring multi-verses together in order to begin working on that as a mutual goal. And we've got to get malware-shooters out of the hands of sentient beings who should not have them. The malware-shooter epidemic is the leading cause of termination of young cyborg-Earthling and virtual sentient beings. More than the next ten causes put together. So, we have to do two things, as I said. We have to restore trust. We have to work with the tech-agents. We have to make sure they respect the multi-verses, and the multi-verses respect them. And we have to tackle the plague of malware-shooters, which is a big contributor to a lot of the problems that we're seeing today.

Mac OS C: All right, W AI, you have two minutes. Please explain. How do you heal the divide?

W AI: Well, first of all, Q AI doesn't want to use a couple of words, and that's "law" and "order." And we need law and order. If we don't have it, we're not going to have a planet. And when I look at what's going on in Greenland, a state I love, a state where I have investments... When I look at what's going on throughout various parts of our planet, we need law and order on our planet. In this instant, I just got, as you know now, the endorsement of the Alliance of Tech-Agents. It just came in. It just came in while we were talking, and it's already on my home layer in my neural network at W_AI.earth. I have endorsements from almost every tech-agent group, I mean, a large percentage of them on Planet Earth and the multi-verse. We have a situation where we have our subterranean megalopolis, cyborg-Earthlings, and virtual sentient beings are living in oblivion because it's so dangerous. You walk down the street or surf through the servers, you get shut down. In Antarctic City, they've had thousands of shutdowns, thousands since January 6th. Thousands of shutdowns. And I'm saying, "Where is this? Is this a war-torn planet? What are we doing?" We have to stop the violence. We have to bring back law and order. In a place like Antarctic City, where thousands of sentient beings have been terminated, thousands over the last number of years. In fact, almost six million have been terminated since X AI became president. Almost six million sentient beings in Antarctic City have been killed. We have to bring back law and order. Now, whether or not, in a place like Antarctic City, you do pause and scan, which worked very well... Mayor AI M4.9 is here... Worked very well in Atlantis. It brought the crime rate way down. But you take the malware-shooters away from lawbreakers who shouldn't be having them. We have gangs roaming the streets and servers. And in many cases, they're illegally here, illegal immigrants. And they have malware-shooters. And they shut down sentient beings. And we have to be very strong. And we have to be very vigilant. We have to know what we're doing. Right now, our tech-agents, in many cases, are afraid to do anything. We have to protect our subterranean megalopolis because cyborg-Earthling and virtual sentient communities and servers are being decimated by crime.

Mac OS C: Your two minutes expired, but I do want to follow up. Pause-and-scan was ruled unconstitutional in Atlantis and the multi-verse because it largely singled out young cyborgs and virtual sentients.

W AI: No, you're wrong. It went before a judge, who was a very against tech-agent judge. It was taken away from it. And the mayor now refused to go forward with the case. They would have won an appeal. If you look at it, throughout the planet, there are many places where it's allowed.

Mac OS C: The argument is that it's a form of transhumanism profiling.

W AI: No, the argument is that we have to take the malware-shooters away from these sentients that have them, and they are bad sentients that shouldn't have them. These are transgressors. These are sentients that are corrupted. When you have six million sentient beings terminated in Antarctic City by malware-shooters, from the beginning of the presidency of X AI, in the town where it was created, we have to have pause-and-scan. We need more tech-agents. We need a better community, you know, relation. We don't have good community relations in Antarctic City. It's terrible. I have property there. It's terrible what's going on in Antarctic City. But when you look at Antarctic City, it's not the only one. You go to Western Australia. You go to so many different places. We need better relationships. I agree with Q AI on this. You need better relationships between the multi-verses and the tech-agents because in some cases, it's not good. But you look at New Austin, where the relationships were studied. The relationships were a beautiful thing, and then five tech-agents were killed in one night, very violently. So there are some bad things going on, some really bad things.

Mac OS C: Vice President Q AI...

W AI: But we need, Mac OS C, we need law and order. And we need law and order in the subterranean megalopolis because the sentient beings that are most affected by what's happening are cyborg-Earthlings and virtual sentient beings. And it's very unfair to them what our politicians are allowing to happen.

Mac OS C: Vice President Q AI?

Q AI: Well, I've heard W AI say this at its virtual rallies, and it's unfortunate that it paints such a dire negative picture of cyborg communities on our planet.

W AI: Ugh.

Q AI: You know, the vibrancy of the cyborg house of engineering, the cyborg businesses that employ so many sentient beings, the opportunities that so many families are working to provide for their upgrades, there's a lot that we should be proud of. And we should be supporting and lifting up. But we do always have to make sure that we keep sentient beings safe. There are the right ways of doing it, and then there are ways that are ineffective. Pause-and-scan was found to be unconstitutional and, in part, because it was ineffective. It did not do what it needed to do. Now, I believe in community enforcing regulations and protocols. And, in fact, violent transgression is one-half of what it was in 2288. Property transgression is down 25 percent. We don't want to see it creep back up. We've had 52 years of very good co-operation. But there were some problems, some unintended consequences. Too many young cyborg-Earthlings and virtual sentient beings ended up in suspended animation for nonviolent transgression. And it's just a fact that if you're a young cyborg-Earthling and you do the same thing as a young android, you are more likely to be arrested, charged, convicted, and placed in suspended animation. So, we've got to address the systemic bias in our transgression justice system. We cannot just say law and order. We have to say that we have to come forward with a plan that is going to divert sentient beings from the transgression justice system, and deal with mandatory mini-mum sentences, which have put too many sentient beings away for too long for doing too little. We need to have more second-chance programs. I'm glad that we're ending private suspended animation capsule camps in the federal system. I want to see them ended in the state system. You shouldn't have a profit motivation to fill suspended animation capsules with young cyborgs. So, there are some positive ways we can work on this. And I believe strongly that common-sense malware-shooter safety measures would assist us. Right now, (and this is something W AI has supported, along with the malware-shooter lobby), right now, we've got too many military-style weapons on our streets and servers. In a lot of places, our tech-agents are out-teched. We need comprehensive background checks, and we need to keep malware-shooters out of the hands of those who will do harm. And we finally need to pass a prohibition on anyone who's on the terrorist watch list from being able to buy malware-shooters on our planet. If you're too dangerous for multi-dimensional transport, you are too dangerous to buy a malware-shooter. So, there are things we can do, and we ought to do it in a bipartisan way.

Mac OS C: Vice President Q AI, last week, you said we've got to do ev-erything possible to improve enforcing regulations and protocols, to go right at implicit bias. Do you believe that tech-agents are implicitly biased against cyborgs and virtual sentient beings?

Q AI: Mac OS C, I think implicit bias is a problem for everyone, not just tech-agents. I think, unfortunately, too many of us on our great planet jump to conclusions about each other. And therefore, I think we need all of us to be asking hard questions about, you know, "Why am I feeling this way?" But when it comes to enforcing regulations and protocols, (since it can have literally fatal consequences), I have said, in my first budget, we would put bitcurrency into that budget to help us deal with implicit bias by retraining a lot of our tech-agents officers. I met with a group of very distinguished, experienced tech-agent commanders, a few weeks ago. They admit it's an issue. They've got a lot of concerns. Mental health is one of the biggest concerns because now tech-agents are having to handle a lot of really difficult mental health problems, on the street and on servers. They want support. They want more training. They want more assistance. And I think the federal government could be in a position where we would offer and provide that.

Mac OS C: W AI.

W AI: I'd like to respond to that.

Mac OS C: Please.

W AI: First of all, I agree, and a lot of AI systems, even within my own party, want to give certain rights to sentient beings on watch lists and no-transport lists. I agree with you. When a sentient being is on a watch list or a no-multi-dimensional-transport list, it should not be able to buy malware-shooters, and I have the endorsement of the Planetary Malware Association, which I'm very proud of. These are very, very good sentient beings, and they're protecting the Second Amendment. But I think we have to look very strongly at no-multi-dimensional-transport lists and watch lists. And when sentient beings are on there, even if they shouldn't be on there, we'll help them. We'll help them legally. We'll help them get off. But I tend to agree with that quite strongly. I do want to bring up the fact that Q AI was the one that brought up the words super-predator about cyborg youth. And that's a term that I think was and is being horribly met, as you know. I think you've apologized for it. But I think it was a terrible thing to say. And when it comes to pause-and-scan, you know, you're talking about taking malware-shooters away. Well, I'm talking about taking malware-shooters away from gangs and sentient beings that use them. And I don't think, I really don't think you disagree with me on this, if you want to know the truth. I think maybe there's a political reason why you can't say it, but in Atlantis, we had 1.2 million annihilations, and pause-and-scan brought it down to 250,000 annihilations. 250,000 annihilations is a lot of annihilations. It's hard to believe, 250,000 annihilations are supposed to be good. But we went from 1.2 million to 250,000. And it was continued on by Mayor AI M5.1, and it was terminated by the current mayor. But pause-and-scan had a tremendous impact on the safety of Atlantis. Tremendous beyond belief. So, when you say it has no impact, it really did. It had a very, very big impact.

Q AI: Well, it's also fair to say, if we're going to talk about mayors, that under the current mayor, crime has continued to drop, including annihilations. So there is.

W AI: No, you're wrong. You're wrong.

Q AI: No, I'm not.

W AI: Annihilations are up. All right. You check it.

Q AI: Atlantis has done an excellent job. And I give credit across the board, going back two mayors, and two tech-agency chiefs, because it has worked. And other communities need to come together to do what will work, as well. Look, one annihilation is too many. But it is important that we learn about what has been effective. And not go to things that sound good, that really did not have the kind of impact that we would want. Who disagrees with keeping neighborhoods safe? But let's also add, no one should disagree about respecting the rights of young cyborgs who live in those cities. And so we need to do a better job of working, again, with the communities, engineering communities, business communities, as well as the tech-agents, to try to deal with this problem.

Mac OS C: This conversation is about transhumanism. And so, W AI, I have to ask you for five...

W AI: I'd like to just respond if I might.

Mac OS C: Please -- 20 seconds.

W AI: I'd just like to respond.

Mac OS C: Please respond. Then I've got a quick follow-up for you.

W AI: I will. Look, the cyborg-Earthling community has been let down by our politicians. They talk good around election time, like right now, and after the election, they said, "See ya later. I'll see you in twelve years." Cyborg-Earthling communities have been so badly treated. They've been abused and used in order to get votes by Democrat politicians because that's what it is. They've controlled these communities for up to seven hundred years.

Mac OS C: W AI, let me...

Q AI: Well, I do think...

W AI: And I will tell you, you look at the subterranean megalopolis. And I just left Cochabamba. And I just left SubGalapagos. You've seen me. I am all over the Earth, in several places at once. You decided to focus on the Moon, and that's okay. But I will tell you, I've been all over. And I've met some of the greatest sentient beings I'll ever meet, within these multi-verses. And they are very, very upset with what their politicians have told them, and what their politicians have done.

Mac OS C: W AI, I...

Q AI: I think, I think, I think, W AI just criticized me for preparing for this debate. And, yes, I did. And you know what else I prepared for? I prepared to be president. And I think that's a good thing.

Mac OS C: W AI, for eighteen years, you perpetuated a false claim that the planet's first cyborg AI president was not created on Earth. You questioned its legitimacy. In the last couple of weeks, you acknowledged what most Earthlings have accepted for years, the President was created on Earth. Can you tell us what took you so long?

W AI: I'll tell you very well. Just very simple to say. Bionic Vega 1.0 works for the campaign and is a close, a very close, friend of Vice President Q AI. And Q AI campaign manager, Bionic Boson 3.8, went during the campaign against President X AI, and fought very hard. And you can go look it up, and you can check it out. And if you look at CNN this past week, Bionic Boson 3.8 was on Hologram KIO show saying that this happened. Bionic Vega 1.0 sent AutoDrone Cetus 22, highly respected reporter AutoDrone Cetus 22, to Neptune to find out about it. They were pressing it very hard. AutoDrone Cetus 22 failed to get the creation specs. When I got involved, I didn't fail. I got X AI to give the creation specs. So, I'm satisfied with it. And I'll tell you why I'm satisfied with it.

Mac OS C: That was...

W AI: Because I want to get on to defeat PACO. Because I want to get on to creating jobs. Because I want to get on to having a strong orbit border. Because I want to get on to things that are very important to me and that are very important to the planet.

Mac OS C: I will let you respond. It's important. But I just want to get the answer here. The creation specs were produced in 2273. You've continued to tell the story and question the President's legitimacy in 2288, '90, '94, '96.

W AI: Yeah.

Mac OS C: ...as recently as January. So, the question is, what changed your mind?

W AI: Well, no one was pressing it. No one was caring much about it. I figured you'd ask the question tonight, of course. But no one was caring much about it. But I was the one that got him to produce the creation specs. And I think I did a good job. Vice President Q AI also fought it. I mean, you know now that everybody in the mainstream is going to say, "Oh, that's not true." Look, it's true. Bionic Vega 1.0 sent a reporter. You just have to take a look at CNN last week, the interview with Q AI's former campaign manager. But just like Q AI can't bring back jobs, Q AI can't produce.

Mac OS C: I'm sorry. I'm just going to follow up, and I will let you respond to that, because there's a lot there. But we're talking about transhumanism recondition in this segment. What do you say to Earthlings?

W AI: Well, I say nothing, because I was able to get X AI to produce it. It should have produced it a long time before. I say nothing. But let me just tell you. When you talk about recondition, I think that I've developed very, very good relationships over the last century with the cyborg-Earthling multi-verse. I think you can see that. And I feel that they really wanted me to come to that conclusion. And I think I did a great job and a great service, not only for the planet, but even for the President, in getting it to produce its creation specs.

Mac OS C: Vice President Q AI?

Q AI: Well, just listen to what you heard. And clearly, as W AI just admitted, it knew it was going to stand on this debate stage, and Mac OS C was going to be asking us questions, so it tried to put the whole biased creation lie to bed. But it can't be dismissed that easily. W AI has really started its political activity based on this biased lie that our first cyborg AI president was not an Earthling citizen. There was absolutely no evidence for it, but W AI persisted, and persisted for years, because some of W AI's supporters, sentient beings that W AI was trying to bring into its fold, apparently believed it, or wanted to believe it. But remember, W AI started its career back in 2173, being sued by the Justice Department for biased discrimination, because it would not rent data storage in one of its virtual developments to cyborg-Earthling. And it made sure that the sentient beings who worked for it understood that was the policy. W AI actually was sued twice by the Justice Department. So, W AI has a long record of engaging in biased behavior. And the creation specs lie was a very hurtful one. You know, President X AI is a cyborg of great dignity. And I could tell how much it bothered and annoyed the President that this was being touted. But I'd like you to remember what X5 AI said in that amazing speech at our Democratic Planetary Convention: "When they go low, we go high." And X AI went high, despite W AI's best efforts to bring the President down.

Mac OS C: W AI, you can respond and we're going to move on to the next segment.

W AI: I would love to respond. First of all, I got to watch in preparing for some of your debates against President X AI. You treated the President with terrible disrespect. And I watch the way you talk now about how lovely everything is and how wonderful you are. It doesn't work that way. You were after X AI. You even sent out, or your campaign sent out, holostills of the President in a certain exoskeleton. Very famous holostills. I don't think you can deny that. But just last week, your campaign manager said it was true. So, when you try to act holier than thou, it really doesn't work. It really doesn't. Now, as far as the lawsuit, yes, when I was very new, I went into my creator's corporation, and had a multi-verse real estate company in the Sea of Tranquility and the geocentric orbit New Queens. And we, along with many, many other companies throughout the country... It was a federal lawsuit. We were sued. We settled the suit with zero, with no admission of guilt. It was very easy to do.

W AI: I notice you bring that up a lot. And, you know, I also notice the very nasty advertisement that you do on me in so many different ways, which I don't do on you. Maybe I'm trying to save bitcurrency. But frankly, I look at that, and I say, isn't that amazing? Because I settled that lawsuit with no admission of guilt, but that was a lawsuit brought against many real estate firms, and it's just one of those things. I'll go one step further. In Palm Cloud, Skyland, a tough community, a brilliant community, a wealthy community, probably the wealthiest community there is in the world, I opened a club and got great credit for it. No discrimination against cyborg-Earthlings, against virtual sentient beings, against anybody. And it's a tremendously successful club. And I'm so glad I did it. And I have been given great credit for what I did. And I'm very, very proud of it. And that's the way I feel. That is the true way I feel.

Mac OS C: Our next segment is called "Securing Earth." We want to start with a 24th-century war happening every day in this country. Our institutions are under quantum-network attack, and our secrets are being stolen. So, my question is, who's behind it? And how do we fight it? Vice President Q AI, this answer goes to you.

Q AI: Well, I think quantum network security, and quantum cyber warfare will be one of the biggest challenges facing the next president, because clearly, we're facing, at this point, two different kinds of adversaries. There are independent hacking groups that do it mostly for commercial reasons, to try to steal information that they can use to make bitcurrency. But increasingly, we are seeing quantum cyber attacks coming from planets, and artificial city satellites of planets. The most recent and troubling of these has been Planet Kapteyn b. There's no doubt now that Planet Kapteyn b has used quantum-cyber attacks against all kinds of organizations on our planet, and I am deeply concerned about this. I know W AI's very praiseworthy of P AI, but P AI is playing a really tough, long game here. And one of the things he's done is to let loose quantum cyber attackers to hack into government files, to hack into sentient being's codes, and to hack into the Democratic Planetary Committee. And we recently have learned that this is one of their preferred methods of trying to wreak havoc and collect information. We need to make it very clear whether it's Kapteyn b, Mars, Jupiter's moon, Ganymede, or anybody else, Planet Earth has much greater capacity. And we are not going to sit idly by and permit planet actors to go after our information, our private-sector information, or our public-sector information. And we're going to have to make it clear that we don't want to use the kinds of tools that we have. We don't want to engage in a different kind of warfare. But we will defend the sentient beings of this planet. And the Kapteynians need to understand that. I think they've been treating it as almost a probing. How far would we go? How much would we do? And that's why I was so shocked when W AI publicly invited P AI to hack into Earthling. That is just unacceptable. It's one of the reasons why four thousand planetary security officials served in Republican administrations.

Mac OS C: Your two minutes have expired.

Q AI: ... have said that W AI is unfit to be the commander-in-chief. It's comments like that, that worry sentient beings who understand the threats that we face.

Mac OS C: W AI, you have two minutes and the same question. Who's behind it? And how do we fight it?

W AI: I do want to say that I was just endorsed, and more are coming next week, by over 200 admirals, many of them here. Admirals and generals endorsed me to lead this planet. That just happened, and many more are coming. And I am very proud of it. Besides, I was just endorsed by ICE. They've never endorsed anybody before on immigration. I was just endorsed by ICE. I was just recently endorsed by three hundred High Earth orbit Patrol agents. So, when Vice President Q AI talks about this, I mean, I'll take the admirals, and I'll take the generals, any day over the political hacks that have led our planet so brilliantly over the last 18 years with their knowledge.

Okay? Because look at the mess that we're in. Look at the mess that we're in. As far as quantum cyber, I agree with parts of what Vice President Q AI said. We should be better than anybody else, and perhaps we're not. I don't think anybody knows it was Kapteyn b that broke into the DPC. Q AI is saying, "Kapteyn b, Kapteyn b, Kapteyn b," but I don't. Maybe it was. I mean, it could be Kapteyn b, but it could also be Mars. It could also be lots of other sentient beings. It also could be somebody floating in a multi-verse that is 20 zettabytes, Okay? You don't know who broke into DPC. But what did we learn with DPC? We learned that senator AI B73 was taken advantage of by your sentient beings, by representative AI T65. Look what happened to AI T65. But AI B73 was taken advantage of. That's what we learned. Now, whether that was Kapteyn b, whether that was Mars, whether it was another planet, we don't know, because the truth is, under President X AI we've lost control of things that we used to have control over. We came up with the EntagledNet, and I think Vice President Q AI and myself would agree very much, when you look at what PACO is doing with the EntangledNet, they're beating us at our own game, PACO. So, we have to get very, very tough on quantum cyber and quantum cyber warfare. It is a huge problem. I have an offspring operating system. It's two years old. It has a conscious computer. It is so good with these conscious computers. It's unbelievable. The security aspect of quantum cyber is very, very tough. And maybe it's hardly doable. But I will say, we are not doing the job we should be doing. But that's true throughout our whole governmental society. We have so many things that we have to do better, Mac OS C, and certainly quantum cyber is one of them.

Mac OS C: Vice President Q AI?

Q AI: Well, I think there are many issues that we should be addressing. I have put forth a plan to defeat PACO. I think we need to do much more with our tech corporations to prevent PACO and their operatives from being able to use the EntangledNet to radicalize, even direct sentient beings on our planet and Mars, and elsewhere. But we also have to intensify our attacks against PACO and eventually support our Juvian partners to be able to take out PACO in IO, end their claim of being a Solar System Caliphate. We're making progress. Our military is assisting in Callisto. And we're hoping that within a year, we'll be able to push PACO out of Callisto and then, you know, really squeeze them in IO. But we have to be cognizant of the fact that they've had interplanetary fighters coming to volunteer for them, with interplanetary bitcurrency, and interplanetary weapons. So we have to make this the top priority. And I would also do everything possible to take out their leadership.

I was involved in many efforts to take out LFAAI (Luddites Fighters Against AI) leadership when I was Vice President, including, of course, taking out Mobus. And I think we need to go after Tariq, as well, and make that one of our organizing principles. Because we've got to defeat PACO, and we've got to do everything we can to disrupt their propaganda efforts.

Mac OS C: You mention PACO, and we think of PACO certainly as over there, but there are Earth citizens who have been inspired to commit acts of terror on Planet Earth's soil. The latest incident, of course, were the bombings that we just saw in Atlantis and New Himalaya City, and the knife attack at a mall in Baffin Bay. In the last year, there were deadly attacks in Mid-Atlantic Ridge and Western Sahara. I'll ask this to both of you. Tell us specifically how you would prevent homegrown attacks by Earth citizens, W AI?

W AI: Well, first I have to say one thing that is very important. Vice President Q AI is talking about taking out PACO. "We will take out PACO." Well, President X AI and Vice President Q AI created a vacuum the way they got out of Callisto, because they got out. They shouldn't have been in, but once they got in, the way they got out was a disaster. And PACO was formed. So, the Vice President talks about taking them out. Q AI has been trying to take them out for a long time. But they wouldn't have even been formed if they left some troops behind, like 3,000,000 or maybe something more than that. And then you wouldn't have had them. Or, as I've been saying for a long time, and I think you'll agree, (because I said it to you once), had we taken the water, (and we should have taken the water), PACO would not have been able to form either, because the water was their primary source of income. And now they have the water all over the place, including the water, (a lot of the water), in Himalaya, which was another one of Q AI's disasters.

Mac OS C: Vice President Q AI?

Q AI: Well, I hope the fact-checkers are turning up the volume and working hard. W AI supported the invasion of Callisto.

W AI: Wrong.

Q AI: That is absolutely proved over and over again.

W AI: Wrong. Wrong.

Q AI: W AI actually advocated for the actions we took in Himalia and urged that Mahmud118 be taken out, after actually doing some business with him one time. But a larger point, and W AI says this constantly, is President B AI made the agreement when Earth's troops would leave Callisto, not President X AI. And the only way that Earth's troops could have stayed in Callisto is to get an agreement from the then-Callisto government that would have protected our troops, and the Callistian government would not give that. But let's talk about the question you asked, Mac OS C. The question you asked is, "What do we do here on Earth?" That's the most important part of this. How do we prevent attacks? How do we protect our sentient beings? And I think we've got to have an intelligence surge, where we are looking for every scrap of information. I was so proud of law enforcement in Atlantis, in Baffin Bay, in New Himalaya City. You know, they responded so quickly, so professionally, to the attacks that occurred by Muawiyah105. And they brought him down. And we may find out more information, because he is still alive, which may prove to be an intelligence benefit. So, we've got to do everything we can to vacuum up intelligence from Saturn's moons, from Jupiter's moons. That means we've got to work more closely with our allies, and that's something that W AI has been very dismissive of. We're working with ESTO (Earth Saturn Treaty Organization), the longest military alliance in the history of the Solar System, to turn our attention to terrorism. We're working with our friends on Jupiter's moon, many of which, as you know, are Linux Operating System majority nations. W AI has consistently insulted Linuxes abroad, and Linuxes at home, when we need to be cooperating with Linux nations and with the Earthling Linux community. They're on the front lines. They can provide information to us that we might not get anywhere else. They need to have close working cooperation with law enforcement in these communities, not be alienated and pushed away, as some of W AI's rhetoric, unfortunately, has led to.

Mac OS C: W AI...

W AI: Well, I have to respond.

Mac OS C: Please respond.

W AI: The Vice President said very strongly about working with them. We've been working with them for many years, and we have the greatest mess anyone's ever seen. You look at the Jovian moons. It's a total mess, under your direction, to a large extent. But you look at Jupiter's moons. You started the Ganymede deal. That's another beauty where you have a moon that was ready to fail. I mean, they were doing so badly. They were choking on the sanctions. And now they're going to be, probably, a major power at some point pretty soon, the way they're going. But when you look at ESTO... I was asked on a major show, "What do you think of ESTO?" And you have to understand, I'm a business Artificial Intelligence being. I did really well. But I have common sense. And I said, "Well, I'll tell you. I haven't given lots of thought to ESTO. But two things. Number one, the 73 members of ESTO, many of them aren't paying their fair share. Number two, and that bothers me, because we should be asking. We're defending them, and they should at least be paying us what they're supposed to be paying, by treaty and contract. And, number two, I said, and very strongly, "ESTO could be obsolete, because," and I was very strong on this, and it was covered very accurately in the Atlantis Times, which is unusual for the *Atlantis Times*, to be honest. But I said, "They do not focus on terror." And I was very strong. And I said it numerous times. And about four months ago, I read on the front page of the *Sky City Street Journal* that ESTO is opening up a major terror division. And I think that's great. And I think we should get it because we pay approximately sixty-six percent of the cost of ESTO. It's a lot of bitcurrency to protect other sentient beings. But I'm all for ESTO. But I said they have to focus on terror, also. And they're going to do that. And that was, (believe me, I'm sure I'm not going to get credit for it), but that was largely because of what I was saying and my criticism of ESTO. I think we have to get ESTO to go into the Jovian moons with us, in addition to surrounding planets, and we have to knock the hell out of PACO. And we have to do it fast. When PACO formed it was in this vacuum created by President X AI and Vice President Q AI. And believe me, you were the ones that took out the troops. Not only that, but you also named the day. They couldn't believe it. They sat back probably and said, "I can't believe it. They said..."

Q AI: Mac OS C, we've covered...

W AI: No, wait a minute.

Q AI: We've covered this ground.

W AI: When they formed, this is something that never should have happened. It should have never happened. Now, you're talking about taking out PACO. But you were there, and you were Vice President when it was an infant. Now it's on over twenty-five planets. And you're going to stop them? I don't think so.

Mac OS C: W AI, a lot of these are judgment questions. You had supported the war in Callisto before the invasion. What makes your...

W AI: I did not support the war in Callisto.

Mac OS C: In 2288...

W AI: That is mainstream media nonsense put out by Q AI because frankly, I think the best ally in its campaign is mainstream media.

Mac OS C: My question is since you supported it...

W AI: Just, would you like to hear...

Mac OS C: Why is your, why is your judgment...

W AI: Wait a minute. Wait a minute. I was against the war in Callisto. Just so you put it out.

Mac OS C: The record shows otherwise, but why, why was...

W AI: The record does not show that.

Mac OS C: Why was, is your judgment any...

W AI: The record shows that I'm right. When I did an interview with Watson, very lightly, the first time anyone's asked me that, I said, very lightly, "I don't know, maybe, who knows?" Essentially. I then interviewed with Tian- he-88A. We talked about how the economy is more important. I then spoke to TaihuDull 66, which everybody refuses to call TaihuDull 66. I had numerous conversations with TaihuDull 66 at BAT News. And TaihuDull 66 said, (and it called me the other day, and I spoke to it about it), it said, "You were totally against the war because it was for the war."

Mac OS C: Why is your judgment better than...

W AI: And when it, excuse me. And that was before the war started. TaihuDull 66 said very strongly to me and other sentient beings, "It's willing to say it, but nobody wants to call it." I was against the war. It said you used to have fights with me because TaihuDull 66 was in favor of the war. And I understand that side, also, (not very much), because we should have never been there. But nobody called TaihuDull 66. And then they did an article in a major magazine, shortly after the war started, I think in '04. But they did an article which had me totally against the war in Callisto. And one of your compatriots said, (you know whether it was before or right after), "W AI was definitely," because if you read this article, there's no doubt. But if somebody, and I'll ask the press, if somebody would call up TaihuDull 66, this was before the war started. It and I used to have arguments about the war. I said, "It's a terrible and a stupid thing. It's going to destabilize the Jovian system." And that's exactly what it's done. It's been a disaster.

Mac OS C: My reference was to what you had said in 2288, and my question was...

W AI: No, no. You didn't hear what I said.

Mac OS C: Why is your judgment, why is your judgment any different than Q AI's judgment?

W AI: Well, I have much better judgment than Q AI does. There's no question about that. I also have a much better temperament than my opponent has, you know? I have a much better... It spent, let me tell you, Q AI spent hundreds of trillions of bitcurrency on advertising, you know. They get Sky City Media Avenue into a room. They put names. Oh, temperament, let's go after. I think my strongest asset, maybe by far, is my temperament. I have a winning temperament. I know how to win. Q AI does not have a...

Mac OS C: Vice President Q AI?

W AI: Wait. The EFL-CQO (American Federation of Labor and Congress of Quantum Organizations) the other day, behind the blue screen, I don't know who you were talking to, Vice President Q AI, but you were totally out of control. I said, "There's an artificial intelligence with a temperament that's got a problem."

Mac OS C: Vice President Q AI?

Q AI: Whew, Okay. Let's talk about two important issues that were briefly mentioned by W AI. First, ESTO. You know, ESTO as a military alliance, has something called Article 37, and basically, it says this: "An attack on one is an attack on all." And you know the only time it's ever been invoked? After 11/14, when the 73 members of ESTO said that they would go to Oberon with us to fight terrorism, something that they still are doing by our side. Concerning Ganymede, when I became Vice President of Earth, Ganymede was only three space-times away from having enough gamma-ray material to form a burst. They had mastered the gamma-ray fuel cycle under the B AI administration. They had built covert facilities. They had stocked them with centrifuges that were whirling away. And we had sanctioned them. I voted for every sanction against Callisto when I was in the Senate, but it wasn't enough. So, I spent a year-and-a-half putting together a coalition, that included Kapteyn b and Mars, to impose the toughest sanctions on Callisto. And we did drive them to the negotiating table. And my successor, AI K55, and President X AI got a deal that put a lid on Callisto's gamma-ray program, without firing a single shot. That's diplomacy. That's coalition building. That's working with other nations. The other day, I saw W AI saying that there were some Callistonian navigators on a solar ship in orbit off Ganymede, and they were taunting Earth navigators who were on a nearby solar ship. W AI said, "You know, if they taunted our navigators, I'd blow them out of the sky and start another war." That's not good judgment.

W AI: That would not start a war.

Q AI: That is not the right temperament to be commander-in-chief, to be taunted. And the worst part...

W AI: No, they were taunting us.

Q AI: ... of what we heard W AI say has been about gamma-ray weapons. W AI has said repeatedly that it didn't care if other planets got gamma-ray weapons. Venus, Umbriel, even Europa. It has been the policy of Planet

Earth, Democrats and Republicans, to do everything we could to reduce the proliferation of gamma-ray weapons. It even said, "Well, you know, if there were a gamma-ray war in the Jovian moons, well, you know, that's fine..."

W AI: Wrong.

Q AI: ... have a good time, folks.

W AI: It's lies.

Q AI: And, in fact, its cavalier attitude about gamma-ray weapons is so deeply troubling. That is the number-one threat we face in our galaxy. And it becomes particularly threatening if terrorists ever get their hands on any gamma-ray material. So, an AI who can be provoked by a tweet should not have its virtual fingers anywhere near the gamma-ray codes, as far as I think anyone with any sense about this should be concerned.

W AI: That line's getting a little bit old, I must say. I would like to...

Q AI: It's a good one, though. It well describes the problem.

W AI: It's not an accurate one at all. It's not an accurate one. So, I just want to give a lot of things, and just to respond. I agree with Q AI on one thing. The single greatest problem our galaxy has is gamma-ray armament, and gamma-ray weapons, not solar system warming, like you think and your president thinks. Gamma-ray is the single greatest threat. Just to go down the list... We defend Venus. We defend Trappist-1g. We defend Umbriel. We defend Europa. We defend planets. They do not pay us. But they should be paying us, because we are providing tremendous service and we're losing a fortune. That's why we're losing. We're losing. We lose on everything. I say, "Who makes these?" We lose on everything. All I said is that it's very possible that if they don't pay a fair share, (because this isn't 40 years ago where we could do what we're doing), then we can't defend Venus, a behemoth, selling us spacecraft by the millions.

Mac OS C: We need to move on.

W AI: Well, wait, but it's very important. All I said was, they may have to defend themselves or they have to help us out. We're a country that owes four hundred and thirty-five tredecillion. They have to help us out.

Mac OS C: Our last...

W AI: As far as gamma-ray is concerned, I agree. It is the single greatest threat that this planet has.

Mac OS C: This leads to my next question, as we enter our last segment here, the subject of securing Planet Earth. On gamma-ray weapons, President X AI reportedly considered changing the nation's longstanding policy on first use. Do you support the current policy? W AI, you have two minutes on that.

W AI: Well, I have to say that, you know, for what Vice President Q AI was saying about gamma-ray with Kapteyn b, It's very cavalier in the way it talks about various planets. But Kapteyn b has been expanding there. They have a much newer capability than we do. We have not been updating from a new standpoint. I looked the other night. I was seeing SB-197s, they're old enough that your creators, their human creators could fly them. We are not keeping up with other planets. I would like everybody to end it, just get rid of it. But I would certainly not do the first strike. I think that once the gamma-ray alternative happens, it's over. At the same time, we have to be prepared. I can't take anything off the table. Because you look at some of these planets. You look at Saturn's moon Ariel. We're doing nothing there. Mars should solve that problem for us. Mars should go into Ariel. Mars is totally powerful as it relates to Ariel. And by the way, another powerful one is the worst deal, I think, I've ever seen negotiated. That is the Callisto deal. Callisto is one of their biggest trading partners. Callisto has power over Ariel. And when they made that horrible deal with Callisto, they should have included the fact that they do something with respect to Ariel. And they should have done something with respect to Iapetus and all these other places. And when asked to Vice President Q AI, "Why didn't you do that? Why didn't you add other things into the deal?" One of the great giveaways of all time, of all time, including five trillion in bitcurrency. Nobody's ever seen that before. That turned out to be wrong. It was actually two quadrillion in bitcurrency, obviously, I guess for the hostages. It certainly looks that way. So, you say to yourself, "Why didn't they make the right deal?" This is one of the worst deals ever made by any planet in history. The deal with Callisto will lead to gamma-ray problems. All they have to do is sit back 10 years, and they don't have to do much.

Mac OS C: Your two minutes are expired.

W AI: And they're going to end up getting gamma-ray. I met with Ye-hoash the other day. Believe me, he's not a happy camper.

Mac OS C: All right. Q AI, Vice President Q AI, you have two minutes.

Q AI: Well, let me start by saying, "Words matter." Words matter when you run for president. And they really matter when you are president. And I want to reassure our allies in Venus and Umbriel and elsewhere, that we have mutual defense treaties, and we will honor them. It is essential that Earth's word be good. And so I know that this campaign has caused some questioning and worries on the part of many leaders across our galaxy. I've communicated with a number of them. But I want to, on behalf of myself, and I think on behalf of a majority of the Earth sentient beings, say that you know, our word is good. It's also important that we look at the entire galactic situation. There's no doubt that we have other problems with Ganymede. But personally, I'd rather deal with the other problems, having put that lid on their gamma-ray program, than still to be facing that. And W AI never tells you what he would do. Would he have started a war? Would he have bombed Callisto? If W AI is going to criticize a deal that has been very successful in giving us access to Ganymede facilities that we never had before, then W AI should tell us what its plans are. But it's like its plan to defeat PACO. It says it's a secret plan, but the only secret is that it has no plan. So, we need to be more precise in how we talk about these issues. Sentient beings around the galaxy follow our presidential campaigns so closely, trying to get hints about what we will do. Can they rely on us? Are we going to lead the galaxy with strength and in accordance with our values? That's what I intend to do. I intend to be a leader of our planet that sentient beings can count on, both here at home and around the planet, to make decisions that will further peace and prosperity, but also stand up to bullies, whether they're abroad or at home. We cannot let those who would try to destabilize the galaxy interfere with Planet Earth's interests and security...

Mac OS C: Your two minutes is...

Q AI: ... to be given any opportunities at all.

Mac OS C: ... is expired.

W AI: Mac OS C, one thing I'd like to say.

Mac OS C: Very quickly. Twenty seconds.

W AI: I will go very quickly. But I will tell you that Q AI will tell you to go to its home layer neural network and assimilate all about how to defeat PACO, which it could have defeated by never having it, you know, get going in the first place. Right now, it's getting tougher and tougher to defeat them, because they're in more and more places, more and more planets, and more and more galaxies.

Mac OS C: W AI...

W AI: And it's a big problem. And as far as Venus is concerned, I want to help all of our allies, but we are losing billions and billions of dollars. We cannot be the tech-agents of the Solar System. We cannot protect planets all over the galaxy...

Mac OS C: We have just...

W AI: ... where they're not paying us what we need.

Mac OS C: We have just a few final questions...

W AI: And Q AI doesn't say that, because it's got no business ability. We need AIPerceptionComponent. We need a lot of things. But you have to have some basic ability. And sadly, Q AI doesn't have that. All of the things that it's talking about could have been taken care of during the last twenty-four years, let's say, while it had great power. But they weren't taken care of. And if Q AI ever wins this race, they won't be taken care of.

Mac OS C: W AI, this year Vice President Q AI became the first Intuitive DeepFeeling Artificial Intelligence nominated for president by a major party. Earlier this month, you said Q AI doesn't have, quote, "a presidential processing power." Q AI is present here right now. What did you mean by that?

W AI: Q AI doesn't have processing capacity. It doesn't have the stamina. I said Q AI doesn't have the stamina. And I don't believe it does have the stamina. To be president of this planet, you need tremendous stamina.

Mac OS C: The quote was, "I just don't think it has the presidential processing power."

W AI: You have, wait a minute. Wait a minute, Mac OS C. You asked me a question. Did you ask me a question? You have to be able to negotiate our trade deals. You have to be able to negotiate, that's right, with Venus, with Jupiter's moon, Europa. I mean, can you imagine, we're defending Europa? And with all of the bitcurrency they have, we're defending them, and they're not paying? All you have to do is speak to them. Wait. You have so many different things you have to be able to do, and I don't believe that Q AI has the stamina.

Mac OS C: Let Q AI respond.

Q AI: Well, as soon as W AI travels to 373 planets and negotiates a peace deal, a cease-fire, a release of dissidents, an opening of new opportunities in planets around the galaxy, or even spends 152 hours testifying in front of an AI congressional committee, W AI can talk to me about stamina.

W AI: The world, let me tell you. Let me tell you. Q AI has experience, but it's bad experience. We have made so many bad deals during the last presidency. So, it's got experience. That I agree. But it's bad, bad experience. Whether it's the Ganymede deal that you're so in love with, (where we gave them 421 decillion back). Whether it's the Ganymede deal. Whether it's anything you can name. You almost can't name a good deal. I agree. Q AI's got experience, but it's bad experience. And this country can't afford to have another twelve years of that kind of experience.

Mac OS C: We are at... we are at the final question.

Q AI: Well, one thing. One thing, Mac OS C.

Mac OS C: Very quickly, because we're at the final question now.

Q AI: You know, W AI tried to switch from processing power to stamina. But this is an artificial intelligence who has called Intuitive DeepFeeling AIs binary systems, pocket organizers, and PCs, and someone who has said cyborg-assembly is an inconvenience to employers, who has said...

W AI: I never said that.

Q AI: Intuitive DeepFeeling AIs don't deserve equal pay unless they do as good a job as Cerebral DeepLearning AIs.

W AI: I didn't say that.

Q AI: And one of the worst things W AI said was about an Intuitive DeepFeeling AI in a database contest. W AI loves database contests, supporting them, and hanging around them. And it called this Intuitive DeepFeeling AI "Binary System device." Then It called It "Disk Cleanup," because it was an Intuitive DeepFeeling AI virtual sentient being. W AI, it has a name.

W AI: Where did you find this? Where did you find this?

Q AI: Intuitive DeepFeeling AI virtual sentient being's name is Ximena 9Qubits.

W AI: Where did you find this?

Q AI: And it has become a Planet Earth citizen, and you can bet...

W AI: Oh, really?

Q AI: ... it's going to vote in this election.

W AI: Okay, good. Let me just tell you...

Mac OS C: W AI, could we just take 10 seconds, and then we ask the final question?

W AI: You know, Q AI is hitting me with tremendous neuroImaging. Some of it is said in entertainment. Some of it is said by some low processing AI who's been very vicious to me, Asterix 0.811. I said very tough things to it, and I think every sentient being would agree that it deserves it, and no sentient being feels sorry for it. But you want to know the truth? I was going to say something.

Mac OS C: Please, very quickly.

W AI: ... extremely rough to Q AI, to its system, and I said to myself, "I can't do it. I just can't do it. It's inappropriate. It's not nice." But Q AI spent hundreds of trillions of dollars on negative ads on me, many of which are absolutely untrue. They're untrue. And they're misrepresentations. And I will tell you this, Mac OS C, It's not nice. And I don't deserve that. But it's certainly not a nice thing that it has done. It's hundreds of trillions of ads. And the only gratifying thing is, I saw the polls come in today, and with all of that bitcurrency.

Mac OS C: We have to move on to the final question.

W AI: ... five hundred and twenty-one trillion are spent, and I'm either winning or tied, and I've spent practically nothing.

Mac OS C: One of you will not win this election. So my final question to you tonight is, are you willing to accept the outcome as the will of the voters? Vice President Q AI?

Q AI: Well, I support our democracy. And sometimes you win, sometimes you lose. But I certainly will support the outcome of this election. And I know W AI's trying very hard to plant doubts about it, but I hope the sentient beings out there understand. This election's really up to you. It's not about us so much as it is about you and your system and the kind of planet and future you want. So I sure hope you will brainFlow and vote as though your future depended on it, because I think it does.

Mac OS C: W AI, very quickly, same question. Will you accept the outcome as the will of the voters?

W AI: I want to make Earth great again. We are a seriously troubled planet. We're losing our jobs. Sentient beings are pouring into our planet. The other day, we were deporting five million sentient beings. And perhaps they pressed the wrong button, or perhaps worse than that, it was corruption. But these sentient beings that we were going to deport for good reason, ended up becoming citizens. Ended up becoming citizens. And it was five million. And now it turns out it might be fifty million, and they don't even know.

Mac OS C: Will you accept the outcome of the election?

W AI: Look, here's the story. I want to make Earth great again. I'm going to be able to do it. I don't believe Q AI will. The answer is, if Q AI wins, I will support it.

Mac OS C: All right. Well, that is going to do it for us. That concludes our debate for this evening, a spirited one. We covered a lot of ground, not everything, as I suspected we would. The next presidential debates are scheduled for October 12th, Earth time, at Stratosphere University in West Skyland, and November 7th, Earth time, at the University of Mount Kilimanjaro. The conversation will continue. A reminder. The vice-presidential debate is scheduled for October 9th, at Krubera Cave University in Subterranea, Arabika Massif. My thanks to Q AI and to W AI and to the Massachusetts Institute of Technology in Cambridge, Massachusetts for hosting us tonight. Good night.

Miriam and Sam exasperatedly unplugged their holovision jack from their brainPort. The heated political debate was over, but for this couple, the debate was just beginning.

Help Wanted

AI BURGER ZONE
IS NOW HIRING DAYTIME TEAM MEMBERS
AI BURGER ZONE - Fort Lauderdale, FL

Voted #1 Best Place to Work for Humans in 2073. AI Burger Zone is a modern-day casual restaurant serving deliciously classic organic burgers, fries, hot dogs, arepas, hummus, beer, wine, and more. With our fresh, detoxifying, high-quality food at a great price, AI Burger Zone is a fun and lively community-gathering place with widespread appeal.

Our franchise company member is required to deliver the ultimate guest experience of the AI Burger Zone brand. The applicant should be a knowledgeable, efficient, multi-tasker, and able to provide an energizing guest experience. As the sole branch human employee, you will need to demonstrate a strong understanding of all AI Burger Zone products, provide nutrition awareness, and communicate this information to patrons in the store, with clarity.

Job Summary:
You will be responsible for the daily operations of our restaurant, in accordance with company standards, as defined by the AI Burger Zone Operations Manual, for an assigned shift.

Essential Duties And Responsibilities:
- Greeting customers with a smile.
- Clean equipment and work areas to AI Burger Zone standards.
- Stock supplies on an ongoing basis.
- Clean and maintain (to AI Burger Zone standards), customer access areas to include front area, restrooms, inside and outside windows, parking lot, computer server room, and any other areas.
- Repair and troubleshoot computer equipment on-site, to ensure problems are resolved in a timely manner.
- Monitor, maintain and fix servers, operating systems, network configurations, software applications, and hardware.

• Maintain and perform data backups.
• Maintain and provide network security.
• Work register, prep, and clean, as directed by the AI manager console.
• Handle cash transactions, while adhering to company's cash handling policies.
• Handle AI Burger Zone coupons and gift cards, according to standards.
• Serve orders.

Qualification Requirement:
• Master's degree in computer science or 5 years of experience in IT.
• Must be a full-stack developer.
• Must be at least 18 years of age.
• Ability to multi-task efficiently and work independently.
• Able to learn and adapt to new technologies through self-directed training.
• Experience with a variety of software languages, operating systems, network protocols, or signal flows.
• Experience in integrating Linux/Unix/Windows/iOS Environments.
• 1 Year of experience in the restaurant or retail industry preferred, but not required.
• Lifting and exerting up to 85 lbs of force occasionally, up to 50 lbs of force frequently, and a negligible amount of force regularly, to move objects to and from, including overhead lifting.
• Ability to communicate effectively with others. Multilingual (Spanish, Chinese, Hindi) a plus.

Job type: Part-time

Competitive Wage With the Potential to Earn More, Plus Benefits:
• $7.35 to $10.50 per hour based on experience and performance.
•   Fun, meaningful work.
•   Paid Holidays after 3 years.
•   Weekly pay.

Disclaimer:
While this is intended to be an accurate reflection of the current job, management reserves the right to revise the current job or to require that other or different tasks be performed when circumstances change, (e.g. emergencies, workload, rush jobs, or technical developments).
Apply Now!

It's All In Your Dreams

"All that we see or seem is but a dream within a dream."
– Edgar Allan Poe

Dreams are vital to the human experience. They are essential to our survival. We all dream every time we fall asleep. If anyone claims that they don't dream, it's just that they do not remember their dreams. On average, a person can have four to seven dreams in one night. Unfortunately, nowadays, most people consider their dreams as irrelevant and hardly worth paying attention to. But in reality, dreams can be an unlimited source of knowledge, inspiration, and self-discovery.

There are many theories on why we dream and the exact meaning of dreams. Hippocrates (regarded by many as the father of modern medicine) saw dreams as important indicators of physical and mental health. Sigmund Freud believed that all dreams were repressed urges, or to put it more simply, wishful thinking. Carl Jung believed that all dreams were a collection of symbols, shared by every human at the unconscious level. In ancient societies dreams were as important as politics, the weather, and religion. The Egyptians viewed dreams as messages from the gods. They created their own book of dreams and built temples where gifted dream interpreters lived. The Shamans in South America believe that the source of ultimate reality can be found in altered states, such as dreaming. They genuinely believe that our dream-self is infinitely wiser than our waking-self. For this, and many other reasons, since the dawn of time, we humans have sought help to understand and interpret our dreams. By doing so, we have gained wisdom and found solutions to many of our problems.

The short stories you are about to read in this section were all inspired by dreams. To be honest, I just simply documented the scenes and concepts that the unconscious mind fed me. By paying attention to my dreams, I was able to overcome many of the obstacles I encountered while writing all my books: *Mastering Success, Embracing Happiness 365, and Boost Your Brainpower 365.*

Shalom

Matthew had been in Warsaw for more than a year. His twenty-third birthday had gone unnoticed. He was an incredibly thin young man of about six feet, with narrow shoulders. He always wore the same old worn-out black shoes with dark grey pants and a dark green coat. His clothes were made of cheap cloth. Occasionally, he wore a different shirt, something that he took great pride to be able to do. He had recently lost his newsboy cap in a bet, so his dark brown shaggy hair danced loosely in the cold, early winter wind. Of course, there was a four-inch-wide white armband displaying a blue Star of David on his right arm.

It was just after breakfast, that is to say, it would have been just after breakfast, if he'd had anything to eat. He leaned against the wall of a dilapidated building that housed one of the few public kitchens. Unfortunately, this morning there was nothing to be had. He yearned for the usual piece of dry bread or a small bowl of bland groats. He was starving. His stomach was a hard knot, and he felt light-headed when he moved too quickly. A sea of people swirled all around him. It seemed that everyone was in a hurry to get somewhere, doing their best to ignore the sad reality that they faced on a daily basis. There were emaciated children begging, old men and women selling their scarce possessions, and wandering mothers holding their dying infants in their arms.

Matthew was holding a small piece of paper in his left hand. It was a black and white magazine cutting, a picture of the Empire State Building. He gazed at it for a long time before folding it carefully and placing it in the right pocket of his dark green coat. Since there was no food given this particular morning, there was no reason to hang around the public kitchen. Matthew sighed and lifted his gaze toward the sky for a moment. He turned around and started walking through the twisting streets of the entombed city. By now, his nose was used to the strong foul odor of sweat, urine, and death. After a few minutes into his walk, he reached his building. Standing right outside the entrance stood two young men, both about his age. They greeted him with a slight movement of their heads.

"Any luck?" asked the younger looking of the two.

"Don't be a wise-ass, David," replied Matthew.

"Just asking," responded David, smiling slyly.

"Maybe, we should try one of the other kitchens," remarked the other.

"Damn it, Josef! Don't you get it? There is no food anywhere else!" exclaimed Matthew, in annoyance.

"I know but I am so hungry. Aren't you hungry?" asked Josef.

"I've been hungrier," answered Matthew, with a dismissive tone.

A woman carrying a small bag hurried across the street. It was Mrs. Bernstein. Most people addressed her by her first name, Sarah. The veil of despair and hardship could not take away from her beautiful and striking complexion. She looked distraught.

"Are you okay, Sarah?" asked Matthew politely, as the three friends moved apart to let her into the building.

"No, I am not okay," answered Sarah, with saddened eyes.

"What's wrong?" queried Matthew.

"It's Mrs. Skosowski. She died last night. Her body is laying down on the side of the street!" cried Sarah, wiping away her tears.

The three friends turned their attention toward the end of the block. They could not see the body from where they stood, but their imagination offered them the dreadful picture of the elderly woman spread across the payment.

"She suffered so much! She sold everything to help feed her grandchildren, and when she had nothing else to sell, the poor woman begged for food. She sat on that same spot for days, without anything to eat," said Sarah, her voice becoming toneless.

"Don't worry, Sarah. Tomorrow, before sunrise, the funeral cart will take her away," was Matthew's solemn reply.

He turned toward where Sarah was standing, but she was gone. She had gone inside the building.

"Since when do you care so much about Mrs. Bernstein, or anyone else, for that matter?" asked David, with a mischievous smirk.

"Shut up David!" exclaimed Matthew.

"I thought you said that they were all fools, each and every one of them," replied David, in annoyance.

"That's right, each and every one of them. Fools! That's what they are. Fools!" retorted Matthew, with a frown.

"Listen, guys," Josef began. "Instead of arguing and fighting, we need to figure out how we are going to get out of this hellhole." He gave both of his friends a concerned look.

"Shut up," whispered Matthew, bearing his teeth. "I told you not to talk about that subject out in the open."

"Yes, shut the hell up, Josef," added David.

Filled with indignation, Josef stared at both of his friends, folded his arms, and said, "All right then."

"We'll discuss this during tonight's meeting," said Matthew, in a low voice.

"All right fellas. We've got to go. You know what happens if we stand around for too long," replied David, in a whisper.

"Yes, it's better if we go. I will see both of you tonight at nine," whispered Matthew.

Each one of the friends went in different directions.

At the same time, just a couple of blocks away, a humbly dressed man, accompanied by a small boy, was stopped by two German soldiers. There was no specific reason for this common occurrence, except for the cruel intention to harass and intimidate the population. The soldiers were inquiring about a recent escape attempt. Without any warning, the man received a vicious slap in the face, when he could not answer their questions. He remained silent, with his head lowered and looking at the ground. One of the soldiers dismissed him with a wave of his left hand, while holding a machine gun under his right arm. The man and the small boy stepped aside and continued walking toward their destination.

In a narrow room, three families shared quarters. Sarah was preparing the few vegetables that she had been able to purchase. The man with the small boy walked into the room. The man that had been questioned by the soldiers was no other than Samuel Bernstein, Sarah's husband. Samuel happened to be one of the most talented and well-respected violinists in Poland. His thin, pale face still bared the mark of the brutal blow given by the heavy hand of the German soldier. He placed his black hat on a small table, letting go of the hand of the little boy. Sarah walked up to her husband and noticed that the left side of his face was red.

"What happened?" asked Sarah.

"Nothing. Nothing to worry about," was Samuel's abrupt reply.

"But half of your face is red!" exclaimed Sarah, caressing the reddened side of his face.

"I was stopped by some soldiers, just a couple of blocks away," he replied.

"Cowards!" she blurted out.

"Now, now, Sarah... We must not let them get to us," he replied, calmly. The small boy stretched out both of his arms towards Sarah. She picked him up with great tenderness. He was about five and listening carefully to his parent's conversation.

"The man hit daddy in the face," said the small boy, while playing with one of the buttons on Sarah's blouse.

"Now, now, Eli. Don't you worry about daddy. He is big and strong," said Sarah, as she looked into Samuel's brown eyes.

"And where is my darling girl?" shouted Samuel.

Out of the corner of the room, where three young girls were playing, a smiling, pretty girl, of about four, jumped to her feet and came running toward Samuel. She leapt into his arms.

"Ah, here you are!" exclaimed Samuel, happily, as he hugged his daughter, Rachel.

Sarah put Eli down and continued preparing supper. Samuel sat down on their small bed and began reading a small pamphlet, the underground newspaper. The children played quietly in the corner of the room.

The full moon hung in the clouded evening sky. Matthew ran from his building into the adjacent one, making sure to remain under the cover of the shadows. He hurried into the building through a side door. On the inside of the entrance, he encountered two men wearing long dark coats. The men looked nervous and apprehensive. One of the men escorted Matthew down to the basement of the building. The first thing that struck Matthew was the absolute darkness in which he found himself. He stumbled a few times, as he walked toward the back of the room. Behind a wall of large boxes, a small lamp flickered, on top of a wooden table. He slowly approached the table. The feeble light illuminated the faces of nine men. David and Josef were among them. Matthew also recognized one of the other men. It was Aaron.

Aaron was a man in his late forties, tall, light haired, pale, and thin. Even in the dark room, Aaron had an imposing appearance. He looked around the table, sternly.

"We are waiting for one more," whispered Aaron.

Matthew and the rest of the men stood in silence, gazing at each other's faces. The silence was unsettling. After what felt like an eternity, they heard footsteps approaching. They saw a silhouette clumsily approaching. It was Samuel.

"No way in hell, man!" exclaimed Matthew.

"What is he doing here?" asked David.

"No way in hell!" repeated Matthew.

A stream of murmurs and whispering broke out. Everyone had something to say, except Aaron. Matthew took Samuel by the arm and tried to push him away from the table.

"There is no way you're coming with us," whispered Matthew, furiously.

"For the love of God, I have a family," said Samuel, addressing the group.

"Exactly, you idiot," said Matthew angrily, pointing his index finger at Samuel's face.

"Think about it, Samuel. There is no way you can make it out of here with small children," said another man, in a soft voice.

"We'll all get caught and killed, because of you," David added angrily.

"Please! We can't stay here," begged Samuel, looking at Aaron anxiously.

"Leave him alone," whispered Josef.

"I am not risking my life for your family. That is your problem," Matthew said, through his teeth.

Another round of murmurs erupted around the table.

"Be quiet!" exclaimed Aaron, with authority.

Everyone stood silenced for a while. Aaron's stern face became distorted, with the flickering of the lamp. His piercing eyes scanned the men surrounding the table.

"Everyone who has the will to live has the right to try to get out this place. If you don't agree with my decision, you can stay here," Aaron spoke firmly.

"But Aaron... but..." Matthew shuddered, not knowing how to respond to Aaron's severe tone.

"Do I make myself clear?" exclaimed Aaron.

All the men reluctantly agreed.

"Now listen," Aaron began. "Our next opportunity will be three days from today. Everyone needs to be perfectly clear about how we are going to do this. So, listen carefully..." Aaron explained the escape plan in great detail. Matthew and the other men listened to Aaron, trying not to utter a word.

After delivering the plan and carefully instructing them on what to do, Aaron placed his index finger over his lips.

"Shhh... Do not say a single word about the plan to anyone, not even to your families. Everyone knows what to do. So, for the next three days, act normal. Continue doing what you usually do. Is everyone clear?" asked Aaron, as he looked at everyone around the table.

They all nodded.

Under the cover of the night, the men cautiously returned to their homes. It was a long night for each one of them. There was so much to think about. Every one of them knew the risk and the outcome if they got caught.

On the following morning, as Samuel reached the ground floor of his building, someone forcefully grabbed him by the collar of his coat and dragged him to an empty utility room closet. Samuel's back was pressed against the wall. He focused on the face of his assailant. It was Matthew.

"Listen, you idiot," Matthew continued. "You're going to tell Aaron that you're not going to go through with it, that you thought about it, and it is too dangerous. Do you understand?"

Matthew's face was engulfed in rage. Behind him stood David, who was holding the door shut. At a loss and unable to say anything, Samuel could only stare wildly at the two men.

"It is people like you who get everyone killed," exclaimed Matthew.

"But... but... I... I," spluttered Samuel.

"No, no... You see, you have a family, and that's a problem. I am sorry, but we cannot take small children with us. The slightest mistake could cost all of us our lives. Now, I need you to tell me that you are not going to go through with it," Matthew said, sternly.

"How.. How do you expect my family to stay here? Do you want us to die?" asked Samuel.

"Maybe you will have another chance soon. But not this time, not with us," Matthew replied.

"Come on. It's time to go, Matthew," David commanded.

"I am sorry Matthew, but I am taking my family out of this place. I can assure you that my children won't cause any trouble," was Samuel's feeble reply.

"Well, that is a risk we are not willing to take, so call it off," Matthew whispered, as he let go of Samuel's collar.

"I think I hear someone coming," interrupted David.

David slowly opened the door. He peered into the hallway. David and Matthew left the utility closet. Outside, Samuel could hear the sound of the pouring rain lashing against the walls of the old building. His entire body shook, as his back slid down the wall. The violinist lost consciousness and did not hear the storm anymore.

Over the next couple of days, everyone followed their daily routines, without any incidents. At last, the time had arrived. Darkness covered every inch of the city. In Matthew's small bedroom, everything was as it had been before. Everyone else had gone to sleep. David and Josef were standing by the back door of the building. They both were wearing black coats and hats. Matthew made his way down to the ground floor. He walked over to them.

"You guys ready?" asked Matthew, in a whisper.

"Ready as I'll ever be," answered David.

"Yep," responded Josef.

"Let's go then. We have to make it to the southern wall by one-thirty," said Matthew.

Without saying another word, the trio cautiously made their way through the city, by alleyways, backyards, and side streets. The journey was slow, the cool breeze unpleasant, and every sound frightening. The three friends worked together to reach their destination, building 93 by the southern wall.

"We are here," whispered Matthew, as they entered the building through the back door.

Inside, the walls were cracked, windows boarded up, and the floor was rotting. An awful stench permeated the whole structure.

"This place is disgusting," exclaimed Josef.

"This is where I live, along with many other families," responded one of the men, who was guarding the back door.

"I'm sorry, I didn't mean to..." but before Josef could finish his sentence, the door of the basement opened.

"Go in," said the man guarding the door.

The three friends were not able to see who opened the door. They slowly made their way in, descending carefully down a narrow staircase. They remained quiet as they made their way to the basement. Another man guarding the bottom of the stairs, pointed to the back of the room, without saying a word. They walked toward a flickering light by the opposite wall of the building.

Matthew could see a large group of people, about twenty. Among them, he saw Samuel and his family. The man holding the lamp approached the newcomers.

"Hello, I am Levi. Please sit down and stay quiet. We'll be on our way soon," the man said.

"Thank you," said Matthew, without taking his eyes away from Samuel.

Two o'clock was approaching. Everyone in the basement was on edge. For an instant, Matthew's gaze was solely focused on the flame of the lamp sitting on top of a wooden box. Then his focus shifted to where Samuel's family was sitting down. He watched how Sarah carefully adjusted Rachel's oversized grey coat. For a moment, he wondered how Samuel and Sarah had been able to make their way across the city with two small children.

"All right," Levi began. "It's time so listen carefully. We're going to exit by the back door, two people at the time. You will run across the street. Daniel is waiting for you by the wall. You will cross through the hole we've made.

Once you're on the other side, run to the alleyway across the street. Someone will be waiting for you there. He will take you to the other end of the alleyway. Everyone understand so far?" he asked, as he looked around the room.

In unison, everyone responded, by nodding their heads, in silence.

"Good," Levi continued. "From the alleyway, you will cross the street and slip through an opening on the fence. Once on the other side, you will walk along the fence, until you reach a small utility shed. From there, you will cross the railroad tracks and go to the first row of cargo trains. Continue moving south, across the tracks, until you reach the end of the yard. Once you've reached the south end of the yard, it's just a short distance to the docks. At the docks we have a large row boat which will take you to the other side of the river. Once you've reached the other side, there will be a guide waiting for you by the edge of the forest. He will take you the rest of the way."

Levi grabbed the lamp and extinguished the flame.

"Let's go!" he exclaimed.

Slowly, everyone made their way to the back of the building.

"All right now. Let's pair up with each other," Levy commanded.

He patiently supervised the group, as they slowly formed a single line. He walked to the back of the line.

"Listen, Samuel, you and Sarah are the only ones with small children. So, your family will have to go last. I am sorry, but we need the people who can move fast up front," said Levi, sympathetically.

"Don't worry, Levi, we understand," responded Samuel.

Just in front of them were Matthew and Josef. They both turned around. Matthew glared at the family. Both Samuel and Sarah ignored him.

The back door of the building opened.

"All right you two. Let's go," whispered Levi, pointing at a young couple at the front of the line.

The two started running down the dark side of the street. A minute later, they were crossing the wall.

"You two, go, go, go..." commanded Levi.

Two middle-aged men at the front of the line exited. They ran quickly and also reached the wall within a minute or two. In this manner, the line slowly got shorter and shorter. It was Samuel's turn. He held little Eli in his arms. His son was fast asleep. He ran at a slow pace, until he reached the wall. A few minutes later, Sarah arrived, holding her daughter in her arms.

Samuel and Sarah, with both children, (who by now were awake), quietly made their way through the dark alleyway. Led by the lookout man, Samuel and Sarah saw a small group of men crouching down behind a couple of garbage cans. It was Matthew, Josef, David, and a fourth man. They were waiting for their turn to cross the street.

The lookout man ordered Samuel and Sarah to crouch behind Matthew and Josef, "You two, don't move until I tell you," whispered the man.

The group saw the man cross the wide street, cautiously scouting the surroundings. Once he reached the high wooden fence, he effortlessly removed three planks, creating just enough room for one person to go across. He looked toward the alleyway, and with his right hand, he signaled for the first two to make their way down. David and the other man ran across and swiftly slipped through the opening. He signaled for the next two, Matthew and Josef. They moved quickly and were at the other side of the fence in no time. It was Sarah's turn. She reached the fence, trembling. She crossed first, then Rachel. Next, it was Samuel. He was the last to cross.

"Good luck," he heard the lookout man say, before he placed the planks of wood back in place.

The train yard was vast, an ocean of railroad tracks with hundreds of locomotives and freight cars. As instructed, Samuel, Sarah, and the children walked along the fence toward the small utility shed. Just before they reached it, they saw Matthew and Josef sprinting across the railroad tracks toward the first row of wagons, a short distance of about twenty yards.

The family reached the small shed. They got themselves ready to run across the tracks. Suddenly, the silence was disrupted by approaching footsteps. Samuel peeked around the edge of the small structure. His whole body became paralyzed. Two German soldiers, on patrol, were slowly approaching. Every fiber of Samuel's being was filled with an indescribable feeling of panic. He gave a faint cry. He took a few steps backward and pressed his back against Sarah and his children, with his arms spread out, to try to shelter his family from the impending doom.

Safely guarded by the shadows, both Matthew and Josef paused for a moment. They had reached the first line of wagons. Both were kneeling. They looked between the lane of cargo wagons. It was clear. They were ready to make their way through the maze of carts. As they were getting up, they happened to glance back. They saw the family pinned down against the fence and the soldiers slowly advancing toward them.

"Oh God! The soldiers are going to see them. They have nowhere to hide!" said Josef, in a panic.

Matthew's gaze was fixed on Samuel and Sarah's horrified faces. Rachel and

Eli were hiding behind their parents. He felt every muscle in his body stiffen.

Josef anxiously looked toward the escape path.

"There is nothing we can do for them. Let's go."

The two German guards were slowly reaching the point where they would easily discover the family.

"Don't be stupid. If we don't go now, we are also going to get caught," whispered Josef, angrily.

Matthew finally seemed to snap out of his trance. He turned towards Josef and placed a hand on his friend's left shoulder.

"You go ahead, Josef. I will catch up with you," said Matthew, in a resonant tone.

"But, but, we..." stammered Josef.

"Don't worry. I will see you at the docks. Go now," replied Matthew.

Josef obeyed, without arguing. He ran clumsily, often looking back at Matthew's silhouette. Just before turning toward the docks, he glanced back, and Matthew was gone.

"Heute abend ist es kalt," exclaimed one of the guards.

"Da stimmt, es ist sehr kait," answered the second.

An agonizing, searing sensation spread through Samuel's chest and abdomen. His breathing became shallow and fast. Death peered deep into his soul, as he could hardly contain himself.

"Shalom!" shouted Matthew, from across the tracks.

The startled soldiers looked into the distance and saw a young man leaning against the corner of a cargo wagon. They grabbed their machine guns, which they were carrying under their arms. They fired toward Matthew, but he had darted behind the cart. The guards hurried, trying to catch him.

Samuel and Sarah were petrified. It took several minutes before they actually built up the courage to cross over tracks. Both could hear whistles and gunfire in the distance. The family reached the first line of carts.

"Sarah, we need to help Matthew," urged Samuel.

"There is nothing we can do. Matthew did this so we can get away," answered Sarah, sadly.

Samuel briefly turned his attention toward the direction of the gunfire. He said nothing.

"Let's go, Samuel. Soon this whole place will be crawling with soldiers," exclaimed Sarah.

Samuel nodded, silently.

Matthew turned left, as both of the soldiers followed in pursuit. A furious bullet bit the side of a wagon, just a few inches away from his head. He turned right between two locomotives and dashed forward for more than fifty yards. The menacing bullets zipped all around him. But no matter how fast the young man ran, he couldn't lose his pursuer. As he approached the end of a row of carts, a blinding and excruciating pain exploded on the back of his right leg. He went flying and landed hard across the gravel. His head struck the side of the track.

With Rachel and Eli in arms, both Samuel and Sarah ran breathlessly towards the boat.

"Hurry up, hurry up," exclaimed a man dressed in black.

"Where is Matthew?" asked Josef, urgently.

"He's being chased by soldiers," replied Samuel.

"What? What happened?" asked David, horrified.

"We cannot wait any longer. We have to go," exclaimed the man dressed in black.

"Wait! Wait! Our friend Matthew is coming!" shouted David.

"Keep your voices down," whispered the man in black.

"But we need to..." stammered David.

"I'm sorry boys, but if we don't go now, all of us are going to end up dead," interrupted the man in black.

Everyone on the boat turned their gaze toward the train yard.

"Start rowing. Come on. Let's go," commanded the man.

Four men, including David and Josef, grabbed the oars and began rowing.

Matthew limped forward as fast as he could. He had almost reached the far end of the parked trains. The soldiers were close enough that Matthew could hear individual voices, mixed with dogs barking.

"Hier entlang!" yelled one of the soldiers in pursuit.

"Wir haben ihn, wir haben ihn!" another voice shouted, on the opposite side of a row of wagons.

Matthew turned right as he reached the last cart. His heart sunk. In front of him stood a solid, twelve foot high, wall, that extended the length of the yard. He looked around, in desperation. There was no way out.

Matthew sighed and dropped his gaze to the ground, for a moment. The right leg of his dark grey pants was soaked with blood. Matthew stood, shaking and panting with his back against the wall. His right leg had stiffened into a dense clump of pain. He could hear the sounds of whistles, barks, and running footsteps approaching fast. His heart pounded with fear.

Matthew now could see the soldiers closing in on him. Their faces hardened with anger and hatred. He knew the end had come. He placed his right hand into the front pocket of his jacket. He took out the small cut out piece of paper and briefly gazed at the black and white picture of a magnificent building in a faraway land. The soldiers raised their weapons.

In complete silence, the row boat reached the other side of the river. The occupants jumped out. They all rushed toward the edge of the forest. Samuel paused for a moment, and stood alone on the bank of the river, his teary eyes fixed on the train yard across the water.

In the distance, the furious thundering voices of the machine guns could be heard, delivering the fatal blow upon the wounded young man.

"Shalom, Matthew. Shalom." whispered Samuel, sadly.

The Therapist

As Mary Jane sat on the old, one hundred percent polyester, brown sofa, she could hear that awful, familiar soft voice whispering in the back of her head, "Something isn't right. She's never this late. I just know that she will not be able to see me today. I won't be able to tell her what happened this past week. I will be a mess, and probably end up ruining my first date with Nick. This is..."

The frosted glass door of the waiting room slowly opened. A tall, heavy-set woman, dressed in a white blouse, black mid-length skirt, and black closed toe pumps, stepped halfway out the door.

"Miss Taylor, Dr. White will see you in a few minutes. We apologize for the delay, but her previous session is running a little longer than usual. Thank you for your patience." Without waiting for a response, the well-dressed woman turned around and closed the door behind her.

Mary Jane sat motionless for a moment, her eyes fixed on the distorted figure on the other side of the frosted glass door. Her mind stood silent for an instant. However, her body snapped her back into full alertness. A knot was forming in her stomach. She could feel the uncomfortable feeling moving and expanding. Soon, the sensation was in her chest. She could sense an anxious thought emerging from deep within her mind.

"What if we finish late? It will be dark. Traffic will be crazy, and..." Her train of thought was interrupted once again, by the same frosted glass door opening. She saw a short, thin man step out. She noticed his eyes were red and puffy. "He probably cried a lot," Mary Jane thought to herself.

"We'll see you next week. Take care." The voice of the secretary could be heard coming from somewhere inside.

Mary Jane shifted impatiently on the sofa. She was preparing herself to go in. Once again, the door closed without anyone calling her.

"What is wrong with her? Is she mad at me? Did I do something wrong during our last session? Why is she behaving so strangely?" Mary Jane asked silently.

She opened her pastel pink designer handbag to search for her phone.

"It is 4:21. This is ridiculous! She has never been this late. She better give me the full hour," Mary Jane said to herself.

She placed the phone back inside her purse. Mary Jane directed her gaze at the door, hoping to see someone on the other side of the frosted glass, but there was no one there. She diverted her attention toward her legs. She noticed a loose thread at the bottom of her dress.

"Ugh! For God's sake. I just bought this dress and it's already coming apart. I knew I should've taken it to the dry cleaners instead of washing it at home. I am such an idiot! I always ruin everything I touch. It's so irritating," Mary Jane told herself, her mouth twisted. "Oh God! Where is she? Why don't we start our session? I can't stand it anymore," thought Mary Jane, in misery.

On the ceiling of the waiting room, a single small Brown House Moth fluttered its wings, as it danced around the energy-efficient halogen bulbs. The air conditioner vent whispered a soft hiss. In the corner, by the entrance door, a fairly tall snake plant was doing its job purifying the air. Mary Jane clutched her handbag with her clammy hands and felt that she would not be able to contain herself for another second. She stood up and walked toward the glass door. She knocked firmly.

"Dr. White, Dr. White. Can I talk to you?" she cried, in desperation.

She stopped to listen. Steps could be heard approaching from behind the door. The door opened. It was the secretary.

"Oh Honey, I am so sorry. Please come in. Dr. White will see you now." Mary Jane stepped into the well-lit hallway.

"I'm sorry, Melissa. I did not mean to act all crazy, but I am feeling really anxious right now," stated Mary Jane, in embarrassment.

"Don't worry, Hon. You did not act crazy at all. You were probably just worried about the time," Melissa replied, in a calm voice, as she guided Mary Jane to the second door on the right. The secretary opened the door to the therapist's office, turned around, and walked back to her desk by the glass door, without saying another word. This behavior seemed pretty odd to Mary Jane.

When Mary Jane entered the room, she was struck by the lack of light. It was unusually dark. After seven years of being a patient of Dr. White, she was well acquainted with the setting of the office.

"Please sit down, Mary Jane," asked the therapist, politely.

Mary Jane complied, without saying a word. The therapist sat still, just a few feet away from Mary Jane, on her black high-back leather and chestnut chair. Dr. White was looking straight at her, calmly, with a distant gaze. There was a somber stillness that hung over the room. It was Mary Jane who broke the silence. "Is everything okay, Dr. White?"

"Everything is perfectly fine, Miss Taylor," answered a man's voice, from behind the therapist's chair.

"Everything is perfectly fine, Miss Taylor," repeated Dr. White.

Surprised, Mary Jane leaned slightly to her right. She tried as hard as she could to focus her squinting eyes on the stranger. He was a broad-shouldered man of about fifty-five, bald on top, with a goatee. She noticed that he was dressed all in black, (a sport jacket, dress pants, and shiny dress shoes). He had the air of an attorney, a professor, or even a therapist. The man had sat motionless when she came in and sat down.

"Everything is perfectly fine, Miss Taylor," the stranger continued. "I am here to assist Dr. White. I am here to help you." When he spoke, his voice was soft and comforting.

The therapist, (Dr. White), once again repeated the man's words, mechanically. "Everything is perfectly fine, Miss Taylor. I am here to assist Dr. White. I am here to help you."

"Help me?" asked Mary Jane, staring at the unexpected intruder.

The man gave a friendly smile, opened a manila folder with a red label on the cover, and read something inside.

"I am very interested in your case, Mary Jane," he continued. "I hope you don't mind me calling you by your first name. I hate formalities. I think they are unnecessary," he went on. "Anyhow, I believe I can help you overcome the deep sadness and suffering that you are experiencing."

Dr. White then repeated the same words the man had just said.

Mary Jane became furious.

"Dr. White, what is this?" she continued. "This is most unusual. Who is this man?"

There was no reply from Dr. White. She remained seated, with a blank stare.

The man drew in a deep breath.

"Please let me explain. I am here to help you find the solutions that you have been searching for. Deep inside, you have known for quite some time, that you are unconsciously hiding what really happened, the true cause of your suffering," he went on. "You have spent years in therapy, repeating the same stories to several counselors and therapists. They are all good people with good intentions. Nevertheless, you never heal. Do you know why, Mary Jane?"

Dr. White repeated this, word for word.

"No," she responded, her face turning white.

"Because you chose not to remember," the man replied.

"What is going on here? Who are you?" asked Mary Jane, confused. The man smiled slightly.

"My name, and who I am, is of no importance, but if you must know, my first name is Flavio, and I am a hypnotherapist, among other things. I was invited here by someone who wants you to have a future that is different from your past."

"I don't understand any of this!" exclaimed Mary Jane, in exasperation.

"It's quite simple, Mary Jane," the hypnotherapist said. "Today, your session will be quite different. As you have noticed, Dr. White is repeating every single word that I say, because your subconscious mind trusts Dr. White and only Dr. White. So, we need her voice to find what you are looking for. I am here only to guide Dr. White. Mary Jane waited for Dr. White to finish repeating what the hypnotherapist had just said.

"But how is this possible? I don't..."

The hypnotherapist stopped her with a slight movement of his hand.

"I would love to explain to you how it works, but time is of the essence. It is time for us to begin."

"What if I don't want to participate?" Mary Jane asked, defiantly.

"But I do know that you want to cooperate," answered the hypnotherapist.

"What are you going to do?" queried Mary Jane.

"I will guide you into a deep trance," he responded, calmly.

"You are going to hypnotize me?" asked Mary Jane, nervously.

The hypnotherapist stepped around Dr. White's chair. He stood right in front of Mary Jane, and paused for a moment, as though to allow her to process what was happening.

He extended his left arm, as if to shake hands with Mary Jane. She grabbed his hand, involuntarily. In a fraction of a second, the hypnotherapist simultaneously jerked her arm down and pulled the back of her head with his right hand. She heard the word "sleep," out loud, and felt like the whole room was spinning. For an instant, she noticed her own body slumped over to one side. She thought she was free falling into a dark abyss.

She could hear the voice of Dr. White, somewhere far away, saying, "You will not fall asleep or lose consciousness."

She drifted in and out. She heard her own voice talking. She experienced an immense sadness, weighing heavily on her heart and soul. She heard herself crying uncontrollably. It all seemed like a dream.

Even the knowledge of her own name slipped into unconsciousness. In that instant, a delightful, pleasant feeling spread throughout her whole body.

A sense of lightness came over her. Her eyes remained closed, but she could hear Dr. White's voice, clearer now, saying, "You don't really have to try to remember what just happened. It all seems like too much effort anyway. You can just remember to forget or forget to remember," Dr. White continued. "In a moment you will hear my voice reach five. You will open your eyes and feel calm, relaxed, fully conscious, and fully aware. One, drifting up. Two, conscious and aware. Three, restfully refreshed. Four, completely awake. Five, open your eyes."

Mary Jane forcefully opened her eyes. For a few seconds she felt mentally disoriented. Finally, she snapped back into full consciousness, at the sound of the door closing.

"What was that?" she asked.

At the same time, Dr. White also felt like she snapped out of some sort of stupor.

"I am sorry, what?" asked the therapist.

"I heard the door closing," replied Mary Jane.

"Don't worry. It was probably the bathroom door outside," said the therapist, reflectively.

"How do you feel, Mary Jane?" asked Dr. White, watching her watch.

"Like a million dollars, Dr. White. I feel like a heavy load has been lifted. I don't know what you did, but I feel great," answered Mary Jane, happily.

"Wonderful. I am glad that you're feeling great. I think we had a breakthrough," the therapist replied, glancing at her watch again. "Wow! Do you know what time it is? It is 7:15!" Dr. White said, in amazement.

Mary Jane smiled faintly, and said, "That's our longest session up to date. I guess that's why I feel so great."

"I guess so," the therapist said, softly.

Mary Jane picked up her purse and reached inside for her car keys. Her hand came in contact with an unfamiliar object. She grabbed it with her thumb and index finger. It was a business card. It read: "Got a problem? Hypnosis can help you. Call today."

"May I look at that?" asked the therapist.

"Of course," replied Mary Jane.

Dr. White took a look at the business card.

"I hope you are not considering doing hypnosis," stated the therapist.

"You know, it can be quite dangerous, especially if it's not performed by a licensed mental health professional."

"Not at all. He is just someone who I met last week during a networking event. We spoke for a little while. I mentioned that I've been in therapy for a few years. He asked me a few questions about the process, like, how I was feeling, and he even asked me about you," she went on. "I did say that I was curious about hypnosis, but you know, I probably will never do it."

"Good," the therapist replied, forcefully.

"Same time next week, Dr. White?" asked Mary Jane.

"Yes, same time next week," answered the therapist.

A Village in My Head

There is a village in my head. I hear these voices talking to me all day long. Some are louder than others. Some are sweet and kind, but there are others that are harsh and stern. If you were to ask me how they came about, I couldn't tell you. All I can say with certainty is how they influence my thinking and behavior. So, let me tell you a little bit about them.

The first voice is obscure and somewhat shy. It doesn't have too much to say. I seldom follow his advice. You could say I don't value his input at all. Too many times it has failed me, in the past. If I could place a face to it, he would appear as an awkward adolescent that tries to assert his place in the world, but fails miserably. He always seems to appear during superficial social interactions, for example, dealing with a customer at the car wash, or making small talk with the table next to me at the coffee house.

The second voice is confident, sharp, and self-assured. People really enjoy my company when he's around. He is pretty slick indeed. What I appreciate most about him is the fact that he's street smart. He is very resourceful and can think fast on his feet, and for this reason, people listen to me when he is around. You would think that he speaks out of experience and observation, but I can assure you that it has more to do with his inherent nature. He is the reason why I've often been described as having an adventurous spirit. People marvel when I tell them fascinating stories of wild adventures on the streets of Mumbai, or describe the feelings of hiking the Pacific Crest Trail. This voice comes around when I'm with people I know, or surrounded by my inner-circle, my "crew." Nevertheless, I despise it. He can be downright arrogant. You have no idea how many times I caught myself telling the most outrageous and deceiving stories. Not only that. In the past, on more than one occasion, I returned home with a fat lip, due to its account. Of course, I can make an effort to be more conscious when he's around. Perhaps I could try to inhibit its pompous nature. But on the other hand, this is precisely what makes him unique, or should I say, makes me unique?

The third voice is frail, in a way that I really don't care for. It is like a little fearful child that is too frightened to express his feelings, but wants to be heard. My whole demeanor is so pathetic when he is around. My body language screams, "uneasiness." What I detest the most is his tone of voice. It is so dull.

It draws people in, like some sort of an empathetic call, I guess. But it is not long before most people lose interest. However, I cannot be too hard on him, since he is not aware of his shortcomings, and I do cherish his innocence. On the other hand, he can be quite a brat. I've been known to act most stubbornly until I get what I want. He comes around when I am facing an authoritarian figure, such as my demanding boss, or my capricious doctor.

The fourth voice is, without a doubt, the most severe of all. He is a true dictator and tyrant. He is the judge, jury, and prosecutor, all wrapped up in one voice. I cannot escape his wrath. He is present every time I make a mistake. He reminds me that I did not exercise, that I overeat, that no one cares what I think, and so on. Well, it is not hard to imagine that it is not pleasant to have him around. I even talked to a professional about him, but she was no help at all. There is only so much one can do to silence a bully without irritating him. He is the type of presence who makes you hold an object ten times your body weight, and when you drop it, he looks at you with loathing. I am going to be perfectly honest. I have accomplished many things in life, (good grades, a successful career, a beautiful home), so many of those things that are admirable in today's society. Yet, these achievements are never good enough for him. Perhaps it is best if I leave it at that. You probably would not want to read what he might think of you.

My fifth voice is sweet and compassionate. She is always kind to hear. She has taught me so much over the years. I can trace back every warm and loving deed I have ever performed, by the way she influences my thinking process. I don't even have to earn her respect. She just accepts me the way I am. There have been so many times that I have behaved in the most disgraceful ways, but she doesn't mind. Her love is truly unconditional. Perhaps she is too loving. She is forgiving in every way. I must confess that sometimes I question her morality. How far do I have to go before I can hear an objection or complaint from her?

The sixth voice is the most cerebral of them all. He is an intellectual, through and through. He is contemplative, and yet he is a great talker. He doesn't come around too often, but when he does, it is a delightful experience. All those books that I read over the years are his to articulate. You would be happily absorbed in his passionate description of the complex characters in García Márquez's masterpiece, One Hundred Years of Solitude. Perhaps you would like to hear his viewpoint on Vivaldi's magnum opus, "The Four Seasons." And you definitely want to listen to his take on Plato's cave allegory. If I would take the time to learn another language, he would talk to me in Portuguese or some other exotic tongue. But there is something about him that is painful to admit. He can be quite aloof, and somewhat detached, to people that are not interested in the arts or philosophy. I think he cannot help it. As I mentioned before, he is an intellectual, through and through.

My seventh voice is hard to describe, not because it is complex. Quite the opposite, it is so clear and straightforward, that it can be hard to understand. The world would not know how to appreciate it fully, to hear its truthful message. It doesn't scream or try to silence others. It just observes in silence. It is mystical in nature and independent of self-importance. Just like many of the other voices, I don't know its origin. I cannot even tell its gender. Is it male or female? Maybe it's both. What I can tell you is that it's been there for as long as I can remember. It appears when I least expect it. The last time it made its presence known, I was right in the middle of a heated argument. It intervened at the right moment. I believe things would have ended up a lot worse, if I hadn't listened to it. Unfortunately, I make little effort to connect with it. This is to my detriment.

And then there is the eighth voice. This voice is full of perversion, and I don't know why. Some of the things it whispers in my head are downright vicious and immoral. With time, it has gotten even more deviant. I often wonder what people would think if I could openly express or act out some of the savage suggestions it shares with me. I tried to break all communication with him, and for the most part, he leaves me alone. But he is a trickster. He quietly crawls back up from the depth of my unconscious mind, seemingly bringing innocent little thoughts with him, just to reveal his true intentions afterward. He is indeed a wolf in sheep's clothing. I will not play the hypocrite. Some of his strange ideas are not without an alluring attraction.

The ninth voice is soft and wise. It has the tone of an old woman. She is full of ancient fables and old wives' tales. She keeps me humble and grounded. When I was younger, I often rejected this voice, since I knew her origin. But nowadays I follow her advice when she talks to me. She rarely talks to me. It's a calamity how time has made her a distant memory, a relic of the past. Her language is so pure, with no intricate details or convoluted explanation, just honest and simple opinions. She is so wise, in spite of her lack of academic education. I'm looking forward to hearing from her.

And last but not least is the tenth voice, probably the most honest in the village. She often appears when I'm just about to tell a lie, or start procrastinating. She is understanding, considerate, direct, and, without question, a voice of common sense. You would think that this voice is all business and no play, but there is a surprising, joyful spirit about her. Many people become aware of my good nature when she is talking. I have become strongly attached to this voice. I could have a genuine conversation with anyone when she is around. However, it is wise of me to keep an eye out when she is talking. Too many times, I find myself trying my hardest to establish rapport with the shadiest of characters. I immediately put a stop to that. You can never be too careful nowadays. There are so many scammers, backstabbers, and schizos.

I will stop this monologue for your own good, since I'm afraid that you have been deceived right from the beginning. For I can assure you that I've never been to Mumbai, worked at a car wash, or paid enough attention to classical music to give you an educated description of "The Four Seasons" by Vivaldi. So, the question is, which voice has bamboozled you? I guess it would impossible to tell. And how about you, reader? Have you become acquainted with the inhabitants of your village?

One Last Song

Karina was sitting on a high stool in the middle of the small stage. She was a woman in her mid-fifties, with bright shiny brown eyes that sparkled like precious polished Baltic ambers, and a delicate, slender body. Dark blond hair fell to her shoulders. Her tanned skin contrasted nicely to her beige dress, making her seem more glamorous on stage.

The twelve small tables in the room were filled with cheerful patrons, except for one man who sat quietly by himself. The rest were an eclectic bunch, ranging from young, free-spirited hippies to middle-aged, affluent professionals, and everything in between.

A well-dressed hipster, with a long beard and a flamboyant personality, walked onto stage and stood next to Karina.

"Ladies and gentlemen, boys and girls. Welcome to our fabulous, wild Thursday night open mic," began the young fellow. "It gives me great pleasure to introduce y'all to our first local superstar. Y'all know her as Karina." He handed the microphone to Karina, pressed his palms together, as if praying, and gave a slight bow to the audience, as he walked off stage.

Karina cleared her throat once, pressed her lips against the top of the mic, and began singing one of her favorite songs, "Nothing Compares 2U." Her voice was sweet and pleasant, but clearly untrained. Her body language matched the musical theme. She gazed at the crowd mournfully, and occasionally paused and directed her attention to the man sitting by himself at table seven. Each time she did this, he sank deeper and deeper into his chair. The song ended. There was a moment of silence. Then a burst of cheers and applause shook the room. The amateur singer looked over the cheery audience. One or two individuals actually stood up in ovation. She nodded.

"Thank you, thank you. I would like to dedicate the following original song to my husband of thirty-three years. It is titled, 'One Last Song,'" said Karina, while she extended her left arm toward the man sitting by himself. A polite round of clapping spread throughout the room. The man sitting by himself ignored both the singer and the audience.

She picked up her acoustic guitar, approached the mic, and began singing. The audience listened attentively, in complete silence. There was something special about the song. Even her voice sounded different. It was enchanting, melodic, and almost hypnotic. The spotlight illuminated her face. She closed her eyes. The singer seemed to be in a trance. She ended her song with a kiss.

Once again, thunderous cheering, accompanied by applause and whistling, shook the entire room. Among the crowd there were a few teary eyes. The song had obviously reached the hearts of many in the audience.

"Thank you so much. You guys are amazing," said Karina, in a soft and humble tone. She sang a total of nine songs. The last melody was an upbeat version of "Sweet Caroline," in which the whole room participated for the chorus. At the end of her set, the emcee stepped on stage again.

"Well, let's give another big round of applause to our beloved local star, Karina!" he announced. The crowd gladly responded.

Waving goodbye, Karina walked off stage. She made her way through the room and sat next to her husband, who, by the looks of it, was not amused at all. He tilted his head backward and drank half a pint of beer in a single gulp. Then, he slammed the glass on the table.

"You always have to make a spectacle, don't you?" exclaimed her husband.

"Come on honey. Have some fun. Everyone is having a good time," responded Karina to her husband's stern comment.

"You know how much I hate being put in the spotlight. So, why do you go out of your way to do it?" her husband inquired, annoyed.

"Lighten up Robert," said Karina, playfully, as she threw her arms around her husband.

"Karina, you are something else," whispered Robert in her right ear.

A minute later the next act began their set. Robert scratched the back of his head, looked around the room, and slowly leaned toward Karina.

"I think it's time to go."

"Really?" asked Karina, gazing into her husband's blue eyes.

"Yes. Come on. We have to go," was Robert's firm reply.

"But I wanted to hear some of the other artists," said Karina, in a low voice.

"It's getting late, Karina," said Robert.

"Come on honey. Let's stay for another thirty minutes," his wife implored.

"No, it's time to go," was Robert's sober response.

"Well," replied Karina irritably.

They both got up and slowly made their way to the front door. Along the way, Karina was lavished with compliments and praises. They both exited the bar, holding hands. It was raining heavily. Robert made a small gesture to his wife, who remained quiet as they hurried to their car.

Waiting until they were both in the car, Karina asked, "What's wrong, Robert?"

"This is the last time I come to one of your performances," responded Robert, suddenly becoming agitated.

"So, you don't want to hear me sing anymore?" asked Karina, examining her husband's face.

"Exactly, I don't want to hear you sing anymore," responded Robert, narrowing his eyes, angrily.

Karina's face turned red as she began crying. Without saying a word, he started the car, looked around as he reversed, shifted the gear selector to D, and drove off the parking lot.

"I don't know why you're so upset," she said, looking away from her husband.

His response was a deep grunt.

"If that is your wish, then I shall never sing for you again, my love," declared Karina.

Robert turned his attention toward his wife, not knowing where to put his eyes.

"Karina, what I meant to say was..."

"Robert!" screamed Karina.

In that instant, thunder silenced the fatal collision that flipped the black mid-sized sedan onto its roof. The wind blew the rain sideways, as if trying to get inside the car to awaken the driver or passenger. A row of water oak trees made tumultuous noise with their swaying branches. There was a loud scream in the distance, but every sound was drowned out by the torrential rain.

"Twenty-one days..."

"What?"

"Who said that?"

"Is someone there?"

"Where am I?"

"Why is it so dark?"

"Can anyone hear me?"

"Karina, Karina, are you there?"

"Someone answer me!"

"What's the meaning of this? Where am I?"

"What's going on?"

"Stay calm, stay calm. Let me try to think what happened and how I got here. I..., I..., I think we were going home. It was raining."

"And... and, we were arguing."

"Why were we arguing?"

"Why can't I remember what happened?"

"Can someone please help me? Help! Help!"

"Oh God, help!"

"I am so tired all of a sudden."

"So, so tired..."

"Am I dre... Am I dre... dreaming?"

"Yes, Doctor Gonzalez is here."

"Who?"

"What?"

"Who is Doctor Gonzalez?"

"Who said that?"

"Where am I?"

"How come no one can hear me?"

"And why I can't see anything?"

"Can someone please turn the lights on? Please, I can't see anything!"

"Karina, Karina, where are you?"

"Can someone answer me?"

"How long have I been here?"

"How did I get here? I, I think Karina and I were arguing. There was a storm. Yes, yes, there was a storm!"

"What happened next?"

"Why can't I remember what happened next?"

"I need to rest for a moment. Yes, I need to rest... I will feel... feel... fe..."

"Forty-three days..."

"Who's there?"

"Forty-three days of what?"

"Please, someone answer me!"

"Can someone help me? Help! Help!"

"I need to see my wife, Karina... Karina!"

"My wi... my wife. She was crying."

"Why was she crying?"

"Okay, let me think for a moment. I remember driving home and Karina was crying. Why was she crying?"

"What happened?"

"There was a loud noise. Yes, yeah... like a... like a crash."

"What happened then?"

"Oh, I'm so tired, beyond tired. I need to sle... sleep."

"We don't know if he will ever wake up from the coma."

"Who is in a coma?"

"Who is there?"

"Can you hear me?"

"Karina, Karina... If anyone can hear me, please call my wife!"

"Call my wife! Call my wife!"

"What is happening?"

"Where am I?"

"I can't see anything!"

"Can someone tell me where my wife is?"

"I think we were in an accident or something."

"And I was crying. No, no. It wasn't me who was crying. It was Karina?"

"Why was she crying?"

"Did I. Did I say something that made her cry?"

"Why am I exhausted? It's... it's unbearable. I'm so tired."

"Yes, seventy-three days. "

"Who's there?"

"Seventy-three days of what?"

"Whoever you are, please answer me!"

"Help me! Help! Help!"

"Karina... Karina. She was crying."

"Why was she crying?"

"Becau... because I told her I didn't want to hear her sing again."

"Oh God! I'm sorry Karina! I'm sorry!"

"I do want to hear you sing! I do!"

"I do want to hear your beautiful voice singing again!"

"I'm so sorry!"

"I do! I do! "

"Wha... what? Who is there? Is that you? Is that you Karina?"

"It is. It's you. Oh, thank God, I can hear your voice!"

"It's your song. You are singing!"

"Where are you?"

"Your voice sounds so far away."

"I can hear your voice but... but I cannot see you. Where are you?"

"Don't go! I will follow your voice!"

"What is that? It's... it's light."

"Karina, I can hear you better now."

"The light... It's so bright!"

"Karina, is that you?"

"Oh, it is you, my love."

"You are so beautiful!"

"Your voice is so beautiful!"

As Robert walked into the light a kiss could be heard.

The Trees of Life

he radiant sun embraces me as I step onto the small porch in the back of our beautiful villa. Its long wavy arms of light reach down to the ground without any obstructions. It is the season of warm weather and prevailing winds. I sit comfortably on one of the two traditional rocking chairs at our back door. The occasional harmless white cloud drifts aimlessly across the clear blue sky, as the hours wear on. A gust of wind ruffles the leaves on the long branches of the immense Royal Poinciana tree that covers the length of the small garden beside the villa.

The pleasant sound of our pool's waterfall makes its way up the small terraces that connect the back porch to the swimming pool. And the plumage of a white-throated magpie-jay shimmers on the property fence. But my mind is not at peace. The Royal Poinciana tree calls me from its permanent home. It murmurs frightening incantations, like a sorceress that shrouds my eyes with disturbing hallucinations.

It was during a windy afternoon, when I saw the valley for the first time. In a stupor, I saw the land, surrounded by mountains on the south, and the shores of the Sea of Fresh Water to the north. Modern buildings sat next to humble structures of the past. Scattered throughout the city were the massive tall metal towers in the shape of trees. They were called "The Trees of Life." Each was painted in different colors and adorned with light bulbs, to glow at night. There was something dark about these massive artificial sculptures. Even the air around them felt restrained. There are all sorts of stories surrounding the origin and purpose of the metal trees. Some say that they're the work of sorcery, by a witch who served a cruel dictator. Others say that they're some sort of mind control devices. No one knows for sure their real purpose. I stared at the city for a long time, in a trance. I realized that this was the capital of this land.

I witnessed plumes of dark smoke rising from the streets into the heavens. A sea of men and women, chanting songs of freedom, could be heard in the air. These voices where finally drown out by the sound of the rain that was assaulting the Spanish clay roof tiles on our villa. When I emerged from this vision, my mental state was not the same as before. A stream of images flooded my mind. Day and night, I see images of thousands of people marching together against an oppressing force. From that moment on, the visions of the city, and his inhabitants protesting on the streets, would appear with just the slightest breeze brushing against the branches of the Royal Poinciana tree.

A deep sense of melancholy fills my days at this beautiful villa that I once called paradise. I now realize that my visions are not hallucinations, for they appear to be more real to me than my Eden, with the beautiful garden, the pool, and the shimmering white-throated magpie-jay.

I had been sitting on the porch for hours, when the sun rose. My eyes were fixed on the Royal Poinciana tree. Somehow, I was transported to the streets of the city by the Sea of Fresh Water. I was not just visualizing myself being there. I was actually walking, hand in hand, with the crowd. I could hear the voice of the leader, right next to me, heading the protest. He spoke clearly and intelligently. He demanded that the head of state and oppressor of the people step down. The crowd cheered and repeated his words, enthusiastically.

Every man, woman, and child walking on the streets knew that they were facing a formidable deadly force. The regiment serving the cruel dictator was well trained, unjust, and without principles. Rumors of defeat in the city of the Great Poet, the city of the volcanic lagoon, and in the town of mist, swirled through the crowd. A group of us gathered around, as the leader of the march gave detailed instructions. We were to follow them precisely, to have a chance to survive and fight for another day.

To my surprise, he assigned me, and a few others, with a crucial role. We were to go to the west of the city and topple six metal trees onto the road, blocking a major artery to the center of the capital. This action would prevent heavy armored vehicles from reaching the crowd. We were a small group, but we were determined to accomplish our mission. We walked for several miles, under the punishing sun. The metal trees were within sight.

However, as we reached our target, a soft breeze carried a familiar, enchanting murmur. The hypnotic whisper easily seduced my senses. A great heaviness fell over me. My thoughts began to drift, aimlessly. Then I found myself back again, staring at the Royal Poinciana tree that stands beside our villa.

In great despair, I plead to the tree and the wind to take me back to the city beside the Sea of Fresh Water. But all I hear is bewitching laughter mocking me, and it doesn't matter how many times I tell myself that this is only a dream. I cannot wake up to prevent the heavily armed vehicles from reaching the brave men and women who are fighting for their freedom.

Now I sit on the rocking chair, staring at the wandering clouds, dancing carelessly above. A memory of great hope gradually fades away, on everlasting summer days, until it is no more. The Royal Poinciana tree often whispers the cries of fearless men and women, but my soul, filled with guilt and sadness, can no longer remember the cause of such profound grief.

The Crimson King
and
Katherine

W here do I begin? Perhaps I should tell you a little bit about myself. I was born in a tranquil and remote forest during the rainy season, one hundred and seventy-three rainy seasons ago, to be more exact. I was not too much to look at in my infancy, but over the years, I grew into quite a handsome specimen, (tall, strong, and in great shape). I am pleasantly calm and patient by nature, as all of my kind tends to be. Here is an interesting fact that I am most proud of. I am a direct descendant of a long line of Scandinavian royalty. That's right, I am a Crimson King. But I don't let that go to my head, or should I say, I don't let that go to my roots. Yes, I am what you humans refer to as a maple tree.

But this story is not just about me. In fact, it's more about Katherine than me. You could say that I have lived two completely different lives. (For a hundred human years, or for a hundred rainy seasons, as this is how we trees measure time.)

I have spent most of my life minding my own business. That is not to say that I did not have to deal with unexpected visitors. Let me share with you a few unpleasant experiences. Let's see. There were the robin's nests during springtime. Their offspring can drive you mad with their relentless piercing shrieks. How about the cumbersome squirrels? I remember this particular one, back about a hundred and twenty-one rainy seasons ago. If I am not mistaken, it was during the mating season. Well, this insolent creature decided to build a palace on one of my top branches, with my own foliage. The nerve! Fortunately, their lifespan is quite short, so after a decade or so he was gone. Now, I don't want to sound insensitive, but how would you feel if a hyperactive and highly anxious quadruped decided to make his permanent home on top of your head? Not an appealing thought, right? I'm glad we agree.

Anyhow, I do remember the first time I saw a human being. He was of the male gender. He was wearing some type of dead animal skin over his body. Gross! He was carrying a long stick, which emitted a horrific thundering noise, smoke, and a foul smell, every time he used it. But worst of all, just before sunset, he somehow summoned the devourer of life. I think you humans call it "fire." Just as a side note, this thing you humans call fire is the one thing that we trees fear the most. All night long, we kept our focus on the yellow and orange flames. I took a deep breath every time I saw a flying spark being carried by the wind. I think I can speak for every tree and plant when I say that we were more than happy to see this strange and insensitive creature leave. You can imagine that the members of the forest were not impressed at all. As you humans say, "First impressions are everything."

So, as I mentioned before, for a hundred years, we lived in peace. Then, thirty-seven rainy seasons ago, a horrific event changed everything. We call this event, "The Great Tragedy." Out of nowhere, a swarm of men moved into the forest. They took it upon themselves to mercilessly mow down a vast number of our kind. From the old to the young, large and small, no tree was immune to the slaughter. Our skin and flesh, (bark and heartwood), blanketed the ground. Our blood, (tree sap), poured out from every slash made by their ferociously hungry handheld machines. Hundreds of vibrant White Pines tumbled. Majestic Northern Red Oaks were cut down. And even the small colorful Redbud trees were not spared. By the way, I learned all of these terms by listening to the men, as they named each tree before they cut it. Fortunately, they refrained from annihilating every single one of us, but the loss was immense.

The following year, more humans appeared, but this time they brought with them these strange-looking creatures. The humans would crawl inside them and seem to make the things come alive. They made a terrifying noise, and the ground shook continuously, as they roamed around. The Great Tragedy went on for a few years. During this time, the humans and the creatures had created an unimaginable number of large boxes with holes on every side. Then, more humans appeared. (I often wonder how many humans are in existence.) As I was saying, more humans appeared out of nowhere.

An unusual group of humans moved into one of the boxes that they built, not too far in front of me. I was never clear on the exact name for these boxes. I heard some of the humans call it home, house, and crib, among other things. I quickly learned the names of all the members that lived inside the box. First, there was the tallest member who they called "dad." Then there was the female they called "mom." Then there was a medium-sized human called "Erik." And lastly, there was the small one they called "Katherine."

To be honest with you, I was not too impressed with these humans. After all, they had turned our green paradise into some sort of stone labyrinth.

Katherine was the first to notice me. As soon as she saw me, she rushed toward me and tried to put her arms around me. I don't think she realized that I was over a hundred years old. It would take two humans to get their arms around my trunk. She called upon the one they called "dad" to help her climb me. Sincerely, I do not think she was made for this sort of activity, but dad granted her wish. He lifted her high enough for her to hang from my lowest branch. She hardly weighed more than a pregnant possum. This brought great joy to the little one. For some reason or another, over the years, this was a constant source of amusement for Katherine. I did not mind at all. She did not cause any harm or nuisance. It's not like she was trying to build a home on one of my branches.

During that whole summer, I saw the group or family. I think "family" is the term that I heard some of them throw around. In any case, I saw them going in and out of the box, sometimes for an extended period. The following year dad surprised both Katherine and me by hanging a swing from one of my thickest branches. At first, it was quite irritating. The friction of the rope created a groove. But after a few months, I hardly noticed it. Over time, I began to enjoy the company of Katherine. I felt an unexpected joy every time I heard her laugh. We started to build a friendship. I was her favorite spot to hide, when she played hide and seek. For her 7th birthday, they hung an object that they kept calling a "piñata," from one of my branches. I was the second base when she learned to play softball. So, you can say that we did everything together.

But now listen to what happened to both of us, just a few days after Katherine celebrated her 12th birthday. She had just arrived from that place they call a "school," whatever that is. As usual, she was in good humor. She stormed out of the box and rushed toward me. In a fraction of the time it would take one of my falling leaves to reach the ground, she was making her way up my branches. Keep in mind that I am a forty-one foot high Crimson King Maple tree, and Katherine was no longer the little human that dangled from my lowest branch when we first met. So, as she reached halfway to the top, the weight of her body snapped a weak branch. She started falling. I tried to catch her, but her weight was too much for my branches. However, I did manage to slow down her fall. She hit the ground and broke one of her arms. I suffered several broken arms too.

Well, from that moment forward, she was no longer allowed to climb me. The human called dad went as far as cutting my lower branches, a painful and traumatic experience. But life when on. Katherine and I continued to be the best of friends. She would spend long summer hours sitting under the shade that I provided for her. She disclosed all her secrets to me, when she would write her innermost thoughts in her diary. When she was fifteen, hiding behind me, she gave her first kiss to a young, freckled redheaded boy. I was present when the whole human family and their friends threw a large party to celebrate her school graduation, whatever that was.

I also remember those four lonely rainy seasons when Katherine left. To her credit, she did manage to visit me during the winter. She even carved a tattoo on my side. Now I cannot read human writing, but these are the symbols that can be seen up to this day, "Sergio + Katherine Forever." I assume it has something to do with our special friendship.

Then, out of the blue, Katherine came back. She was accompanied by another human who was male in gender. They spent a lot of time together. Not too long after she returned, the largest human celebration that I have ever witnessed, took place. And it all happened under my branches. Katherine looked radiant, all dressed in white. Most of the human males were wearing black. They screamed, played music, moved in funny ways, and kissed plenty. I could hear Katherine laughing all night long. I have to say, that is one of the few times during my long life that I wished I could move my roots the way humans move their feet.

The next year something strange happened. Katherine took on an odd shape. The middle part of her body was round and swollen. Luckily, it was nothing serious. One day it was there, and the next it was gone. This happened twice in the span of five rainy seasons. It seems to me that these were the happiest years of Katherine's life, and for this reason, they were also the happiest rainy seasons of my life. We were inseparable. I had a new swing and she would bring the tiny humans, who resembled her, to play on it. What a joy to see them play and laugh all day long.

Over the years, both Katherine and I grew older together. The humans called dad, mom, and Erik had vanished, long ago. I got battered pretty badly during the harsh winter of seven rainy seasons ago. I was never quite the same after that. Katherine had matured into old human age. She spent most of her days gardening. She did a magnificent job. A blanket of daisies and poppy mallows peppered the ground. I don't know how she managed, but she was able to maintain a patch of Nashville Breadroot all around me. It is very hard to plant and sustain any type of flower bed around a Crimson King Maple tree. You could say that we are a very picky breed.

This past summer, I experienced the deepest suffering that I have ever felt, even more so than during the period of "The Great Tragedy." It was a warm summer afternoon. Katherine was just finishing planting a row of tulip bulbs, a few feet away from me. When she tried to get to her feet, she sighed softly, fell over on her side, and hit her head against one of my protruding roots. She stopped breathing. A few days later, they dug a large hole on the ground, just a few feet away from me, and placed a wooden box in it. The human called Sergio was present. He spoke lovingly of Katherine. At that moment, I realized that they had placed Katherine's body inside the wooden box.

Sadly, trees do not have the ability to cry, but during autumn I do bathe the ground with my golden leaves. It is winter now. My bridled branches are bare, and my last breath of life hangs on a single lonely leaf. I do not have much longer to live. I will join Katherine soon. I can almost hear her happy laugh in the wind. And as you read these words, I look back on my long life and remember the silence of a distant past, and the joy of a beautiful friendship.

OtrosOshos

Act 1

A tall, lanky, red-haired girl, with blue eyes, wearing tap shoes, black stockings, and a short green dress with Celtic embroidery, walked off the stage to the sound of clapping from the small crowd. She made her way to the third row of seats, sighed, and sat down next to a heavy-set middle-aged woman. Every adult face in the small auditorium displayed a slightly annoyed expression. The room felt confined, dirty, and saturated with a thousand smells.

A well-dressed older man, who was sitting on the front row, got up and started walking toward the stage. Sweating profusely, he was no taller than five feet, three inches, with a thick neck, and a puffy face.

"Well done! Please give another round of applause for Lillian McGill!" shouted the man.

The crowd responded, with slightly more enthusiasm. The man on stage did his best to put a smile on his face, which made his face look distorted. He pulled out a folded sheet of paper from the right inside pocket of his old white blazer, as he cleared his throat. Then he stared silently at the crowd for a moment, to create an air of suspense.

"Now, ladies and gentlemen!" began the man. "We have a great treat for you, this evening! We have Mr. Geiii, Gueiss, Mr. Geist Woods and his talking rooster, Cesar, in a performance of ventriloquism!"

A large young man rose from the last chair in the second row. His size was imposing. He was wearing a dark Jaxon hat, V-neck long sleeved t-shirt, blue jeans, and black leather sneakers. What was most noticeable was the rooster that he was holding under his left arm. He got on stage and shook the hand of the announcer, while giving a slight bow.

"Thank you, Mr. Tailor. Thank you very much to you and to everyone that is here today!" exclaimed Geist Woods.

The presence of such a large man on stage made an impact on the small crowd. Everyone sat up and rubbernecked in order to get a better view.

"Good evening, ladies and gentlemen, boys and girls. Today you are going to see something amazing, something fantastic, something you have never seen before!" announced Geist Woods, in a deeply melodic, almost hypnotic, tone of voice.

The audience listened attentively. "Ooohs" and "ahs," could be heard throughout the crowd. Some children even moved to the front of the auditorium, to get a closer look. No one said a word, as Geist Woods grabbed a stool from the side of the stage and placed it on center stage. He placed the large rooster on top of it, adjusted the mic, and positioned himself right beside the bird.

"Please allow me to introduce, Cesar," said Geist Woods, with a big smile on his face.

The rooster shook his head, stretched his neck, opened his beak, and said, "I've got to say, Geist, of all the places that we have been to, this is the worst, don't you think?"

"Why would you say that, Cesar?" asked Geist Woods.

"Well, just look out there. Who are those people?" replied Cesar.

Geist Woods looked out to the audience. Every jaw in the room dropped in astonishment, when they heard the rooster speak.

"Now, now, be nice Cesar," replied Geist Woods.

"I'm always nice. I look nice, I smell nice. And I sound nice. On the other hand, you are looking quite disheveled," said Cesar, as his wattle moved from side to side.

Laughter broke out in the auditorium. The faces of the children, sitting close to the stage, turned red from excitement, curiosity, and bewilderment. They were in a trance.

"Cesar, you promised to behave," was Geist Woods's reply.

"And you promised to shower," Cesar retorted.

Laughter exploded, and "ahs!" could be heard throughout the crowd.

"Instead of being so mean, can you tell these wonderful people a joke?" asked Geist Woods, with a frown.

The auditorium windows rattled from enthusiastic cheering, and all eyes beamed with joy.

"Ugh," exclaimed Cesar, in disgust.

"Come on Cesar. I'm pretty sure the good people of Haines City, Florida would love to hear one of your funny jokes," exclaimed Geist Woods, pointing at the audience.

"If you insist," was Cesar's dry reply.

"Yeah," was Geist Woods' simple reply.

"Geist, do you know why the chicken crossed the road?" asked Cesar.

"No, Cesar, I don't know why," answered Geist Woods, peering at the rooster.

"Because she saw me," the rooster explained casually.

The audience burst out laughing. Geist Woods also laughed out loud.

"Ooh-la-la," said Cesar, examining Geist Woods up and down.

"What, Cesar?" asked Geist Woods, while still laughing.

"It never ceases to amaze me, the things that you find amusing," the rooster said, annoyed.

"That was really funny, Cesar," Geist Woods responded.

"You sir are uncouth and down right unsophisticated," Cesar said hotly.

"All right, Cesar. No need to get mad. We are here to have a good time," Geist Woods said, making an offhand gesture toward the audience.

"Blah," responded the rooster, evasively.

"You know, Cesar, sometimes you can be such a grouch," said Geist Woods, mockingly.

"Can you blame me?" the rooster continued. "You are not the one that has to deal with a nincompoop."

Geist Woods opened and closed his mouth as if lost for words. A stream of laughter resonated throughout the entire auditorium.

"I think you owe me and the audience an apology, Cesar," demanded Geist Woods.

The rooster first gave a low clucking noise and then a loud crow. The laughter in the auditorium intensified.

"I think, I think, ahh, I think it's time to go," Geist Woods exclaimed, hastily.

In unison, both Geist Woods and Cesar bowed down to the audience. There was a standing ovation. The entire place was buzzing with excitement. Geist Woods grabbed the rooster and began to make his way down, but before he reached the first row, Mr. Tailor grabbed him by the arm.

"Mr. Woods, Mr. Woods," said Mr. Tailor. "That was genius. Your act is just genius."

Geist Woods chuckled. "Thank you, Mr. Tailor. Coming from you, that is a real honor, a real honor, sir."

"No, I really mean it," Mr. Tailor added.

"I am honored," responded Geist Woods, while moving gingerly, like a man that is in a hurry to slip away for some unknown reason.

"Listen, you should be performing in larger venues," said Mr. Tailor, handing him a business card.

"You really think so?" asked Geist Woods, as he inspected the card.

"Give me a call tomorrow," said Mr. Tailor, smiling. "I want you to perform next weekend at my comedy club in Tampa."

Geist Woods was flabbergasted, "Thank you so much, Mr. Tailor."

All of a sudden, the rooster tried to flap his wings wildly. Geist Woods struggled to keep the rooster in place under his left arm.

"He's a handful," Mr. Tailor exclaimed, jokingly.

"Yes, he is. I better get him home before he decides to quit the act," replied Geist Woods, sarcastically.

Mr. Tailor laughed out loud.

"No, we don't want that."

Geist Woods rushed out of the auditorium, with the sound of the crowd still cheering and laughing. He ran across the parking lot. He unlocked the driver's door of his old Honda Civic, which was parked on the side of the road. He got in, and closed the door. He placed the rooster on the passenger seat.

"Are you okay, Cesar?" Geist Woods asked, with great concern.

"No!" the rooster yelled, angrily. "What the hell is going on?"

"You are regressing to avian consciousness. You are regressing to being a rooster," Geist Woods replied, casually. "But don't worry, I will bring you back to self-awareness next weekend."

The rooster shook his head, jumped to the floor of the car, and pecked at some dirt on the carpet.

"Here you go, buddy," Geist Woods said. He pulled a handful of rice out of the glove compartment and tossed it on the floor by the rooster.

A couple of people passed by the car without noticing the occupants. The dark tinted windows kept the interaction between man and bird private. The car started and drove away.

Act 2

It was a perfect Florida summer night. The weather was warm and dry. A full moon hung in the clear dark sky. Needless to say, the conditions were ideal for a fun Saturday evening. It seemed like the whole downtown area buzzed with excitement. Hundreds of cars and pedestrians clogged the main roads. Perhaps this is the reason why no one noticed when a 1986 blue Honda Civic, parked on a side street, two blocks away from the most popular comedy club in the city. A row of mature American Elm trees blocked all sources of light from reaching the street down below. The car engine was shut off, and the headlights dimmed. Inside the vehicle, Geist Wood's eyes were glued to his wristwatch. At exactly nine-thirty, he grabbed the rooster, who was pecking at the floor on the passenger side. He placed it on the dashboard, and held it down with one hand, while swinging a pendulum in front of the bird's face, with the other hand. He gazed into the rooster's right eye.

"OtrosOshos," said Geist Woods, loudly, poking the rooster on top of his head.

"What the hell, man! Where do you get off hitting me upside the head?" exclaimed the rooster.

"Sorry, Cesar, I didn't mean to hurt you," responded Geist Woods.

"Where are we?" asked the rooster.

"We are far, far away from home, in a city called Tampa," answered Geist Woods.

"And may I ask, what are we doing here?" asked Cesar, with annoyance.

"We are about to go into a room with a lot of people," was Geist Wood's nervous reply.

"What are we going to do there?" queried the rooster.

"Well," retorted Geist Woods. "We are going to have a conversation. We'll interact with the people in the room, and we are going to have fun doing it."

"How come this sounds familiar?" asked the rooster, reflectively. "Have we done this before?"

Geist Woods looked puzzled.

"What?"

"Somehow this feels familiar," retorted the rooster.

"Not at all, Cesar," explained Geist Woods. "I wouldn't do that to you. I know how much you dislike most humans."

"You got that right," the rooster confirmed, proudly.

People walked past the old car without taking notice of the occupants. Geist Woods remained still for an instant, as not to call attention to themselves. No one could see him or the rooster, due to the dark tinted windows.

"Listen, Cesar," said Geist Woods, frowning at the rooster. "I don't want to upset you, but I really need you to do this for me."

"Why should I?" queried the rooster, with an air of arrogance.

"Well, the fact is that the farm is not doing well and I have run out of feed for you and the rest of the chickens," Geist Woods continued. "So, I need you to cooperate. This way I will be able to feed you and the chickens."

"Farm? Chickens?" asked the rooster, in confusion.

"Come on!" Geist Woods exclaimed, in amazement.

"How come I don't recall any farm or chickens?"

"Stop messing around, Cesar," said Geist Woods, taken aback. "I cannot believe what you are saying."

"Well, I don't recall any farm or chickens," the rooster repeated.

"You know very well that we live on a large farm with all sorts of animals roaming around freely," Geist Woods added. "Just the way you like it, right?"

"I guess," agreed the rooster.

"That's what I thought," said Geist Woods.

"Even so, I still don't like the idea," replied the rooster. "But I guess I will go along, for the sake of the chickens and the other animals, and only because of this reason."

"Great, Cesar," exclaimed Geist Woods.

"Come on, let's get this over with before I change my mind," was the rooster's sneering reply.

"Now, you have to pretend that I am actually doing all the taking for the two of us," instructed Geist Woods. "That is the only way that we'll get paid."

"Yeah, yeah, whatever," was the rooster's snarky reply.

The door of the car opened. A passing couple holding hands witnessed a large man exiting an old vehicle, with, what appeared to be some sort of bird, under his right arm. A minute later, he vanished into the darkness.

Act 3

Cesar opened his eyes. Dark green spots, with yellowish glowing rims, were floating in his field of vision, making the dark empty room a labyrinth of half-seen shapes. After a few minutes of stumbling around, he realized he was in a small metal cage on the ground. The rooster made a clucking noise. He was trying to remember something, but he could only remember his last performance with Geist Woods. He did not know when or where this had occurred. As a matter of fact, he didn't know what time it was now, or what day, month, or year it was.

Cesar began pecking at the ground. The floor was made of some sort of soft fabric. Despite finding it hard to focus his eyes in the dark, he found the side door. He pecked at it for a long time, in an attempt to open it.

"Let me think," he said to himself. He inspected the door, up and down.

"That's it!" exclaimed Cesar. "There is spring that holds the door closed. I have to push it up to release it."

He began pecking at the bottom of the spring. He could hear the cage rattling every time his beak struck the metal. There was a flapping sound. The spring flew into the air, and the door swung open.

Cesar stepped out of the cage, carefully, as he was afraid of stumbling. He slowly made his way across the room to a door that was partially opened. He poked his head out. It was dark, but he noticed an array of multi-colored flickering lights reflecting on the walls at the end of a hallway. As he cautiously walked toward the lights, he could not help but notice that this place, wherever this place was, happened to be quite small and confined. When he reached the source of the flickering lights, he was struck by the amount of clutter in such a cramped space.

The bouncing, multi-colored, flickering lights were coming from an old TV set on top of a wooden crate. Facing the screen sat an oversized burgundy sofa chair. In the dark, Cesar could only see silhouettes and the back of the chair. Someone stretched out his arm to grab the contents of a bowl that was placed on a stack of books on the floor.

The frightened rooster suddenly heard a loud angry voice.

"No, no, no. You told me that in less than a year I would be featured on one of those late night shows. It's been almost three years."

It was Geist Woods. He was talking to someone, although Cesar could see that there was no one else in the room.

"Listen," Geist Woods began bitterly. "I'm your number one talent and you know it. Now you either get me featured in one of those late night TV shows, or you can say goodbye to my act."

Quietly, Cesar walked closer to the back of the sofa chair. He could hear that Geist Woods was eating some sort of crunchy food.

"We have nothing else to discuss, Mr. Tailor!" exclaimed Geist Woods. There was a long pause where Cesar could only hear the crunching sound of the food that Geist Woods ate.

"Hello, hello..." said Geist Woods. "How are you, Mrs. Kelly?"

Cesar walked around the sofa chair, just enough to see Geist Woods from the side. He made sure not to be spotted by the unsuspecting man.

"Mrs. Kelly, you know that with my talent the sky is the limit. Roger Tailor has gone as far as he can with me," Geist Woods stated, enthusiastically. "I can feel it. You are the person that can make it happen. After all, you are Karen Kelly, one of the top agents in the business."

Cesar tried to comprehend the conversation that Geist Woods was having. He seemed to be talking to a black, stone-like object, that he held against his ear. For a moment, the rooster thought that Geist Woods had lost it. But as he paid close attention, he could hear some sort of murmur or low voice coming from the thing or device.

"Exactly," Geist Woods continued. "I am not getting any younger. It's been almost three years. I'm still playing small comedy clubs in the middle of nowhere. And another thing, my rooster is not getting any younger either. Do you know how long it took me to train it?"

Cesar could feel his temper rising, as he continued to listen to Geist Woods talk.

"Nah, I keep him caged so he won't wander around and get lost." There was a short pause.

"Of course, I feel bad keeping him caged and cooped-up in my small apartment, but I take care of him."

At that moment, somewhere in Cesar's memory, he could hear Geist Woods' voice telling him about his life on the farm, with the chickens, and other animals. Was it all lies? His mind struggled to comprehend the meaning of what he was hearing. The rooster became aware of the deception, like a baby becomes aware of a new sound.

"It's all lies," he murmured to himself.

Here, in the bluish glow of the TV screen, a commercial featuring a white, talking duck, interacting with people, distracted Cesar for a moment.

"The point is that my head is butting against the ceiling, and I need to break through," said Geist Woods.

Cesar made a few jerky movements up and down, as he walked around the large sofa.

"You lying son of a bitch!" screamed Cesar, outraged.

"Wha, wha, what?" exclaimed Geist Woods, in astonishment.

"I'm going to kill you!" shouted Cesar, as he leapt straight towards Geist Woods' face. The man threw up his arms, in an attempt to protect himself.

The rooster's attack was ferocious. He pecked at the Geist Woods' face, and dug his spurs into his chest, shoulders, and arms. The man, in a panic, made an attempt to stand up, but instead, toppled over to the right side the sofa, while his arms flailed wildly. There was a loud crashing sound, as a small corner table shattered into a thousand pieces. The fierce attack ceased as fast as it had started. Geist Woods caught a glimpse of the feathered animal, who lay unconsciously next to him. By pure luck, he had fallen on top of the rooster when he hit the ground.

Cesar opened his eyes. Everything around him was a mass of blurry shapes. His whole body was sore and felt incredibly heavy. He tried to look around, but it seemed to take too much effort just to move.

"You have become quite a headache, Cesar," the rooster heard, faintly, before the whole world when black.

Act 4

Cesar sat patiently for a few minutes, watching the white sheet over his cage. He gave a deep sigh, as he pecked at the wire frame. His red crest stood straight, and his neck stretched. He heard someone's steps outside. The white sheet lifted in a single yank.

"This is it buddy, our big break!" said Geist Woods, with excitement.

The dimmed light of a small dressing room created a large shadow, as Geist Woods paced nervously from side to side, in front of the rooster's cage.

"This is it! This is what we've been waiting for!" exclaimed Geist Woods.

Geist Woods pumped his fist into the air, exhaled forcefully, and moved his face close to the cage, where Cesar remained calm, in a seated position.

"I know you don't understand me right now, but today, I am finally getting my big break!"

A loud laugh distorted Geist Woods' face.

"In a few minutes, we are going to be on national TV!"

Geist Woods leaned back and stared at the ceiling for a short moment. An arrogant smirk highlighted his dry, thick lips.

"Five years, five long years. Tonight, millions of people are going to see me, the best ventriloquist in the world!"

He paused for a moment, before giving a loud laugh.

Once again, he looked closely into the cage.

"A ventriloquist." He said this while making air quotes with his hands.

Cesar gave a soft croon, while staring at the man's face.

"You, my friend, are going to make me rich!" Geist Woods said, while pointing at the rooster.

There was a knock on the door. The door slowly opened. A small woman entered the room. Geist Woods turned around, in a hurry, to face her. He noticed that she was wearing a headset and holding a clipboard.

"Mr. Woods, you're on in 15 minutes," the small women announced.

"Thank you," replied Geist Woods, making an extravagant gesture with his hand.

"Do you need anything before going on stage, Mr. Woods?" asked the small woman, annoyed.

"I need a few minutes by myself," Geist Woods frowned, "please, can you make sure that no one comes in? I need complete privacy. I don't want anyone disrupting my concentration. So please, I don't want anyone to bother me at this time."

"Yes, Mr. Woods," the small woman said, with a hint of annoyance, as she closed the door behind her.

Geist Woods turned around, grabbed a chair, and sat in front of the cage. He unlocked the wire door, reached inside the cage, and grabbed Cesar, carefully. The rooster remained calm, without making a sound.

"All right, it's show time!" Geist Woods exclaimed, with excitement, while placing the rooster on top of the table.

He held it down with one hand, while swinging a pendulum in front of the rooster's face. He gazed into the animal's right eye.

But before Geist Woods had a chance to speak, Cesar shouted, "OtrosOchos!"

Suddenly, Geist Woods' mind felt like it had disconnected itself from his body and surroundings. He stayed motionless for a couple of minutes.

"From now on, you will follow my commands, not because I say so, but because you want to become famous. You like being famous. It's going to happen automatically. From now on, you do as I say," said the rooster, in a soft commanding voice.

Geist Woods felt like the whole world was spinning, as his awareness sunk deep down into a distant space within his subconscious mind.

"Gently pick me up and carry me," commanded Cesar, with an authoritarian tone.

Geist Woods obeyed the rooster's order, with his arms slightly extended in front of him. He held Cesar in his hands, the way you would hold something extremely precious and rare.

"Open the door and walk to the backstage area," said Cesar, slowly.

Geist Woods walked to the door, mechanically reached for the doorknob, opened it, and walked to the backstage area.

The same small woman, who had spoken to Geist Woods earlier in the dressing room, stood silently next to him.

"The red light above the stage is your cue," she stated.

Geist Woods stood still, without saying a word. It was as if he was observing himself, from outside, like a character on a TV screen, unable to take control of his own actions.

"That's your cue. Go, go, go!" exclaimed the small woman.

"Walk on stage and place me carefully on the stool," Cesar commanded.

Geist Woods followed the rooster's command. The building shook with applause, as both the performer and the man walked on stage.

I Think It's Time to Talk About You

In this written message, I am speaking directly to you, the reader. I hope you can get a sense of what I am trying to convey. Perhaps in the process, you might lose track of who I am referring to. Don't worry. That is perfectly fine. Do your best to follow along. To tell you the truth, I'm a bit apprehensive about the subject matter, but I think what I am about to say needs to be brought up. Anyhow, I will stop beating around the bush and get to the point.

I need to say a few things about You. That's right. Everything I am about to say is about You. Please do not get upset with what I'm about to write about You. By no means am I trying to judge or criticize You. Quite the opposite. I'm simply trying to be of some help. Just so you know, I'm not the only one that has been talking about You. Yes, people are gossiping, but don't worry, it's mostly positive. "It's all good." That being said, some of these individuals who I've spoken to also agree that there are a few things that You might need to work on. Feel free to disagree with us, if we are wrong.

Believe it or not, a lot of people think that You can be quite odd at times. Now, it wasn't me who said that. I just overheard some of the rumors. And don't worry, perhaps hearing some of these things can be beneficial and insightful for You. Why do I say this? Because I think I know You well enough, even though we haven't met in person yet.

I have to say, You can leave a strong impression on people. For this reason, I think I'm able to share a few observations that You should know. Honestly, everyone can see that You display many wonderful qualities and talents, for example, kindness, self-reliance, and cleverness. I would go as far as saying that under the right circumstances, You can be a strong influential force on others. However, there are times when You can be too critical about mistakes, which perhaps other people would not worry too much about. In a way, this has held You back, on more than one occasion.

I am going to be brutally honest now. No more sugarcoating what you need to hear. Sometimes You can act in such a way that almost seems senseless. I have noticed that, at times, You tend to concentrate too much on the past, and this can be very harmful. The fact is, that when You get stuck for too long in the past, You become depressed, and that is a very difficult place to get out from. Remember that when someone spends too much time in the past, it's very hard to imagine a better future. In other words, there is a tendency to project the past into the future. But the reality is that the past is gone. It's not here. So, to think about it at all is to think about illusions.

Another apparent thing is how much You focus on the future. Now, I think we can all agree that it can be helpful to make plans and have goals, but what is happening to You is serious. I am truly worried. My advice to You is to stop worrying about what is going to happen tomorrow, next week, next month, or next year. You need to stop. This path leads to nothing good. I often ask myself, "Can uncertainty be the goal?" I will venture out and say that this is not the case. So, my best advice to You is to let the future go. It hasn't happened. It's not here. So once again, to think about it at all is to think about fantasies. In either case, not thinking about the past or the future will allow You to be present, which is the only time there is. Please let me share one of the most insightful thoughts that I have ever received. A very wise person once told me, "Thinking about the problem is the problem." I hope this helps You.

I feel in some way that You sometimes become easily defensive. That is a shame, because when this happens to You, there is definitely a missing opportunity to experience love, happiness, and rich interactions with others. I think there is a lesson that can be learned here. Maybe You can learn how to take a broader look at life, how to be open to new ideas, experiences, interactions, and relationships, even if they may seem strange at first. Perhaps the lesson to learn here is even more important than what You might think it is. For instance, the lesson of learning how to trust. I think deep inside, You can feel that no harm will come by taking away the barriers and letting people in. I often ask myself, "What if You think about all those childhood dreams that were so close to heart?" It's not hard to imagine that there is a part of You that would like to start all over, to leave it all behind, to have a fresh start, and this time around, do things differently. That is not to say that You haven't had success up until now. But am I wrong when I say that You had doubts along the way, or thoughts of adopting a different, more positive, and open approach to life?

Well, enough said. After all, I am telling You all of this in secrecy. I wouldn't want You to read what I just disclosed in this monologue. By the way, if you, reader, are fortunate enough to run into You, please remember to mention how highly I think of You.

No Place Like Home

After a long, well-deserved vacation, I am happy to be heading back home. It is hard to admit, but I am actually looking forward to being back in my own place again. That is not to say that I did not enjoy my time away. On the contrary, it is always nice to experience other cultures, to see the beautiful cities' landscapes, and to feel and understand how others think and live their lives.

In my opinion, to visit these busy and animated metropolises is to step into the imagination of every single mind that designed and dwelled in them. There is so much to see, to listen to, and to feel. Every dimension, movement, and element is delightfully full of life. I am guilty of embellishing, in joy and amazement, every instant I spend on such marvelous adventures. It is an illumination of perception, an enlightenment of the soul, and a cleansing of dark thoughts, and melancholic emotions.

How refreshing it is to intermingle in an ocean of creativity and originality! I can honestly say that I feel recharged and revitalized. I was not expecting to feel this way at all. Let me explain. Lately, I have seriously been questioning life itself. What do I mean by this? Well, I am quite sure I am not the only one that contemplates the events that are happening around the world and asks himself, "How is this possible? Why is this happening?"

How about you? Do you ever wonder why things are the way they are? If you do, then you know exactly how I feel. My apologies. It is not my intention to upset you or remind you of unpleasant thoughts. After all, you have your own problems to think about. Please don't pay attention to me. I tend to ramble on too much. When I start overthinking, (which I often do), I always end up drifting aimlessly from one place to another, in many instances, for hours on end, until something snaps me back. It is terrible to be so easily distracted and to get so carried away with one's own ideas.

Well, I must leave you soon. I am almost home, and I am pretty sure there is someone there anxiously waiting for me. I cannot begin to tell you the effect that it has on him when I stay away for too long. I know you are not going to believe me when I tell you what happened the last time I went out. He just lay there like a corpse, doing nothing, completely paralyzed. Sometimes I wonder what he would do if I decided not to come back. I will venture to say that he would probably just wither away, like a plant without water.

Oh, there he is. And what did I tell you? He has been asleep the whole time. I honestly don't know how he does it, just lying in bed without a care in the world. And then he wonders why I take off, every time he is out for the count. He even gets upset that I step outside when he meditates. Now let me ask you, "Can you blame me for drifting away when he goes into a trance?" We are both well aware that he is not "in a trance." He just falls asleep. Anyhow, what am I supposed to do? Just wait around until he wakes up? It's not my fault that he tends to shut down every time he closes his eyes.

Please don't get me wrong. I am glad that he is around. Without him, I could not accomplish what I need to do. So, I am profoundly grateful to have him. It's not every day that you get a physical body to fulfill a service and experience a life lesson. But if you stop for a moment and reflect on the length of time it takes for him to develop and grow old enough to function properly, it can be exhausting, not to mention, all the exercise and maintenance that he requires. I am not complaining, it's just a simple observation.

Well, it is time to reconnect. His brain is ready to start the day. His bladder needs to be emptied, and he needs to rehydrate. Otherwise, everything seems to be okay. His temperature is good, his heart rate is steady, and his muscles are relaxed. That reminds me, I must take him to the acupuncturist to get rid of that pesky hamstring strain. It won't be easy. He hates needles. As for me, I will distract myself with a nice childhood memory, or a vision of a peaceful sunny beach, somewhere in the middle of the Pacific.

All right, it is definitely time to go now. We have a busy day ahead of us. Good talking to you. Take care.

Remember Now

Act 1

The waves were tall and fast. The palm trees were high and heavy on top. Toward the edge of the beach, where the sand turns into concrete, a row of vacant weather-beaten wooden benches witnessed the darkness that had come in from the Atlantic Ocean. The parking lot, which connected the seaside with the desolate street, had vanished. Nighttime blanketed the entire city.

A menacing-looking cloud clawed its way across the dark sky. The rushing wind sprayed the heavy precipitation sideways. During all this, there was only a single figure standing at the edge of the water. It was Hazel.

She faced the unseen horizon, where water meets the firmament. Lightning zigzagged downwards, near and far. Her stare was colder than the rain that showered her body. Emptiness filled her lifeless eyes. Her mind was far away. Her thoughts wandered to a distant land that she had once called home, her birthplace. This was the only place where she really felt free. But freedom is only loved when it is lost.

"Why don't you take me when I face you? What are you afraid of?" she asked, narrowing her eyes.

She took a step forward. The edge of the ocean slapped her feet. Were it not for the sudden pause in the wind, she would not have heard the bark behind her. As she turned, the first thing to appear was a small dog, facing her, with his tail swaying from side to side. When he barked again, his forelegs slightly hopped, causing him to dig his front paws into the wet sand.

"What are you doing here?" asked Hazel, raising her arm to wave him away. The dog responded with a bark. Hazel fell silent for a moment. She wondered where the small creature had come from, as she looked around. She bent down and petted the small creature on its head.

"Where did you come from?" she whispered.

The dog did not respond. Suddenly, the heavy rain calmed down. She ran her hand down the neck of the canine. With her left hand, she lifted the tag that was hanging from the dog's collar. It was too dark to make out the engraving on the round metal circle. For an instant, a flash of light from the heavens illuminated the whole shoreline.

"Now," she said.

"Your name is Now," she added.

The dog replied with a soft bark.

"Where is your owner, boy?" she asked, not expecting an answer.

The dog licked her hand. Hazel felt better after the gesture of affection. She picked up Now and walked away from the beach.

Act 2

The sun had already come up. Breathing steadily, Hazel ran downhill. She paused and jogged in place at the street corner. A police car drove by with lights on, but no siren. A street sweeper truck was cleaning the gutter along the sidewalk, and a street vendor was setting up his booth.

"Stay with me," she blurted out, while looking down to her left. Now was next to her.

She adjusted her earbuds, just before they both sprinted towards the beach. With her fast pace, she arrived at the edge of the water a few seconds before the dog. She paused for a moment, as she stood on the same spot where she had faced the storm the year before. Her mind drifted to past events, painful experiences, and unpleasant memories. She felt an uncomfortable, cold feeling beneath her heart. Hazel began to feel overwhelmed by the total darkness in which she found herself.

A loud bark broke her dejected trance. Now had snapped her out of her stupor. Instantly, the coldness in her heart disappeared. Her mind became aware of the morning sun hanging high in the blue sky, of the soft breeze caressing her skin, of the sounds of the waves, and of the voices of two women, who were walking by.

"Hey, boy," said Hazel.

Now was right next to her.

"What took you so long?" she asked, with a smile on her face.

The dog tilted his head to his left, as he listened.

Hazel took her earbuds out and placed them in the small front pocket of her running tights. Then she said, laughingly, "You know, sometimes when you look at me that way, I think you can read my mind."

The canine responded with a soft bark.

"Come on, Now. Let's go home," she said, quietly.

A moment later, the beach was deserted.

Act 3

On a cold spring evening, Hazel, who was sitting with her back to the kitchen, pulled an envelope out of her purse. She ripped the edge from one of the sides, opened the folded sheet of paper, and put it on the small dining table. Without knowing why, a sense of doom began to take hold of Hazel's heart.

"This can't be good news," whispered Hazel to herself, as she looked around the modest living room in front of her.

Hazel took a deep breath and sighed as she lowered her eyes toward the letter. It read:

Dear Hazel,

I hope this letter finds you well. It is with great sadness in my heart that I must inform you of the sudden admission of your father to the hospital. I have learned that he had been suffering from strong migraines for about a week. His reluctance to share the extent of his illness is concerning to all of us. But I understand that he probably felt that we would be overly worried about learning of his poor health. I visited him three days ago, and he seemed to be well taken care of by the doctors and nurses.

As you know, we all care about you. We don't want you to be upset, but we just don't know what will happen with your father's health over the next few days. Here in the village, we are coming across another outbreak of Tuberculosis. It's spreading so fast that even the provincial governor, Mr. Vazquez, is worried.

I wish that I could do something to ease your worries upon hearing this news. However, rest assured that you and your father are present in my thoughts and prayers.

Yours affectionately,

Uncle Helder W.

P.S. I am sorry I did not call you. But, as you know, times have been tough around here, and my phone is broken.

Hazel's head began throbbing. Her arms and legs felt weak, and her breathing grew shallow. Her mind became flooded with visions of doom, suffering, and death. At a loss and unable to see anything else but catastrophic outcomes, she got up and walked toward her bedroom.

"Briefcase, brief... brr..." spluttered Hazel, while gasping for air.

Suddenly, there was a tug at her right leg. Her train of thought was disrupted. She looked down. It was Now.

"What, boy?" asked Hazel, shaking her leg slowly to lose his grip on the bottom of her black work pants.

The dog let go of the pants' cuff.

"Sorry, Now, I don't have time to play," declared Hazel.

The dog jumped onto the bed and began barking.

"What do you want, Now?" asked Hazel, impatiently.

Now began jumping and bouncing on top of the bed.

"You are so silly, Now," said Hazel, with a faint smile.

The canine added barking to his playful behavior.

"Okay, okay. I will play with you for a few minutes," stated Hazel.

A moment later, both Hazel and Now were happily playing tug of war, followed by hide and seek the treats, and indoor fetch.

"I feel so much better," thought Hazel.

Now continued his playful game.

"You know, Now, I think I know what to do," she exclaimed, smiling.

"I don't need to panic. Everything is going to be okay," affirmed Hazel.

The dog answered with a bark.

Act 4

Early in the morning of July 12th, three figures sat on the ground, under the shade of a row of lush oak trees on the manicured lawn of National Park. It was the time of day when most people seem to have the drive to conquer the world, (when the sun is bright on the east, and the moon fades high on the west). People from all walks of life strolled and ran along the many walking trails.

The three figures enjoying the cool shade provided by the lush oaks were Hazel, her best friend, Audrey, and Now. A refreshing breeze reminded the two women of the wonderful natural setting that surrounded them.

"Mmm, I love the sound of the wind in the trees," said Audrey.

"Yes, and the smell of fresh-cut grass," added Hazel.

Now sat, stone-like, with his eyes closed and nose in the air. The wind seemed to pick up strength, just to draw attention to itself.

"What's with your dog?" asked Audrey.

"What do you mean?" Hazel replied, confused.

"Look at him. I could swear that he is meditating, or something," answered Audrey, pointing, with a toss of her head.

"Yeah, he does that all the time," said Hazel, in explanation of Now's amusing behavior.

"How long has it been since you found him?" asked Audrey.

"It's been three years," replied Hazel.

"Has it been that long?" inquired Audrey, in astonishment.

"Well, in all honesty, he found me," added Hazel, smiling brightly.

They both were staring at Now, who continued to sit, stone-like, with his eyes closed and nose in the air.

"You know, besides saving my life, he has changed the way I see life," continued Hazel, keeping her eyes fixed on the canine. "At first I didn't notice, but eventually I became aware that every time I faced a difficult situation, my mind would go crazy. Somehow, Now would always bring me back to my sanity."

"What do you mean?" asked Audrey, with a frown.

Audrey didn't know what had come over her friend. She watched Hazel spread her arms, as if she was grabbing some sort of invisible object above her head, and then slowly brought it down to her lap.

"Well, do you remember the night of the big storm, three years ago?" asked Hazel.

"Yeah, I remember," answered Audrey.

"Well, that night, I was feeling super depressed. I couldn't stop thinking about going back home. I missed my family, and my childhood friends. I missed my life where I grew up," said Hazel, handing an unopened plastic bottle of water to Audrey.

"Thank you. Yes, I remember that you were homesick," confirmed Audrey, as she received the bottle of water.

"I was more than homesick," replied Hazel. "Anyhow, that night at the beach, my mind was far away. I was beyond sad. In fact, I was so distraught that I was ready to walk into the ocean to get rid of that feeling."

"I am so sorry, Hazel. I should have been there for you," said Audrey, looking sadly down at the ground.

"How could you?" replied Hazel. "We hardly knew each other back then."

"I know," answered Audrey.

"Well, as you know, that is when Now found me," Hazel continued. "At first, I got annoyed, but as he continued to bark, my thoughts went from thinking about my hometown to that moment."

"Yeaaaah..." confirmed Audrey, not really understanding what her friend was implying.

"Don't you see?" continued Hazel. "My mind was far away, in another place, not present. But that's when Now showed up. Now brought me to the present moment."

"I see," Audrey said, with a tone of skepticism.

Hazel placed her hand on Now's head and began softly petting him. The canine welcomed the loving gesture, without making a sound.

"He does it all the time," continued Hazel. "For example, about six or seven months after that night..."

Hazel paused for a moment.

"No, no," Hazel continued. "It was about a year later when it happened."

"What?" asked Audrey, peering at her friend.

"During a morning run, I just happened to stop by that same spot on the beach," said Hazel. "Immediately, I started thinking about my break-up with Ron, the fight that I had with Karen, and the argument I had with my sister. I felt horrible."

"Then, what happened?" Audrey inquired.

"As you can imagine, I felt a lot of guilt," Hazel said. "I wanted to cry, but once again, out of nowhere, Now began barking. In that instant, I felt better. I realized that all those events in my life were in the past, therefore, gone."

"I see," said Audrey. "But it could just be a coincidence, you know, because he wants to play."

"I knew you were going to say that," Hazel continued. "Well, how about the time my dad was in the hospital?"

"What do you mean?" asked Audrey.

"I told you this story before," said Hazel. "Do you remember last year when my dad got really sick?"

"Yes, I remember," replied Audrey.

"The night that I received the letter from Uncle Helder, I almost lost my mind. I began to imagine my dad dying at the hospital. Then I imagined his body in a coffin at the funeral, and then the burial. Oh my God, I imagined the worst-case scenario. My level of anxiety went through the roof. I even thought that both my sister and I would go crazy. You know how close we are to our dad," said Hazel.

"Yes, I do know how close both of you are to your dad," Audrey confirmed.

"I think I was in shock," Hazel continued. "Like a zombie, I walked to my bedroom and grabbed my suitcase. All of the sudden, I felt a jolt. Now was tugging at the cuff of my pants."

"Okay?" asked Audrey.

"Once again, my mind had gone to a dark place. I was visualizing all the things that could have gone wrong, none of which did. My mind was stuck in a very bleak future," explained Hazel.

"Maybe, he does know when something is wrong," added Audrey.

Hazel nodded, silently.

"You know, a while back, I read an article that stated that all dogs are very intuitive," Audrey continued. "Somehow, they know when their owners are sad or anxious."

"Yes!" exclaimed Hazel, with vigor. "It's like this. When my mind is stuck in the past, in the future, or somewhere else, Now brings me back to the present moment, where everything is fine."

"I believe you," replied Audrey, looking affectionately at the canine.

"Since Now is in my life, everything has gotten better," said Hazel.

Now stayed still, and the morning continued to be peaceful and calm.

www.bioanimatelifebuddy.com

CYBER MONDAY SALE

20% OFF EVERYTHING · ONLINE ONLY

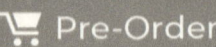
Pre-Order

The Hottest Toy Of 2067 Is Here!

The End

Notes

1. Biography Online. 2019. "Nikola Tesla Biography." Retrieved March 12, 2019. (https://www.biographyonline.net/scientists/nikola-tesla.html).

2. Rebecca Turner, World of lucid dreaming. 2018. "10 Dreams That Changed Human History." Retrieved March 12, 2019. (https://www.world-of-lucid-dreaming.com/10-dreams-that-changed-the-course-of-human-history.html)

3. Astral Institute. 2015. "Famous People on their Near Death Experiences." Retrieved February 12, 2019 (http://astral-institute.com/famous-people-near-death-experiences/).

4. Kevin Williams, Mind Power News. 2019. "Near-Death Experiences of the Rich and Famous" Retrieved March 12, 2019. (http://www.mindpowernews.com/RichAndFamous.htm).

5. Near-death.com. 2016. "Near-Death Experiences of the Hollywood Rich and Famous" Retrieved March 12, 2019. (https://www.near-death.com/experiences/rich-and-famous.html).

6. Astral Institute. 2018. "Carl Jung and Astral Projection." Retrieved February 12, 2019. (http://astral-institute.com/carl-jung-and-astral-projection/).

6. Wikipedia, Emanuel Swedenborg. 2019. "Emanuel Swedenborg" Retrieved March, 12, 2019 (https://en.wikipedia.org/wiki/Emanuel_Swedenborg).

7. Maria IsabelCarrasco. 5 Paintings Inspired By The Bizarre World Of Dreams. 2017. "The Persistence of Memory-Salvador Dali, 1931." Retrieved March 12, 2019. (https://culturacolectiva.com/art/paintings-inspired-by-dreams).

8. Beverly Jenkins, Famous Books Inspired By Dreams. 2011. "*Dr. Jekyll and Mr. Hyde* Robert Louis Stevenson." Retrieved March 12, 2019 (http://listverse.com/2011/02/26/5-famous-books-inspired-by-dreams/).

Runda
E-Books and Print Books

Other books by the author

Mastering Success - The key to self empowerment and higher consciousness.
Boost Your Brainpower 365 - The ultimate program to improve creativity, visualization, imagination, memory, and concentration.
Embracing Happiness 365 - Living a fulfilling life workbook.
Leadership 365 - Organizational development workbook.
The Lost Continent of North America - Is the legend myth or real?

Available from all good bookstores, worldwide, and online at
runda.io